The Memory Collectors

Also by Dete Meserve

Good Sam
Perfectly Good Crime
The Good Stranger
The Space Between
Random Acts of Kindness

The Memory Collectors

A Novel

DETE MESERVE

This is a work of fiction. All of the names, characters, organizations, places and events portrayed in this novel are either products of the author's imagination or are used fictitiously. Any resemblance to real or actual events, locales, or persons, living or dead, is entirely coincidental.

Copyright © 2025 by Dete Meserve

All rights reserved.

Published in the United States by Crooked Lane Books, an imprint of The Quick Brown Fox & Company LLC.

Crooked Lane Books and its logo are trademarks of The Quick Brown Fox & Company LLC.

Library of Congress Catalog-in-Publication data available upon request.

ISBN (hardcover): 979-8-89242-072-3
ISBN (paperback): 979-8-89242-242-0
ISBN (ebook): 979-8-89242-073-0

Cover design by Meghan Deist

Printed in the United States.

www.crookedlanebooks.com

Crooked Lane Books
34 West 27th St., 10th Floor
New York, NY 10001

First Edition: May 2025

10 9 8 7 6 5 4 3 2 1

To my siblings, Devorah, Hannah, David, Zehavah, Rifka, and Mac—who've walked with me through the twists and turns of time, always believing in new beginnings.

I am sitting here wanting memories to teach me to see the beauty in the world through my own eyes—

> Ysaye Barnwell

Part One

The Jump

Chapter One

Elizabeth

The first image isn't dreamlike as many say it will be.

My sister, Debra, is talking with me. Her words are soft and low, as if we've been in conversation for a while. She wears her signature star necklace, and her thick brown hair is tied back in a braid.

The details take my breath away.

We're at a wooden table in a courtyard. Mounds of red and purple bougainvillea spill over its stone walls. Rose-fingered sunlight drifts through the leaves of a guava tree, which fashions a canopy over our table. I draw in a slow, soothing breath of salty air. The ocean is nearby.

It feels so damn real.

My sister's voice, which started out thin and muted, sharpens into focus. She's talking about a young girl's attention problems, and I realize she's telling me about one of her students. Disappointment surges through me. I didn't come all the way here to listen to my sister talk about a student.

But no promises were made. No guarantees. Aeon Expeditions promises a journey into our past but does not guarantee that what happens will be meaningful.

My sixty minutes here will race by, so I turn my attention back to Debra. I can't help but marvel at the things that I once took for granted. Her familiar smile is softer, gentler. A delicate laugh lights up her face. There's an elegance about her—high cheekbones, strong jawline—that I didn't notice in real life.

Yet this is real life.

I ask my sister how old she'll be on her next birthday and her eyes cloud with confusion. I should know how old she is.

"Thirty-eight," she says.

I've come twenty-two years into the past. *Twenty-two years.* The thought is so mind-bending that I cover my eyes with my fingers and fight back tears.

Even though I've already lived this once before, I'm filled with awe. I bring to this ordinary moment the experience of living twenty-two years beyond it. Of knowing all the joy and love and loss and brokenness that will come after.

I notice everything.

Breakfast is laid out on the table. Orange juice in tall glasses. A bowl of cut fruit. Bright yellow napkins.

I reach for the white porcelain teapot before me, its warmth radiating deep into my hands. The liquid flows into my cup and its lemon aroma hovers in the air. Everything is more vibrant the second time around.

I wonder if this feeling will go on forever. Every item. Every moment. Everything I'd once taken for granted taking on new meaning.

I don't remember this conversation with my sister, but I recall being here in Santa Barbara, California, at a family reunion with her, our two sisters, and all our kids.

Our kids.

"Mommy," I hear a little voice behind me say.

I turn in my chair and before I can even make sense of what I'm seeing, I feel the tears well up. My heart is dancing and crying all at once.

"Can you help me with my Transformer?" he asks.

I can't speak. My lips are trembling, and my mouth won't form any words.

My son Sam is barely four here. Strawberry blond with a little boy haircut and big brown eyes. I reach out to touch his freckled cheeks. Smooth and round.

He turns to me, a surprised look in his eyes. Why don't I answer?

I take in every bit of him. The navy-blue cotton shorts and white T-shirt. The scuffed Converse. His chubby fingers grasp a plastic action figure.

"I need help," he says, then takes my hand in his and gently pulls.

My voice is thick with tears. "You want help with this one?" I say, pointing to his toy.

He shakes his head. All serious. "The *other* one. Optimus Prime. Over there." He points to a blanket under a sprawling oak tree where his toys are laid out.

"Are you crying?" my sister asks. "And your face is really red."

"I'm fine," I say, wiping my eyes. A flushed face is a common result of the time travel, but this feels like more than a side effect.

Sam takes my hand in his and walks me to the blanket. He drops to his knees, grabs one of the toy robots and gives it to me. "This one. I can't make him transform."

I sit beside him, feeling a sense of wonder about my body, which bends and stretches in ways that I'd long forgotten. It's strange how I don't remember ever marveling at my body when it was this age. I'd always been disappointed in its penchant for having curves where I wanted it to be flat.

I don't remember how to transform this robot into a truck—what this toy is supposed to do—but I try.

"Bad guy or good guy?" I ask.

"Good."

I steal a look at the toy to make sure I look like I'm trying to figure it out, but my eyes can't and won't leave his face. There's a pink stain on his cheeks from the heat and the sun. I lean in and kiss his hair, breathe in the familiar little-boy scent, and tears prick my eyes once more.

He lifts one of the figures with a purple emblem on its chest. "This one is bad," he growls.

I bring him close and squeeze him tightly. In this moment, he is still mine. I have the power to soothe and comfort him. To protect him from what's to come.

"I'm having trouble transforming him," I say. "Maybe you want to try again?"

He nods and takes it back. I watch as he thinks his way through this puzzle, as if my closeness has somehow made it easier for him. Seconds later, he's morphed the robot into a truck. He holds it up to me, proudly. "Transform!"

I watch him play, and, in this moment, I'm the one transformed. I'm free from all the worry that I wasn't the best mother when he was little; that I was always too tired or not paying enough attention or never enough fun. I bring into this moment that this stage in his life will end all too quickly. That I won't be forever worn and weary and wondering what I did wrong or if I could've done better. And that's when I see the beauty of it all. The joy of his giggles and his love for me that knows no bounds. The littleness of his body that once exhausted me, but now I desperately cling to.

In the future, I no longer get to buy sippy cups or crayons or children's toothpaste. We won't go to the library or playground or buy ice cream cakes. I don't get to run to the shoe store with him because his feet have grown seemingly overnight or get to take him shopping at the toy store to find a birthday gift for one of his friends. I no longer have drawers filled with birthday cards and wrapping paper for impromptu invitations, nor do I have stashes of colored markers and stickers in case he can't find anything to do.

"Can we play hide and seek?" he asks.

"You want to hide?"

He nods because he always loves hiding more than seeking. He drops his truck onto the blanket. "Close your eyes! No peeking."

I cover my eyes but cheat and peek through my fingers. I have so little time with him.

"Ready or not, here I come!" I shout, then start looking around the courtyard, pretending I don't know that he's hiding behind a tree in the corner. "Where did you go?" I call out.

The tears fall. *Where did he go?*

This beautiful little boy will grow and go to school. He will gaze at the stars and want to be an astronaut someday, get his driver's license, meet his first love and take her to prom, go to college and earn his teaching certificate, then begin his dream job teaching astronomy to high school students. Then he will be forever gone, his future erased in a senseless accident.

Yet here he is, standing beneath the tree, his body trembling with excitement, a huge smile on his face, delighted that he's found a hiding spot he thinks I can't find. Bursting with life. Years and years of joy and laughter and love still ahead of him.

The future with all that it brings is held at bay as I scurry around the courtyard twice and then pretend to spot him for the first time. "There you are!"

He laughs and races from behind the tree, then plants a baby powder-soft kiss on my cheek. "You couldn't find me for a long time."

"I know," I say. I hold him close to my heart. "It's been a very long time."

* * *

If you could spend an hour in your past, what would you do?

This is the first question on the Aeon Expeditions application, and the most common answer is surprising. The hour we want to relive is not our wedding day or the day our children were born. It's not even the joyous moments of a Sunday dinner with family or a Christmas with presents under the tree. And despite how altruistic we think we might be, very few people admit they'd spend that hour giving justice to Hitler or Stalin or any other evil icon. No, the most common answer is that we want to spend a few more moments with someone we lost.

I'm just one of millions who gave this answer. I'm also more broken than I admitted in the application. I still have hours, sometimes days, where I don't believe Sam's gone, as if his death is a story I've been told or a movie I've seen. Each day brings the agony of knowing that for the rest of my life I'll live with arms outstretched for a son who's no longer there.

I read somewhere that a baby's cells remain a part of their mom long after they are born, take their first steps, learn to speak, go to school, get a job, and become a parent themselves. Maybe that's why I can't let go of him. Why Sam still feels like he's always with me.

Live long enough and you accumulate losses.

My dad used to say that a lot when I was in my twenties and back then I thought: *Why does he say such depressing things?*

That's because I hadn't lost anything back then. Or perhaps it was also because other than my singular life, I hadn't gained anything either. I hadn't met my future-husband Mark at a friend's wedding and tumbled head over heels in love. I hadn't lost my first pregnancy, a baby we'd hoped to name after my grandmother Violet, in a miscarriage at sixteen weeks. I hadn't given birth to beautiful Sam, who wouldn't exist if my pregnancy had worked the first time.

I had no idea back then that once you love something—anything—all you can ever be sure is that you're going to lose it someday.

Now I'm crying. After my hour was up, I was extracted to the present and even though I've stepped outside of Aeon Expeditions into bright sunlight, I still can't escape the shadows.

From the outside, Aeon could be any industrial building—a fortress of reinforced steel with a curved hangar-like roof. Its walls, painted in muted sage and desert sand, blend seamlessly into the Southern California landscape. No casual observer would guess at the extraordinary things that happen within.

Minutes later, a staff psychologist joins me outside. She has a soft, forgiving face that looks like she's accustomed to seeing people at their worst. "I'm Dr. Kim. How're you feeling?"

The silence expands between us as I find my words. My body trembles and I feel the pulse of grief return. "It's not a broken bone I can show you. But it's real. This pain."

This experience has destroyed my sense of reality. Grief had taught me that I won't hear Sam's voice or see his beautiful smile or experience the light of his silly giggle. He won't run to me or wrap his little arms around me and squeeze. Grief had shown me that living means he is no longer here.

Then, a jump in time and none of that's true.

I spent an hour with Sam, holding his hands, watching him run and play and laugh. I held and tickled his body, kissed his soft cheeks a thousand times, sang ridiculous songs, then cuddled and snuggled him. My heart was full. Nothing else in the world mattered. And in my next breath, it seemed, the sixty minutes evaporated, and my entire world collapsed.

"I'll never stop missing him," I whisper.

"It's common to feel profound grief after a visit with someone we have loved and lost," she says softly. "Give yourself time to recover and get back to normal."

I don't want to recover. I want to recapture the feeling of being with him and hold on to it, like perfume in a bottle, so I can always come back to it. I don't want to go back to a "normal" world where Sam isn't in it.

In the months after Sam's death, I'd fallen apart, acting like a madwoman, exhausting everyone in my life who cared about me until I came to the point where I began to nurse the idea that I was ready to embrace death. To cling to life seemed a betrayal of Sam, who I could only connect with in death. I dulled the pain with wine. And pills. Then both. When I hit rock bottom, I was kneeling on the cold bathroom tile, my head flung over the toilet basin, my hair dragging in the foul water, and my body rocked with spasms as I vomited the cocktail of pills and cabernet I'd consumed an hour earlier. I was sobbing, the kind of uncontrollable tears that made me gasp for air. It felt like my grief had no end. And in that moment, I had a kind of epiphany. Not a religious one, I don't think. A clear, calm thought that seemed as though it had winged itself into the room and lighted on my shoulder.

This wasn't only about losing Sam. It was also about me.

It was only when I allowed the truth to squeeze in that I began to see what I'd kept hidden from myself all this time.

It's my fault that Sam died.

It was my birthday, the milestone fifty, and my husband Mark was in what he called a "technology monastery"—he and a team of twenty-two engineers holed up day and night on a ranch in Ojai, California, working on plans for the technology that would later become Aeon Expeditions. A group of friends had taken me out for a birthday lunch, then Sam and I made plans to grill some steaks together later that night. Ten minutes into the meal, he glanced at his phone and said hurriedly, "Sorry, Mom, I have to go."

"Where're you going?"

He stood. "I've got to meet someone."

"Come on. Stay a while. Talk to me."

He was silent for a long moment. I thought this meant he was finally going to tell me why he'd been so distant, leaving the house at all hours of the night, often not returning until hours later. "Just because Dad ignores us doesn't mean I have to be here with you every second."

His words felt like a punch to the gut. "What're you saying?"

I should have kept quiet then. Instead, my anger flared. After all the things I'd done for him as a mother, after being there for him when his father couldn't, how could he talk to me with such contempt? "You're just like your father. You do whatever you want."

"I'm not Dad."

I waved my hand at him. "Just go then."

He seemed so young as he hurried to the front door, his head bowed. But also, so very old. Like he was embarking on a doomed journey.

He shut the door behind him with a firm *thunk*, and I went about the business of cleaning up the celebration dinner that neither of us had eaten, hating myself for my harsh words. Wishing I'd handled it differently.

I never got the chance to say I was sorry.

When the police called me hours later, I couldn't understand what they were saying. How could Sam be gone? I tumbled end over end. Nothing made sense.

Then the questions slithered in.

Why was the pistol we kept in the safe missing, along with three thousand dollars in cash? Police never recovered the gun or the cash. The same night that Sam was killed in the accident, someone stole our speedboat from the slip at the harbor. It never turned up. The police blamed it on an uptick of thefts that summer, but that didn't explain other nagging questions.

Why had Sam been walking on that lone stretch of highway close to midnight? Why was his car parked miles away? Why were his last minutes spent with a drug dealer?

The coroner didn't find any drugs in Sam's body or in his possession, so maybe this late-night meeting wasn't about drugs. I couldn't find any other connection between them. They hadn't gone to school together. There were no emails or texts between them. It crossed my mind that maybe Sam had a burner phone where he kept those communications secret. I never found one.

My sister Debra brought up the possibility that the two had met on a dating app. Maybe Sam was gay, and I didn't know it. And the reason he was on that secluded road was that he was hiding his relationship.

I cried. Not at the possibility that Sam was gay. I would've accepted it, even though admittedly I hadn't seen signs of that. It broke my heart that Sam might have felt he had no choice but to keep it a secret.

Here's what I know. If I hadn't lashed out in anger, he would not have been on that stretch of highway when that car spun through the curve and took his life. He would be still alive.

The psychologist touches my shoulder reassuringly. "You okay?"

I have the sense that she thinks she knows about death. But she only knows it from a distance, from comforting people like me. She doesn't know that when death takes away your son, the five stages of grief and everything she learned in college are blown to pieces.

Still, I must stop crying. Not just because my ex-husband, Mark Saunders, is the founder of Aeon Expeditions and it will get around the company that I was a mess after my jump. But I don't want this psychologist to conclude that I'm not emotionally stable enough to embark on my second trip, scheduled for late this afternoon.

The waiting list for a jump is so long—sometimes years—that only a handful of people in the world have ever been granted a second one. It is far easier to get into Harvard than it is to get your first time travel slot. The odds of getting a second one, especially when you're the founder's *ex*-wife, are about the same as winning the Powerball.

When I heard the voicemail from Mark telling me he'd scheduled a free second jump for me, I was surprised. I hadn't spoken to him much since our divorce nearly three years earlier, so it made no sense that he'd given me this exceptional gift.

I'd returned his call right away. "How'd you do this?" I asked. There is a limited supply of time travel slots, and the jumps themselves require so much energy and manpower that they aren't cheap to produce. Then there's the byzantine application and selection process that kicks out 98 percent of applicants in the first round. Millions try to circumvent or appeal the process each year and are still rejected. Giving me a second trip, even though Mark is the founder, is a Herculean feat.

"It *was* complicated," he admitted.

"Why then? When we're not together . . ."

"I was hoping you'd call me back," he said slowly. "And you did."

My voice was filled with disbelief. "You gave me a trip that's impossible to get because you *hoped* I'd call you back?"

"I miss you, Elizabeth. And if you're willing, I want us to get together when you return. You can tell me all about your trip."

So, there is a catch.

"And . . . if I don't want that?" I ask.

"Then the trip is still yours."

"Are you okay?" the psychologist asks, bringing me back to the moment.

I speak calmly, disguising the pulsing ache. "I'm grateful that I got this time with him," I say quietly, hoping that expressing gratitude instead of despair makes me appear more stable.

My softened tone seems to work. "Let's get you ready for your next jump," she says, then guides me back inside.

Chapter Two

Andy

She's beautiful. And unlike many of my recent dates, she looks like her Hinge profile photo. She has the kind of striking beauty that turns heads. Big blue eyes set wide apart. Shimmering blonde hair that would make Barbie self-conscious. Even her name, Fiona, is beautiful.

In about five minutes, she'll mention *Christmas with the Kranks* and I'll hear about every scene, every line she loves, and she'll relate them to me breathlessly like she's a sports announcer giving me the play-by-play.

Then she'll try to convince me that she talks to ghosts. Regularly. After that she'll say that her psychic told her we're a great match, but that I harbored some "dark secrets." She hopes that secret isn't that I'm a vampire. We'll laugh about that. Over dessert she'll tell a harrowing account of meeting what she's sure was an alien at her cousin's barbecue.

Scratch that. The truth is, I don't remember exactly what she said about her cousin's barbecue because I'd been distracted. *Morose* might be a better word. Earlier that day, the thriller novel

I'd slaved over for fourteen months was rejected by the editor who'd already published five of my books. Her words had felt like a thousand swords impaling my heart: "We liked it. We just didn't love it." After that, exhaustion had crept into my bones, and I'd been unable to focus on anything.

"Are you okay?" Fiona asks.

"Sure, why?" I say, but the words come out slowly.

"You're crying."

I touch my face. Tears are rolling down my cheeks. A common side effect of the time travel.

"Sorry, I just need some air," I say, wiping my face. "Would you excuse me?"

I amble through the restaurant toward the front door. My mind is a still a mess, but this much I know: I've jumped into Café Fiore in my hometown of Ventura, California, a beach town that's about the size of renowned cities like Santa Barbara. As I pass by the hostess stand, I stop to glance at the date on the reservation screen on her computer. There it is. August 20, 2025.

My heart pounds so hard it's like a drumbeat in my chest. I've come three years into the past. I've hit the jackpot.

This is the summer I met Kate. The summer my world turned upside down.

I only have an hour in the past, so I hurry to the door. I place my hand on the doorknob and try to turn it, but it won't move. Have I lost strength? My skin pricks with anxiety. Every second matters. My patience frayed, I yank on the handle again.

The hostess runs up. "Sorry, is the door stuck again? Let me try for you."

She presses her slim frame against the door, pulls up on the handle, and flings it open.

The gentle summer wind, sweetened by honeysuckle, floats in, beckoning me. Outside, café lights crisscross the boulevard, and couples stroll beneath their warm glow.

I step over the threshold and begin to run. *There are only fifty-eight minutes left.*

I hurry through the four blocks to Kate's apartment, the distance feeling endless despite my speed.

My heart is thrumming double time as I imagine seeing her again. As her apartment building comes into view, reality sets in.

August 20. Kate and I haven't met yet. We haven't had our batting cage and Indian food first date on August 22. I haven't taken her to the karaoke bar on Main Street where I'll discover she can belt out a pop ballad with a voice like Taylor Swift. (Okay, I'm biased.) We haven't walked on Hobson Beach beneath the silvery moonlight.

She has no idea who I am.

* * *

"Buy Apple and Microsoft stock when you get there," my dad said when I told him I'd been granted one of the impossible-to-get travel slots.

My cousin Brad slipped me a list of all the World Series and Super Bowl winners in my lifetime so I could memorize them, bet on a game, and win big. A couple of thousand people on social media have given me the same advice.

But we can't get rich by knowing the future.

We can't bring any physical object from the past. Not our dad's antique watch. Or any sentimental item we've got our heart set on. We can't secret away the Willie Mays baseball card that's worth a quarter of a million dollars today. And no, I can't buy some valuable stock, squirrel it away in a safe deposit box, then look for it in when I return to the present.

It won't be there when I return to the future.

That's because the way we enter and exit the past creates a reset when we return. A whole row of quantum physicists headed by Dr. Fabio Costa at the University of Queensland explained the process at the Aeon Expeditions orientation, using the recent discovery of closed time–like curves, the theory of relativity, and some very complex math to demonstrate that whatever we jumpers do in the past will bear no effect on the future. I'll admit I didn't understand most of what they presented, but the gist of it is this:

No matter what we do in the past, the future we return to remains unchanged.

"Say you go back to spend an hour with your grandma," Dr. Costa said, projecting a giant, yet generic, photo of a smiling grandmother. "Every small decision you make creates variations. The things you talk about with her will be different than what happened the first time you lived through this event. In that hour, you might convince her to go for ice cream, which didn't happen the first time. You could even go somewhere new—anywhere—that didn't happen before. No matter what you do and what happens in that hour, when you return the future is never changed."

So why bother? If nothing I do here changes anything—if nothing I do here matters—why spend a small fortune for sixty minutes in the past?

Because I want one more hour with Kate.

In my present life, my girlfriend wants to move in together. Lauren's an architect at a firm that specializes in historic preservation, she has a love of books that rivals my own, and she likes to text me sweet messages during the day to tell me she's thinking about me. But when we were putting down the deposit on an apartment we planned to share, my hands shook so badly I could hardly sign my name. A week later, when she talked about getting a dog together, my heart pounded with panic, and I ended making up a ridiculous story about dog allergies to get out of making what felt like the next level of a commitment together. I finally had to admit to myself that as perfect as Lauren is, I had never been able to get over Kate Montano.

I'd met Kate at my friend Jonathan's party on August 21. I'd popped into the party, not planning to stay long, and presented Jonathan with a Bordeaux made by a seventh-generation winemaking family—exactly the kind of gift he expects. I was planning to sip some of the expensive Blanton's Bourbon he always served, stay for an hour or so, then make a swift and quiet exit.

My shot of bourbon in hand, I'd wandered into the living room where a woman in a red dress was playing Sinatra's "Fly Me to the Moon" at the piano, arranged to sound like a modern blend of swing and pop. I walked up beside her and sang softly, in what I hoped was a not-too-terrible voice:

You are all I long for, all I worship and adore.
In other words, please be true.

She turned to look at me, her face illuminated by the peachy glow of the candles on the piano. "Thanks for singing."

That's all she said. And yet, I felt something click, as if everything that had happened in my life before had been leading me to that very moment. I was held by the intensity of her eyes, unable to draw a breath.

"What would you like to hear next? Maybe something by Chet Baker?" she asked.

Sure, I wanted to say. Instead, I found myself gazing at her for a long moment, feeling strangely giddy, my usual charm replaced with fumbling awkwardness.

"What would you suggest?" I said, my face burning.

"How about 'There Will Never Be Another You?'"

I nodded and as she began to play, everything around me muted. The cocktail chatter. The clink of glasses. All I heard was the music she made with that piano. I'll never forget the feeling of being with this beautiful stranger and the overwhelming sense that her music was weaving the story of our future life together.

This is the memory I have on forever repeat.

Kate was brightness and effervescence in a time when everything in my life was barely slogging along. Nothing I wrote seemed ready or good. My word count dwindled, and I began erasing sentence after sentence of my work-in-progress. Unhappy with a paragraph, doubting the adjectives. I'd take hours on one scene because the words weren't flowing. I'd begun to think that I'd lost all my storytelling abilities and that I was doomed to find another career, but I couldn't fathom what that might be. I'd scared myself by looking at job listings and realizing I'm not qualified for anything else but the thing I could no longer seem to do.

My last girlfriend had dumped me four months earlier, saying I was depressing and no longer fun. She was right. My every emotion hinged on whether my writing was going well, how book sales were going, what my royalty statements looked like, or the state of my reviews on Goodreads and Amazon. And since those things were miserable then, I drank too much and generally moped around my apartment unable to find the motivation to do much of anything except write.

After our get-to-know-you first date, Kate was on my mind even when we weren't together, and when we were, I felt my heart leaping out of my chest. It's a cliché to say that I never felt more alive, but that's the only way to describe it. When I was with her, I became fun again. In our five days together, we made pasta at two in the morning and tried paddleboarding at Mondos Beach. We got drunk in the tasting room of a craft winery in town and dried out while listening to Puccini and eating sushi in her living room. I smiled all the time because I couldn't believe something this good was happening to me.

My writing flowed. Day after day I'd bang out two thousand words, far more than my usual. It felt as though I was summoning a story from another realm.

And the music. It floated through her apartment all the time. Cool jazz. Elegant string quartets. Homesick blues. Solemn Gregorian chants. Big sweeping concertos. Gut-wrenching opera. Some of it I loved, and much of it felt strange and new, even though it'd been around for centuries, but all of it was crazy and wonderful when I was with her.

Five days later, we were walking on sun-drenched Faria Beach and I told her that I was falling for her.

Who falls for a girl in less than a week? That's the stuff of romance novels, not real life. Before meeting Kate, I'd thought love and romance were commodities manufactured to sell books, songs on Apple Music, and greeting cards. I'd have scoffed at anyone who told me they felt this way about someone after only knowing them a few days.

I was utterly wrong about that. And this part I remember with crystal clarity. "I'm falling for you too," she said as she wrapped her arms around my neck, enveloping me in her jasmine scent as the tide rolled in beneath our feet.

I thought we were becoming a couple.

Until she didn't show up for the picnic she'd planned for Emma Wood State Beach on August 26. At first, I thought I'd misunderstood the date or the time. I even walked thirty minutes up the coast to Solimar Beach in case I was in the wrong place. She wasn't there either.

Then she didn't respond to any texts or calls. Emails went unanswered. Our relationship was new enough that I didn't know how to contact any of her friends.

Sometimes I'd panic and think that our whirlwind romance was as imaginary as the characters I wrote about in my novels. I'd flip through the dozens of photos of us on my phone to remind myself that what we had was real.

Weeks sped by and I found myself filled with the ache of missing her, wondering what happened but feeling powerless to do anything about it. I imagined her calling to say that she'd been in an accident and was laid up in a hospital somewhere, so I answered every call, even the ones that were obviously spam. She never reached out.

"Face it, Andy," my friend Jonathan had said. "You've been ghosted. Happens to the best of us."

After that, I went in for therapy sessions, trying to get over her. How hard could that be? I had only known her for five days.

"We're wired for love," my therapist had said. "What you're feeling is just a cocktail of happy hormones—dopamine, oxytocin, serotonin—which create a sensation that's a bit like a hit of cocaine. That's why it's so difficult to break the addiction to her. These feelings will fade the more time you're not together anymore."

I tried to make that be true. Really tried. I tossed away any reminders of her. Even the striped T-shirt she'd left in my apartment, which still smelled of her perfume. I'd stopped listening to sad breakup songs. I hung out with friends, threw myself into my writing, and spent a week on a beach in Mexico, but none of that made me forget her. I'd always find myself wondering if I'd done something different, would we still be together?

Eventually I used those feeling of desperation and addiction and loneliness to bang out a novel that ended up being a smash success, hitting all the bestseller lists in English-speaking countries before being translated around the rest of the world. *He's Gone* was unlike anything I'd written before, a thriller based on a true story that played out a mile from my apartment the winter after Kate disappeared. A dead body washed up at the pier in Ventura, California. In real life, the discovery of the decomposed, bloated body with a gunshot wound to his neck sent a shock wave through sleepy Ventura. In a place best known for its easygoing beach lifestyle, finding a dead body was unimaginable, something you might expect in a fetid corner of a big city. Not here.

The police couldn't make any identification of the man or come up with any suspects. In my novel, a cop who'd been dumped by "the one" investigates the crime and realizes he's living vicariously through the details he's uncovers about the dead man's love life. And, unlike the rest of my novels, with their happily-ever-after romantic endings, this one didn't end with the cop finding a new love—I was done with romance forever—but instead closed with a gruesome twist that readers loved.

The success of the book gave me more opportunities to meet women at book signings and readings. I'd tried my hand at dating. Or something that resembles that. I quickly tired of the first date and the more daunting second date. I just couldn't power through the awkward introduction phase. It'd been so easy with Kate.

I thought I'd deleted everything that could remind me of us. Then I found some photos on my phone and flipped through them. *We were so happy.*

Now, standing in front of her apartment building, the memories fade. I pinch myself. If I'm lucky, I'm about to experience being with her *again.*

To anyone else, the six-story monolith coated in a smooth light-gray stucco looks like just another apartment complex along this palm-lined street. But to me, it's filled with our memories, as if the things that happened here are stored in its walls and windows and I can play them back. My eyes fall on the arched doorway framed by decorative tiles out front, and the memories come rushing in: Our first kiss beneath its sheltering canopy well after midnight. The morning I surprised her on the doorstep with *Great Expectations*, a novel she'd told me she'd always wanted to read.

My head spins, and the tears come fast, stinging my eyes. Everyone cries within the first minutes of their jump. But these tears aren't just a side effect.

I glance up at her apartment building. Golden light filters from her second-floor window. White curtains flutter in the summer breeze, reaching into the night, an invitation, it seems.

I watch her shadow pass by the window and my throat tightens. The first time around, we'd spent five days together, practically inseparable. Tonight, she doesn't know me. We're back at square one, and all my plans feel like a blur of harebrained ideas that will never work.

Without Jonathan's party, how will I get her to talk to me?

Chapter Three

Logan

~

I feel dangerous today.

I'm rising to the occasion. Nothing can stop me.

Today is the day I'll make shit happen.

If my boss will shut the hell up.

My phone pings with a notification that my AutoDriver will be here in three minutes to take me crosstown. And this is the very moment my loud-mouthed supervisor decides to rant about my Aeon Expeditions trip. In the six months since I was selected, the guy never yakked about the trip once. Sure, he complained about me getting to work late and put me down for taking too long to help customers, but mostly the guy seemed to forget I even existed. Now, with the seconds winding down to the big moment, he stands over me while I finish up at my desk, a deliberate power move to make me feel small.

"Where'd you get the money anyway? You got a side hustle going on I should know about?"

"I have ways." I shrug like it was easy to come up with the money even though the truth is I've tapped most of my savings and maxed out two credit cards for this trip.

"Waste of money," he says. "Five figures for what? Sixty minutes in the past? That's some bullshit there."

My phone pings again. The AutoDriver is out front.

Rage on. Stay focused.

I make a move toward the elevator, but he blocks my way. "They're using you, Logan. You're a guinea pig."

"You don't know what you're talking about," I say with conviction.

Inside the elevator, my confidence fades. My boss is a blowhard who drinks too much Jim Beam, talks too much about conspiracy theories, and mocks anyone who disagrees with him, but he's right about this one thing. I am broken. And why they've chosen me out of the millions of applicants makes no sense.

First off, I answered yes on three health eligibility questions. Even one "yes" usually meant an automatic rejection.

Do you have a chronic medical condition, including a history of mental illness?

Have you ever had a concussion, brain injury, or any brain or spine surgery?

Have you ever had any dependency on drugs, alcohol, or tobacco?

And I failed the fitness requirement of being able to climb seven flights of stairs in ninety seconds.

Not surprisingly, my application was declined. I called in sick to my job at the courier company and spent the day sulking and scrolling through story after story of successful jumps—every single one of them flaunting how the experience changed their lives.

My anger and jealousy fueled a couple of half-baked ideas to convince Aeon Expeditions to change their minds. I didn't have to put any of them into play because two days later, an email swooped into my inbox that said: *Your Aeon Expeditions trip application has been moderated and approved.*

Now I'm lying inside a ginormous machine Aeon Expeditions has named the Sam 5000 that looks like an MRI on steroids married a cement mill. Because of what my boss said, I'm thinking about guinea pigs. Specifically, the guinea pig I had when I was eight. Rocko took a big risk, busted out of his cage, got trapped in the toilet, and died. Hope that isn't my fate here.

The room is meat locker cold and not even the stack of heated blankets they heap on me can stop my teeth from chattering. Travel to the past is not yet an exact science. They can't yet control into what time we jump. We could find ourselves in the middle of having our diaper changed, reciting our wedding vows, or slogging through an hour-long algebra exam.

I heard about one guy who jumped and found himself on the crapper in an outhouse in Mexico on a family vacation. He had food poisoning and spent the entire sixty minutes in misery. He asked for his money back, but Aeon refused. Nothing's guaranteed.

The lights dim, then blink out.

It's pitch dark before a jump. My heart thumps in the presence of such darkness. My eyes open wide to collect light and when not a single particle of light penetrates, my brain makes up light. Stuff.

Flickers of white light pulse at the fringes of what is my vision. These grow into simple geometric patterns, then images floating around the room. There's a bathtub being steered by an old man in a metal helmet. A parade of squirrels wearing backpacks and snowshoes marches across a snowy field. The hallucinations are so consuming they look and feel like my brain has exploded.

And there's a smell. Spices. Fresh fruit. Vegetables. Scents that thicken to the point where they feel like I can touch them.

Some travelers believe that if you think about *when* you want to go to during this pre-jump sequence, you'll jump to that time. The scientists say this isn't possible. This isn't a simulation. You're not walking through your memories. Your consciousness is traveling back in time into your own body.

I don't really understand most of it, but the way the engineers explained it, our consciousness is converted into a signal that can be moved through space-time without the energy requirements it would take to move our bodies. In the same way we use signals to communicate to our machines on Mars, our consciousness—complete with all our memories and emotions—can travel into our bodies in the past.

At first only the billionaires and a few major celebrities did it. Movie stars. Basketball champions. Tech giants. The price tag was so steep that no one else could afford it. When every one of them returned safely from the first Aeon Expeditions jumps, investors rushed to finance it, the tech improved, costs dropped, and for the first time, mere mortals like me could dream about being selected to take a trip.

The machine lurches and spins for a moment. At least, it feels like that. Even though in reality it hasn't moved at all. My consciousness is the only thing moving.

Bang. Inside my head is a loud sound, like fireworks going off. And then I'm impossibly hot, as if the temperature shot up two hundred degrees in five seconds. Then I feel the worst pain in my chest as my body feels like it weighs a thousand pounds, a massive stone hurtling through space, and slamming into . . . what?

I blink my eyes open and I'm at a street corner. *Standing.*

I feel the frenetic beating of my heart. All of this is impossible. That's what my brain says.

It's before sunrise, and the air is crisp and cool. The horizon is lit up neon orange, giving the rugged mountain range in the distance an iridescent glow. The mountain peaks seem to touch the sky, reaching toward the heavens.

It's so quiet that I can hear the steady buzz of a neon sign behind me. I turn to look.

MOTEL: Mt. Whitney

I've hit the jackpot. I am, at most, a fifteen-minute drive away from the trailhead to the highest mountain in the United States, Mount Whitney. I draw in a deep breath of the dry mountain air, a mixture of pine needles and sage, and choke up in disbelief. I'm dizzy with wonder.

I notice a small group of people gathered down the block, backpacks slung over their shoulders. I'm wearing one too. Then the details rush in. I'm about to get on a bus to take me to the trailhead to Mount Whitney's 14,505-foot peak.

I walk a few steps toward the group. I feel like I'm walking on air, my steps light and unsteady, as if I might float away any moment. A quick glance at my legs and my hiking boot–clad shoes, and I start to cry. Big, hysterical, blubbering sobs that make me stop in my tracks.

I am walking.

I'm someone who rarely cries, so these thick tears are foreign and yet strangely inevitable at the same time. They've been locked inside since the old me died on August 25, 2025. The day I became paralyzed.

* * *

I'm racing down the street toward the bus, my legs pumping as fast and as hard as my body will take me. My feet hit the pavement, the bracing mountain air whips through my hair, and a single, intoxicating thought slips into my head: "I am running!"

Rage on.

I scurry up the stairs onto the bus. Some dude has chucked his backpack in the aisle, so I leap over it, a feat that after three years of being unable to run or jump feels like utter magic.

I head down the aisle and scan the faces of the passengers. One woman with short blonde hair scans the tattoos on my arms and neck, eyes me suspiciously, then quickly looks back at her phone.

I'm used to people ignoring me, especially girls. Living in a wheelchair, strangers looked past me, often straight through me, not seeing that I was still someone who wanted the same things they did. Even my old friends have begun to look past me, moving on, too busy to make time for me anymore.

I slide next to a guy about my age with brown hair pulled into a sad knot at the back of his head. His heavy eyelids make me think he'd partied too much last night, a crime that he'll pay for on this morning's hike.

"Hey," I say. "What's the date?"

"Saturday," he says.

"What month? What day?"

"Is this a test or something?" He shrugs. "August twentieth."

Then it hits me like a ton of bricks. This is the last big hike of my life.

The bus races along the highway in the dawn light, hurtling me miles away from the jump-in. Crap. I can't go too far because we're not supposed to go more than ten miles from where we are jumped. That's to ensure that Aeon Expeditions can bring us back. They have to locate our life-signature, a signal unique to each of us, not unlike a fingerprint but on a subatomic level. The technology is in the early stages, so finding that digital fingerprint is like sifting through octillions of grains of sand on a beach. We're easier to find if we stay close to where we came in. In the orientation, they'd told us that we'd experience excruciating pain if we went more than ten miles from the jump-in point.

I yank the cord above my head. "Can I get off here?" I shout.

Several other hikers turn to stare at me. We're in the middle of the dusty scrub and chaparral, still miles from the trailhead. Only a crazy person would ask to be dropped off here.

"Only stop is the trailhead," the driver shouts back.

I brace myself for the pain. Can it be worse than the trauma of being in a broken body, of being exhausted, or sensing strange things that aren't actually happening to my legs? Could it be worse than feeling like I'm in an ice block from the waist down?

We get closer to the trailhead, and I feel that familiar flutter of excitement in my chest that I get every time I'm about to start a hike or a swim or a ride. But no pain.

They lied to us.

* * *

Holy shit, I didn't expect this.

It's five in the morning and I'm on the hike to Mount Whitney on one of the bazillion switchbacks that will ultimately lead me up to Whitney's summit. It's surreal looking out from the pitch-black trail in the middle of the night and seeing lots of tiny little lights in a line spiraling up the mountain.

This is because many people start their day hikes to Whitney early, and the whole trail is more like a party bus than a wilderness hike in solitude. Ahead of us are a couple of hours of steep climbs and descents that will pummel even the most experienced hikers and require near-constant decision-making to navigate an endless gauntlet of rocks and chunks of granite.

I didn't dare dream that I'd get to relive this trip. I'd have been happy if I were swimming in a pool or riding a wave on my surfboard. Even a stroll down the street would have been better than where I was.

Problem is, my body is a bundle of misery. I've got acute mountain sickness—nausea, dizziness, and a pounding headache—and the only ways to get over it is to slow down or leave this line and hike down a thousand feet or so. My legs, my stellar physical fitness—none of that matters because even Olympic athletes get AMS.

"You doing okay?" a guy behind me asks. I turn around and in the predawn light, I can't make out anything but his red flannel shirt illuminated by his flashlight. "You're slowing down a lot."

"Yeah," I say. "AMS flare-up."

He withdraws a metal canister from his pack. "Here, take a couple of hits of oxygen."

I place the plastic mask over my mouth, press the lever and a few seconds of cool oxygen fill my lungs, refreshing me with each breath. Still, my body feels heavy, like I have a hangover.

"Hate to say this, but if you're already feeling like crap, you shouldn't go any farther."

I'm sick of people telling me all the things I shouldn't do. Why do others assume anything about me? In the future, I'll lose a kidney and suffer a dislocated left clavicle, eight broken ribs, and a severed spine, all of which will leave me in intensive care for thirty-three days and in rehab for another seventy. I'll spend months wallowing in dark places, cursing and screaming at my broken body, fighting for my life and limbs and organs, visualizing again and again my body slicing through the waves in the ocean, my feet scaling a mountain, and my legs cranking through a hundred-mile bike ride in a day.

Some stranger with an oxygen can isn't going to gaslight me out of this. "I'm fine."

When I'd completed this hike the first time around, I've been the first in the group to summit, blasting my way there and back in under five hours. But the way I'm feeling, I've got to take it easy. I slow down so much that eventually I'm toward the back of the line where all I can do is concentrate on putting one foot in front of the other, avoiding rock scree, my every step deliberate and precise. I practice gathering my energy and letting it go. Gather. Release. Gather. Release. This is a trick that works for me even in a wheelchair.

Then I try to act like I'm going to battle against this mountain. To fight something mean. It's working. And in my haze of relief, another feeling floats through. Amazement. They haven't extracted me. More than an hour has zipped by and I'm still here with full use of my legs.

"Hey," a woman's voice behind me says. "You have any idea how much farther it is to the top?"

My head whips around, and a girl around my age is talking to me. Sweat glistens on her face, but she smiles through it. She wears a down jacket with the hood pulled over her head. And hiking pants. The kind the athletic-wear stores sell as "performance and style," but they're flimsy and won't last for more than a hike or two.

"Maybe eighty or ninety more," I say.

"Hoping that's minutes, not miles?" She sighs. "I'm terrible at this hiking stuff."

"No one can be terrible at hiking."

She may think she's terrible at hiking, but I suck at this small talk stuff. Still, she laughs.

"Yes, they can, and you've met her. I'm Haley." She puts out her hand and shakes mine. "Starving. Should've brought more snacks. You got anything to share?"

"I've got some chocolate that might help the next mile or so go easier."

"Belgian chocolate?"

I look up at her. "You think I'm on Mount Whitney with Belgian chocolate?"

She laughs. "I'll take whatever you got."

I shrug off my backpack and dig to the bottom, moving aside the lightweight foldable saw I always carry and past the baggie of dried birch bark I use as a fire starter on longer hikes, and pull out the bar of Hershey's chocolate.

I'm blown away she's talking to me. She's not looking past me, like so many girls do when they see me in a wheelchair. And she's not giving me a look of pity or talking to me like I'm a child.

I break off a piece and hand it to her. "Let's get you caught up to the rest of the group. Don't want you falling further behind."

"That might not be so terrible," she says.

After years of being invisible in a wheelchair, I don't know what to make of her comment. Is it a compliment? A joke?

An owl hoots from high above a nearby fir tree. "See, even the owl agrees with me." She smiles at me. Straight white teeth.

Why don't I smile back? Or at least laugh. I'm no good at small talk.

"I don't think I'm going to make it to the summit," she says.

"Give it time and your feet will find their own way on the path," I say, softening my tone. "You have to let go of the pain and the fear that you won't make it."

"Thanks, Yoda."

I turn to look at her and, in the soft morning light, I'm captured by her face. It feels like I've just woken from a long nightmare and I'm seeing things, everything, for the first time. The last three years in the chair, I'd given up hope that I'd ever know what it was like to have a girl like me again. The few times I hung out at a bar or party, it was as if I existed in a separate dimension from everyone else. It'd been almost impossible to talk to anyone, much less date anyone.

"I was making a *Star Wars* joke," she says.

"Yeah, I get it."

"It's just that you sound mighty wise about this hiking thing. You got a name?" she asks.

"Logan. Sandoval."

She pushes her hands into her jacket pockets. "You walk like you were born in these mountains."

"Not exactly. I hike a lot, though. Bike and swim too. How about you?"

"Absolutely none of that."

"None of that? Then what brings you here?"

She sucks in a deep breath. "I'm on a kick to do things that scare the heck out of me. And a hike where there'll be coyotes and mountain lions in the dark kind of fits the bill."

"We're up too high to see any coyotes. Probably not going to run into any mountain lions either."

"Well, they exist in my imagination," she says with a laugh. "And how I convinced myself to do this hike was that if I made it back alive, I would kiss the beautiful, flat cement sidewalk at the entrance. And then I'll treat myself to my favorite food."

"Belgian chocolate?"

"Tacos. Tacos are kind of my love language."

"Mine too."

She smiles at me. "Will you look at that, I *do* have something in common with a mountain man."

The way she says *mountain man* sounds like she might be into me. I'd forgotten what it feels like to be attractive to anyone, and I'm liking this more than I expected. Now I'm just gazing at her and letting the silence grow. *Say something!*

"See, you took your mind off that incline," I manage. "And now we're almost there."

Her eyes widen and she stares over my shoulder. "Will you look at that?" she whispers.

I turn around and maybe twenty feet away is a deer, grazing on the chaparral. He looks up at us briefly then goes back to his meal. Like we're not even there. The rest of the hiking group is too far ahead of us to see him, so it feels like he's giving a little show just for the two of us.

"I've never seen a deer this close," she says.

Truth is, I've seen many deer up close like this, but experiencing it with her, I can't even describe the feeling. Like the closest thing to magic.

"Did you know that deer have great night vision because they have tissue in their eyes that acts like a mirror and magnifies light?"

My smile comes easily now. "Who are you, Steve Irwin's daughter or something?"

"I kind of binge watch the Discovery Channel."

The wind picks up then, rushing past our ears and whistling through the rocks. The deer takes off, disappearing into the brush.

"I think seeing a deer in the wild just shot to the top of my favorite things list," she says as we start hiking again, pressing against the wind. "How about you? What's on your favorite things list?"

"Waiting in line at the DMV," I say, a lame attempt at making a joke.

"Funny," she says. "Although did you know there's a secret DMV office across the street from the capital in Sacramento? It's for lawmakers only. Room 121."

"How do you know random stuff like that?"

"I'm a bartender. At Celestine in Ventura. People tell you crazy stuff when they've had a few drinks. Most things I ignore—like their dreams about Freddy Krueger or the guy who claimed he installed all the locks at the White House—but some of what they say is interesting. And I file it away."

"So, what else is on your favorites list?" I ask.

"Jigsaw puzzles. Big ones. You into that?"

"Haven't done a puzzle since I was in elementary school."

"Didn't think so. Someone who hikes in the mountains like you do, well, you look like this is where you belong."

She's right about me. But suddenly the thought of doing a puzzle with her seems attractive. Very. And the way she's paying attention to me helps me take a big step out of my comfort zone. "I might want to try my hand at it."

Her expression shifts. Like she's maybe imagining us doing a puzzle together and liking the idea.

In the distance we hear cheering and joyful shouts echoing against the sky. Some of the group has already summited, but I'm not disappointed that we're so far behind.

Haley points ahead to the trail that's all but disappeared and the steep and craggy incline.

"I don't know if I can make it," she says, her chest heaving. The air is colder here, and her exhales are accompanied by visible puffs of steam. "My heart is already jumping out of my chest."

I hold out my hand to her. "You'll make it. I'll make sure of it."

She hesitates a moment, then slips her hand in mine. Even through our gloves, her hand feels buzzy and warm. My heartbeat, already pounding from the altitude, quickens even more. The last thirty yards are practically a straight incline. Then we get to the part that's known as the "chute to the summit," which requires us to use our hands and feet up a narrow gully. I hike up a few steps, then extend my hands to her, offering her a firm grip to pull up on. My muscles are burning and my lungs are straining to breathe the impossibly thin air, so I know it must be hard on her too, but somehow she channels her inner mountain goat and makes it to the summit.

The view takes my breath away. It's hard to know where to look—there are panoramic views of vast forests of pine and fir with jagged mountain peaks rising high in the sky in every direction. In the distance, some of the mountains have patches of snow and ice even in August. My eyes scan across the smooth surface of Lone Pine Lake and the feeling of awe is indescribable, even though I've done this hike before.

"I'm never going to forget this," she whispers.

I turn to look at her and feel like I've taken a cheap shot to the chest. She's removed her hood and she's beautiful. The first time around, I didn't even notice her on the trail. I'd been so caught up with pushing to be the first to summit Mount Whitney that I'd missed out on all of this. Sometimes I'm an idiot.

"If we make it back down the mountain, want to have tacos with me?" she asks.

"We'll make it down the mountain."

"Is that a yes?"

"You sure you want me to have tacos with me? I mean, I don't want to get in the way of your victory celebration. And that kiss with the sidewalk you're planning."

She laughs. "You gave me chocolate. Of course I do."

Chapter Four

Brooke

I am half alive. Any sense I've ever had of being a person someone might love has vanished. Sometimes I feel like a zombie that's been stabbed in the heart with a pitchfork, but rather than dying, I just stagger about aimlessly. I want to disappear from the present where I can walk in daylight's brightest gold, but all I feel is muted shades of gray.

That's what I wrote as part of my application, one of millions that Aeon Expeditions receives each year. Most people hoping for a shot at sixty minutes in the past write long, well-crafted essays about tragedies and loss. Longing and nostalgia. A cottage industry of coaches will help you polish your essay to help improve your odds of being chosen. Because even if you can afford the cost, you still must become one of the .001 percent accepted.

I was rejected. And not just because my essay was maudlin. The notice read:

Your application was noncompliant with our acceptance policies. Specifically for the following reason: We currently do not permit travelers who have served time in prison.

I knew my 900-day stint in jail made me ineligible, but I'd hoped my story would be compelling enough for them to reconsider. Unfortunately, a rejection was permanent with no possibility for appeal, or so the email said.

Yet, a week and two days after my rejection, I received a notice indicating that my status had been modified.

Congratulations. Your Aeon Expeditions trip application has been moderated and approved.

I searched online and couldn't find anyone who'd admitted to being rejected then was later approved. It had to be a mistake, but I wanted to see how far I could push it before Aeon Expeditions caught on. I clicked *Accept*.

I worried my way through every one of the orientation sessions, anxious that someone on the admissions committee would discover the error and demand that I leave. I had crazy dreams where men in uniform removed me from the meetings while all the other travelers looked on in shock. None of that happened. I'd sailed through the training sessions without anyone questioning my eligibility.

Now I'm sitting beneath a cascading crystal chandelier in Aeon Expedition's elegant, lavender-scented lobby. A video of Aeon founder Mark Saunders plays on one of the large monitors. "Here at Aeon Expeditions," he says, "we don't change time. But time changes us. What will you discover when you look back with fresh eyes? The most important part of your journey happens after your hour is over."

My heart races as I realize I'm less than thirty minutes away from my jump, if I can successfully get through the final questions with the admissions representative, Jordan.

"Have you taken any medications in the last twenty-four hours?" she asks.

"No," I answer softly. It wasn't easy. Without my sleeping pills, I'd only managed to eke out two hours of sleep.

Jordan tilts her head and stares at her screen. She pushes a lock of beachy blonde hair away from her face. "Huh. The system won't allow me to submit your responses."

My heart pounds a thousand times a minute. *This is when they're going to find out. This is when they kick you out.*

She taps a few more keys, frowning, and looks at me through red-framed glasses over sharp blue eyes. "Something's not right."

Is my trip canceled?

"Oh, I get it now," she says finally. "It looks like you haven't indicated your designated driver."

I sigh with relief. We need a live human driver—not an AutoDriver—for the ride home because every traveler is seriously disoriented when they return. So much so that early travelers had gotten lost in the quite standard bathrooms on the premises and had to call the travel coaches to help them find the way out. Some jumpers had insisted they were fine, driven out of the parking lot, and promptly crashed their cars.

"James Dalton," I answer. "My husband," I say brightly, although James isn't thrilled that I'm embarking on this trip. He thinks we have more pressing things to work on together and he's right. But an Aeon Expeditions trip is so difficult to obtain—and nontransferable—that he ultimately agreed I had to take it.

Jordan confirms his contact information, then presents me with a white plastic bracelet printed with a scannable code.

She snaps it on my wrist. "Congratulations, you're on your way."

For the first time in a very long while, I'm filled with anticipation and excitement about what's ahead. My hopes aren't too grand. All I want is one hour of relief. One hour where I can escape the pain and the guilt and numbness of being me.

Popular wisdom says that rehashing the past keeps you stuck there, but Aeon's research disagrees. Underneath the tagline, "Revisiting the past is the way to move forward," Aeon publishes glowing testimonials from people who say their lives got better after their jump. I want that.

"This is an expensive and, at best, temporary fix," my therapist had warned me. "It might even be dangerous for you. There are other treatments that will help you."

I'd tried them, and nothing worked for very long. Cognitive behavioral therapy. EMDR. I'd experimented with Amazonian ayahuasca. I'd played the drums to reach a trance. None of them dulled the persistent hopelessness. Sure, they softened my anger and irritability and smoothed out my mood swings, but nothing could change the reality that I'm nothing less than a monster.

How could I be capable of something so unforgivable?

A feeling of unease settles on me as Jordan escorts me into the dimly lit, sterile environment where my jump will take place. The machine is a monstrous, cylindrical beast with a tunnel so narrow that I've read that it has even induced claustrophobia in submarine veterans who are accustomed to tight spaces.

A technician in blue scrubs instructs me to lie down on the metal table and with an efficient click, the table slides into the gaping maw of the machine. Seconds later, the technician exits, his reassuring presence replaced by a roaring silence. My heart pounds.

The giant vault of a room slams into darkness. All color has vanished, and I am staring into complete and utter blackness.

The machine roars to life, emitting bone-rattling thuds, screeches, and a high-pitched whine. Suddenly I feel like an invisible vise is clamped around my neck. My body is trembling, like it did when I was in labor, and my heart feels like it's going to explode out of my chest. Something is wrong.

I feel like I'm going to die.

The room spins or perhaps I'm the one spinning. I cannot tell up from down. All sounds have disappeared.

I feel the rhythmic clenching of my heart and my lungs ballooning inside my ribs.

I am dying.

In front of my eyes are abstract patterns, bright amoebas, yellow clouds, and animal prints. Hallucinations. Even when I squeeze my eyes shut, I still see them.

A drop of what I think is water falls from above and touches my forehead, and I flinch as if I've been hit by a hammer.

I blink and I'm sitting on a soft leather couch. I'm in the living room of my home on Hillcrest Drive. It's a beautiful space with cathedral ceilings, a limestone fireplace, and a forged iron chandelier soaring above.

I'm surrounded by dozens of people dressed for some happy occasion. Judging from the short sleeves and summer tans, it's late summer in California. A woman in red is playing the piano.

I glance at my phone on the coffee table: August 20, 2025.

I've come three years into the past, where I'm hosting my end-of-summer party—our last gathering before school and work schedules scatter us all.

A surge of anxiety and disappointment. I'd longed to jump to a time where my mistakes were years ahead of me. But they are less than five days away.

The man next to me on the couch is wearing a silky blue shirt. Armani. He has thick wavy hair and handsome features, eyes a steely blue. In his right hand is a glass of whiskey on the rocks, untouched. He's the boyfriend of someone here, but I can't remember who.

I also can't hear what he's saying. I think he says something about a dragon, but that doesn't make sense. This could be because the room is crowded with so many people. I also sense that my hearing is hushed, as though every sound is being piped through a metal straw.

Aeon Expeditions warned us that it takes a few moments for everything to settle in. Some jumpers have trouble with their eyesight or hearing. Others struggle with balance. Everyone has a tough time speaking in the first few minutes.

They urge us to say just a couple of words when we arrive. Baby steps. Not too fast or you'll sound like you're drunk. Or having a stroke.

I feel someone touch me on the shoulder, and I turn to see my friend Isabella handing me a glass of white wine. "You look like you need this," she says with a smile, then disappears back into the party.

I set the wine down. In my present state, I don't dare take even a sip.

I'm a stranger in my own body. I glance at my hands, and they look like they always have, down to the freckles on my left wrist, but they don't feel like me. My mouth feels dry, my face flushed, as if I'm running a fever.

And yet, I feel like myself again. Myself. After three years of profound sadness, and the lowest depths of self-loathing, I feel . . . normal. The perpetual knot in my stomach, the tension in my forearms, the nausea—all of it is gone.

I don't have to wait for the meds to kick in. Or slog through an hour with my therapist to banish the deep vein of shame.

My spirits soar. I am me again.

Suddenly the sounds rush in. The man in front of me is telling me about a sushi place he's just discovered, not a dragon. The woman at the piano is playing a Frank Sinatra song. "Fly Me to the Moon"? In the corner by the window, a group of friends are laughing about something my friend Amy is saying.

How I love the sounds of a party.

My eyes scan the room, past the faces of my friends gathered here, sharing jokes, gossiping, and catching up on each other's news, until I find the ones I've been aching to see.

My husband, James, is sitting next to my daughter, their faces warmed by the soft evening light filtering through the bay window. She's only eight here, wearing the pink floral dress my friend Alba made for her, and whispering something into James's ear that's making him smile.

My heart squeezes. *This is what it's like to be with them before . . .*

A choked moan escapes my lips, and then I feel the sting of tears on my cheeks. I'm told this happens to every single jumper.

Uncontrollable tears. A side effect of the journey. But it's more than that for me.

I see my life as it was. And I realize.

I had everything.

* * *

My friends insist on making plans. A dinner party at the new Italian restaurant to celebrate Claire and Steve's twentieth wedding anniversary. A girls-only trip to Santa Barbara. As my sixty minutes ticks away, I make plans for a future I won't be living.

It's difficult to relive years in the past. I don't always remember what happened in the days before this party. Most of us have incomplete memories of the things we've said to our friends or any plans we've made or problems we might have shared. These simple details are the things we forget. The fluff of life that our minds discard in favor of memories with more significance.

My friends run down their weekly efforts to stay in shape, debating the merits of gym memberships, personal trainers, and Pelotons, and their voices rise when they chronicle their mammograms, colonoscopies, and hearing tests.

We're grateful for everything good that happens to us. And proud. We're holding down jobs while raising kids, taking care of meals, doctor's appointments, meetings with teachers, and braving the monotony of the driving to and from soccer practice or music lessons.

We don't dwell long talking about monotony. Not when there are parties ahead and so much to dish about. There's the wine-soaked end-of-summer party Brad and Megan Kaplan always throw at their beach house, which has now become a compound because they bought the house next door too.

"And don't forget Lisa's party on the twenty-fifth," my friend Juliette says, sending a chill through my body.

August 25th is the last day I'll know what happiness feels like.

She prattles on, but I'm barely listening. My heart is pounding, aching and painful, with the knowledge of what lies ahead. "She hired the owner of Firestone Walker Brewery to bring a selection of craft beers for a tasting. Craft beer is on trend, I think. You'll be there?"

She stops, expecting an answer.

"I don't think so," I say. But how will I explain why I want to skip a party for a friend I've known for twenty years? "James and I have other plans."

She looks at me in surprise. From across the room, I see Olivia yawn and slip out of the living room.

"Would you excuse me?" I ask, putting a stop to any questions. "I want to put Olivia to bed."

I hurry to catch up with Olivia, winding my way through the party and murmuring to my guests along the way:

Good to see you.

I'm so glad you're here.

We need to catch up soon.

I'm putting on an act for all of them, pretending everything is fine even though I know that five days from now—August 25—I'll do something that will shock every one of them.

I finally manage to slip out of the living room, drifting through the rest of the house. A decade of happiness is here in the hushed dining room where James and I hosted countless brunches and Thanksgiving dinners at the long fruitwood table that once belonged to my grandparents. We'd bring in branzino, rockfish, and salmon from the restaurant I own and present course after course of oysters, chowders, salads, and pastas until well after midnight when Olivia and our friends protested that they couldn't eat another morsel.

And the reason we bought this house was the kitchen, a dream space for someone like me who'd always wanted to open a restaurant someday. A sleek new oven with a steam function for baking bread. A pantry the size of a bathroom. This is where I taught Olivia to bake her first cake. Where she brought her friends to make lemonade from the Meyer lemons we grew in the backyard. And this is where the dream of opening a restaurant began, first with a few recipes I'd created and perfected, then later with blueprints and designs that James and I rolled out on these marble countertops and marked up until we finally landed on the layout of a thoroughly modern *Cheers*-style bar area to attract the younger crowd but also a section of cozy booths where families and friends could linger.

I rush upstairs and pass by the small office that overlooks the garden. The scent of mint wafts through an open window, and I stop in my tracks, sinking into my life in the past. I glance over the framed photos of my life with James and Olivia that line the sideboard beneath the window and can't help but marvel at who I was when I'd lived this life. Someone who was determined to get what she wanted: a married life, a child, a dream restaurant, and a beautiful home. Someone who was loved by so many.

There's a photo of me with James and Olivia, snapped on a beach in Hawaii. Our sun-kissed faces aren't looking at the camera but at each other, laughing about something I can't remember. I always feel the reality of time's undertow in this photo. In the brief instant the photographer snapped it, I knew I would look back on this moment someday and wish to relive it.

We led idyllic lives then. In the evenings, we walked with Olivia on this quiet residential block of single-family homes. We passed out cookies baked at the restaurant to neighbors. On Sunday mornings, Olivia would set up a lemonade or ice cream stand with her friends, then we rounded them up and headed a few blocks to the beach, where they built sandcastles until the sun set.

"Everyone's wondering where you went," my friend Isabella says. I whirl around to see her standing in the doorway.

"I'm on my way to find Olivia. To tuck her in."

"James just carried her up to her bedroom," she says. "She kept nodding off, even though she really wants to stay awake."

I race down the hall to find her.

* * *

My daughter is beautiful.

It's not because of her big blue eyes or her freckles, the last glimmer of her childhood sprinkled across her cheeks. It's the way she's looking at me. As if I'm her favorite person. I've forgotten what it feels like for her to gaze at me without disappointment or confusion but with trust in her eyes.

"Layla and I built a sandcastle on the beach today," she says, as I help her get into her pink pajamas. "It was this high," she says, pointing to her knees. This is what we do, the two of us. I listen as she tells me about any moments she's spent away from me. She wants to make sure I know every detail. As if the moments don't count unless I know about them.

I glance at one of her clay art pieces lying on her floor next to the half-finished Lego house and the hamper piled high with her paint-stained clothing. The first time I'd lived this moment,

I'd straightened everything, put it all in its place, and made plans to push my exhaustion aside and tackle the laundry late at night. Now I see them as they are: masterpieces of the fleeting moments of childhood.

"It's beautiful," I say. "What you're making is beautiful."

And now I'm crying. At how much I have. And how much I lost. As she arranges her stuffed animals at the foot of the bed, I close my eyes for just an instant, and the memory flashes before me. August 25. The night everything changed.

I see the curved stretch of the two-lane Pacific Coast Highway. On my right side was the ocean. Normally the moon illuminates the foam on the waves, but that night it was pitch black. On the other side were stands of stately trees that screen the highway from the railroad tracks and the hills in the distance.

I was driving the posted forty-five miles per hour as the narrow lanes bent and curved, following the contours of the beach. A pale flash flicked across my vision, catching me off guard. Was it a person? An animal? A shadow? I had no idea. Panic surged through my veins and my reflexes kicked into overdrive. I jerked the wheel, veering into the bike line. As I fought to regain control of the vehicle, I heard the screech of my tires and a *thump thump* against the side of my car. I wrenched the steering wheel with all my might and guided the car back onto the empty highway.

I slowed but didn't stop. It was dangerous for a woman to be alone on the empty highway at this late hour. By the time I returned home, my breath was coming in rapid gasps, and I was trembling at the idea of what I might have done. I poured myself a glass of wine to calm my nerves and considered going out to the garage to look at the damage to the car, but I couldn't bring myself to go out there.

The next morning, James returned home from a business trip to San Francisco, discovered the bent front fender and the crushed headlight and asked me what happened.

"I lost control of the car and clipped something. An animal, I think," I said, fighting back tears. I didn't think it was anything more than that.

He inspected the crumpled front panel and looked up at me with concern. "You're okay, though?"

"I'm okay," I'd said. But what was roiling inside me was worse than any physical pain. I went into the bathroom, closed the door, and threw up. *What had I done?*

Later that day, the *Ventura County Star* reported that one man had been found dead and another was injured on the Pacific Coast Highway in what appeared be a hit-and-run. The California Highway Patrol was searching for the driver. A feeling of dread unspooled in my stomach.

Did I do this?

I remembered the impact and then I lost a few minutes in my memory. The *thump thump* was the last thing I could recall. The rest was hazy. Pure shock.

James texted me the story: *Bad night on the PCH.*

That's a dangerous stretch of road, I texted back. Then I wrote a couple of sentences about my plans to petition the city council to fix the problem. I'd convinced myself that what I was saying was true.

It wasn't easy saying nothing, doing nothing. It began to creep into my mind that maybe I was responsible. I squelched that anxiety by throwing myself into restaurant work, creating elaborate meals for James and Olivia, and telling myself that I really did hit an animal. Someone else was to blame for the hit-and-run.

I didn't know about the cameras. The motion-activated night-vision watchful eyes on the beach house by the accident site. The cameras captured a car driving by, hitting two figures, and disappearing into darkness. The local ABC affiliate reported that the California Highway Patrol was searching for the driver.

I thought about coming forward. Confessing. I wanted to start by telling James, but every time I'd get the nerve to say it, my body would freeze up and I couldn't go through with it. I knew it would ruin James and Olivia's lives if I confessed to leaving the scene of an accident that cost one person his life and seriously injured another. I'd convinced myself that my silence was protecting them.

I erased my search history on my laptop. That was my only real cover-up. I didn't want police to see that I'd consistently scoured the Internet with keywords like "hit-and-run" and "Pacific Coast Highway."

I didn't take the car out of the garage—I walked or used an AutoDriver—and I panicked anytime James raised the garage door to get his car out, fearful that neighbors might catch a glimpse of my wrecked front end and ask about it. I told James I was scheduling the car for repair but didn't follow through.

I could never escape what I'd done. Even the simple mention of a car or an accident or a friend talking about the Pacific Coast Highway would trigger a brutal wave of guilt.

Three days later, two uniformed officers from the California Highway Patrol arrived on my doorstep at 8:35 on a Friday morning. They asked an avalanche of questions and photographed the car.

I cried to James about my exhaustion from being interrogated for something I didn't do. We talked about hiring a defense attorney friend to fight this. I created a lengthy narrative of my innocence to my friends.

The night-vision cameras had captured a near-perfect photo of my license plate, and eventually I confessed. I was convicted of involuntary manslaughter and sentenced to serve 900 days in the county jail. When Olivia found out, she broke down.

"Why did you do this?" she cried, her words separated by choked sobs.

I went to take her in my arms and soothe her, but she pushed me away and ran out of the room. I collapsed, as if someone had punched me in the gut.

I wrote her letters from prison nearly every day, but she rarely answered. I asked for video chats, and she turned those down too. She didn't want to visit me. When I missed school events, she told her friends that I was sick. She couldn't admit I was in prison.

I was devastated, but I couldn't deny the shame and embarrassment I'd brought into her life and James's.

I was released from prison two months before this Aeon Expeditions trip, but what I'd done continued to haunt me. I rarely left my home. And when I did, I drove slowly and uncertainly. I'd see vague figures in the road, slam on the brakes, and realize that nobody was there. A bug hitting the windshield made my panic bloom. And then there was this ghostly voice that I'd been hearing inside me since the day of the accident: *You may think you're a good person. But when it comes down to it* . . .

I looked for books to guide me through this, but there are no self-help books or support groups for those who have unintentionally killed someone and injured another. To kill someone—even in an accident—is taboo. The perpetrator—there is no better word—is responsible for the accident, no matter our benign intentions.

I sought out therapists, but the first one I met with ended the session by saying that she "wasn't set up to deal with something like this." Eventually, I found one who put me to work writing letters to the two victims—letters our attorney would never let me send—to express my feelings about what happened.

There was an impossible chasm between me and James. We were polite but trapped in silence, our conversations limited to coordinating meals and managing Olivia's schedule. What happened had not only taken my breath away, but my words.

It was shocking how much Olivia changed in the three years I was in prison. She was a full five inches taller and wove her hair into a French braid all on her own. She'd moved on from wanting to play simple games like hopscotch with me to more serious pursuits like reading and playing soccer. I'd missed out on all the milestones and the daily joys and struggles of being her mom. I was unsure how I fit into her life anymore.

I was also frozen out of friendships that once seemed unbreakable. The truth had come out and none of my friends cared what my intentions were. I'd killed someone. I'd paralyzed another. They mistakenly believed they had to choose a side in such a tragedy, and they chose the victims over me. I wanted them to understand the depths of my pain, but all they could see was the mistake.

On the darkest nights, I'd hear that voice again and think that I'd be better off dead. Certainly, James and Olivia's lives would be easier if I wasn't around. I'd thought about ways to make that happen, but I was never brave enough to follow through with them. The Aeon Expeditions application, like buying a lottery ticket, felt like the only possibility of relief.

"The cookies, the ones with the cinnamon, they were really good," Olivia says, bringing me back to the moment. She settles under the covers. "Will you lie down with me?"

"Of course," I say, eagerly.

I tuck her in, then crawl through the sentinel of dolls lined up at the foot of her bed and snuggle beside her on her soft flower print sheets. The orange stuffed kitten she'd named Luna nestles in her arms.

I flick out the bedside lamp, and the soft light from the dollhouse in the corner casts a warm glow throughout the room. "Would you sing me a song?" she asks.

I draw a deep trembling breath, certain that I'll sound like I'm crying, and she will ask why.

"Let me think . . ." I say, buying time.

Her princess clock, the one she made from a kit my sister gave her, *tick tick ticks* off the seconds we have left together. I look out the window, trying to hold the tears at bay. The sweet scent of night jasmine floats into the room.

My breath shaky, I begin to sing:

Sleep, my child, and peace attend thee
All through the night

"Are you crying, Mommy?" she asks.

"No. I just have something in my throat," I say, then continue:

Guardian angels God will send thee
All through the night

"You're crying," she says. "You're definitely crying."

"Okay, I'm crying because I'm so happy to be here with you."

"Me too."

She grasps my hand in the dark, and a wave of warmth pulses inside my chest. It's a long time before I can sing again:

Soft the drowsy hours are creeping
Hill and vale and slumber sleeping
I my loving vigil keeping
All through the night

I'm no longer strands of guilt and hurt stumbling through life. I'm a mother, holding her child, singing her to sleep. Then this perfect, wondrous moment slips away like quicksilver, and she is asleep, her chest gently rising and falling. Lying here with her is to remember who I was before my life changed in a split second.

I glance at my watch. More than sixty minutes have flown by. I'm sure of it. Have I miscalculated? How can this be?

I do the math again and my heart pounds with joy.

It's been eighty-five minutes, and I'm still here.

In the past.

Chapter Five

Elizabeth

~

My second jump has been delayed.

"A few of the readings are out of range," an engineer says through the intercom.

I shift in the dun-colored mammoth machine in a room so cold that my teeth are chattering even though there's a device delivering warm air through a blanket that surrounds me.

"We're working to correct the problem," he continues.

By "we" he means a control room of twenty-five engineers who manage and monitor every aspect of our jumps. There's no room for error. Even a minor miscalculation or a lapse in concentration could kill us.

My ex developed Aeon Expeditions with some former colleagues who were also engineers at NASA's Jet Propulsion Laboratory, so Aeon's control room is modeled after the same one that JPL uses to launch rovers to Mars as well as deep space telescopes and infrared observatories that orbit the sun. The space is off limits to jumpers, but thanks to Mark, I'd visited the dimly lit room with rows of computer stations arranged in a semicircle facing an enormous screen. The atmosphere inside is tense and formal—most of the engineers are too nervous to even sit down. When there's a problem, there's no shouting or upheaval. As the crawl of numbers on all their screens turns crimson—a red alarm—the brightest minds in the world will buckle down and focus on solutions. Quietly.

In the early years, Mark never even mentioned he was working on time travel, just that it was a technology to harness recently discovered closed-time curves in space. I didn't grasp what that meant, but I could see that Mark was obsessed. Soon he was trotting around the globe raising billions and consulting with the world's best physicists, neuroscientists, and engineers. He was in China when I was thrown in the hospital with pneumonia and in India during Sam's high school graduation.

A year before Sam died, Mark was giddy with excitement when a fleet of trucks, their cargo wrapped tightly under multiple tarps, made their journey from somewhere deep in the mountains of Colorado to a set of hangars his company had built just outside of the Camarillo, California, airport. Even then he didn't say what they were creating. Later he would say that he didn't want me to hold the burden of keeping a tremendous secret like this.

The official announcement of Aeon Expeditions' launch came one week after Sam died. The groundbreaking invention received a massive amount of global media attention. Public interest exploded to the point that time travel—or jumping, as the media called it—was all anyone talked about. I didn't care. Sam's death made me feel like I was sick with an incurable disease that was silently, slowly suffocating me. I was visiting every kind of doctor, trying every pill, and exploring every therapy from acupuncture to yoga, but nothing took the breath-stealing ache away.

While Mark was meeting with experts in physics and engineering, confirming the technology's safety and feasibility to a zealous media and fanatical public, all I could do was try to remain standing. If I remembered to breathe, that was an accomplishment.

"We'll get through this," Mark had said. As if we would ever be the same again. I resented him for his ability to move forward when I was waiting out my life, counting the days until some event I didn't care about came and went, as if I was enduring a checklist of things you do when your life has ended but you're still breathing.

Our relationship took an irreversible turn. We no longer knew what to say to each other. The only person in the world who could possibly understand my pain couldn't share his own grief and didn't have time for me to share mine.

My grief snowballed into rage one Friday night when he called to say he wasn't coming home but was instead boarding a plane to New York to meet with a group of Nobel Prize winners in electrochemistry, physics, cognitive science, and a whole host of other specialties. I shouted into the phone, "I wish you had died instead of Sam!" Later, I regretted those vicious words. But in the moment, I felt the power and the relief in expressing the horror of my bottomless grief.

I asked him for a divorce a week later. He fought it, begged me to consider grief and marriage counseling for the two of us, but I resisted every one of those ideas. Losing Sam had transformed us into opposites, and it felt like our marriage was over. "All great discoveries demand sacrifices in exchange for uncertain outcomes," Mark had said at the unveiling of Aeon Expeditions. Our marriage was one of those sacrifices.

The lights blink out, and the jump sequence finally begins. Something is wrong. Everything is different from my first jump. There's a low rumble I hadn't heard before. A metallic taste in my mouth. I hear someone screaming, and it isn't until I feel my hands on my throat that I realize the screams are my own.

After that, the hallucinations take over: processions of eyeglasses filing down a street, thousands of empty oyster shells, fighter planes buzzing around. What seems like seconds later, my vision fills with gray static and my blood pounds in my ears.

Then I'm standing at my kitchen sink. My hands are covered in soapsuds as I rinse off a juice glass beneath a stream of cool water from the faucet. The refrigerator hums in the background. I look up and the sun is hanging low in the sky above smooth ocean waves.

"Mom, have you seen my sandals?"

I whirl around.

Sam is standing in front of me. And all the love I've ever had for him swells in my heart. That's the only way to describe this sensation. He's in his early twenties here, tall and slender, and except for the thick waves of black hair that grows so quickly he can't keep it in check, he's a near carbon copy of Mark.

The small child I met again a few hours ago has disappeared and in his place is a young man. I am lost in this sensation. Sam's voice. His very physical presence just inches from me. I turn to look at him and start to cry. And crumple to my knees.

"You okay?"

He reaches for my hand and helps me up. His eyes search mine for an explanation, but all I can do is choke up with more tears.

My words are sloppy like I'm drunk, a side effect of the time travel. "I just got a cramp in my leg is all."

Sam helps me to the kitchen table and pulls out a chair. I'm in a silent battle with my body to adapt to this new time. *Hurry.* There isn't a second to lose.

As I watch him move around the kitchen to get me a glass of water, I'm filled with sudden emotion. Clarity. I am in awe to have been part of his birth, his emergence into the physical world. The years spent being his mother have been the most awesome gift. Without the darkness and weight of grief, the feeling is heightened. Light.

I want to say, "I will always love you, Sam." I resist the urge to blurt out my feelings. He would find that strange.

He hands me a glass of water. "Better?"

I try to figure out when this is. His face is clean-shaven, so he's no longer in college. He shaved his scraggy beard a few weeks before graduation in preparation for job interviews.

From the way the golden sunset dances through the windows and onto the dark wood of the kitchen floor, it looks and feels like the end of summer. I notice an iPad on the table and tap the screen. August 20.

My eyes fill with tears.

We are in the last few days of Sam's life.

* * *

This hour in the past is everything I'd hoped it would be. Sam and I are walking Main Street with our Australian shepherd, Sting, and I'm listening to him talk. How many days and nights my grief had consumed me. How many times had I longed for this simple feeling.

The sun has set, and the moon is hidden behind thick clouds, so the only light is the soft glow of the old-fashioned streetlamps.

The streets are hushed and empty. We've talked about his job search and the interviews he's been on, along with how many revisions he's made to his résumé. He shares his anxiety that it's August and he hasn't landed a job yet.

"An awesome job offer is coming your way," I say, because it's true.

I love hearing him talk . . . not just the timbre and cadence of his voice but also the way he thinks through problems aloud.

This is going to sound wrong, but I hope this feeling lasts. Because it's only in this pain that I understand how much I have. How blessed I am to be in this body and in this moment and in this time with him. I hope this feeling holds and that I won't forget the beauty, the air filling my lungs when I'm with him, and the joy of being with him. When you know how easily things can be taken away from you, you appreciate them more.

A man rushes by carrying two champagne bottles and a third one tucked under his arm.

"Beautiful dog," he says to Sting, who looks back at him like he loves being admired. When the man is farther down the block, Sam says, "There's something you're not telling me." His words settle in the cool night air and swirl around us.

"What do you mean?"

"You're . . . you're not sick or anything, are you?"

My voice shakes. "No, I'm not sick."

Although I feel like it. This second trip has been hard on my body. My face is hot, like it's blistered with sunburn, but an earlier glance in the mirror showed blotchy redness, but no blisters. The right side of my head throbs with a headache, but I assume this is just an aftereffect of the travel.

"And everything is okay with Dad?"

"Yes, of course," I say, but I don't know. His father is somewhere in Ojai right now, working round the clock with his team of engineers to iron out the final kinks in the technology that will eventually become Aeon Expeditions.

I've missed this Sam so much. The softhearted young man who was always worried about everyone else. When he was six, he found an injured bird on the beach and brought it home. He nursed that little bird with the blue head and red chest back to life, making it a nest of soft fabrics inside a cardboard box, and feeding it around the clock. More than once, I found him outside in the middle of the night, sitting by the box on the patio table, engaged in lengthy pep talks with the ailing bird. Eventually the bird was strong enough to fly away, and Sam mourned the loss of him for days. I can't help but be in awe at this chance to be with him and his soft heart again.

"If there is something, you know, going on . . . you can tell me," he says. "I'm not a kid anymore."

I consider telling him that I'm from the future. But what good would it do for him to know that all his plans—the job, the apartment, the car—will never come to pass?

"Why do you think something's wrong?"

He shrugs. "I don't know. I guess it's the way you look at me. Like you want to tell me something."

I glance at my watch. More than an hour has passed, and I haven't been extracted. Can that be right? My mind whirs, recalculating the lapsed time. It's been eighty-five minutes.

Then a new thought emerges. This gifted time—whether it's seconds or minutes—presents an opportunity that I hadn't grasped until now.

Maybe I can say all the things I wish I'd said the night he died.

I place my hand on his shoulder. "Let's go home."

* * *

We're sitting in my kitchen now, the two of us, and it's nearly midnight. My eyes are heavy, but I don't dare sleep because any minute I'm worried Aeon will fix whatever problem they're having and whisk me away from Sam and into the despair that is my life in the future.

I notice the pumpkin pie, his favorite, on the counter. I must have purchased it in the last few days. "I'm starving," I say. And it's true. It's the first time in a long while that I've had any real appetite. "Would you like some pie?"

"Sure," he says,

I take my time preparing it, knowing this will be the last time I'll make anything for him. I immerse myself in the sacredness of the moment, the gift of being to do this for him. Even as my heart is heavy, I try to keep my actions light and quick, as if it's perfectly ordinary to be cutting up pumpkin pie at this late hour.

I notice things I never did. The way the lights falls on his face. A lock of hair over his right eye. I'm aware of the softness of the air, the way the kitchen smells of pumpkin and cinnamon. Then I pray.

Bring him love. Bring him life. Bring him joy.

The words feel bigger now. Bigger than this room. Bigger than my heart.

I turn around and my mind is a jumble of emotions and words. I preface all of them by saying that I'm not sick or dying. I just want him to hear what's on my mind.

I know I'm looking at him differently. I can't hide it. I'm thinking there's a way you look at someone when you know you're never going to see them again. Your eyes widen and linger on their face, memorizing every detail.

I draw a deep breath and tell him that I've loved him from the day I knew I was pregnant with him. How long I prayed for him and dreamed I'd become a mother. His mother. How proud I am of all the pieces of his heart that make him who he is.

With tear-stained laughter, I forgive him for throwing a baseball at me and smashing the living room window back in third grade when he was angry because I took away his video games. I tell him not to feel bad for disappointing me with his grades in middle school or for our regular appointments with his high school principal because he wasn't always doing his English homework. I ask him to forgive me for the times I was impatient and frustrated with him.

I tell him that I think he's beautiful and that it would break my heart if he ever thought he wasn't good enough or smart enough. I tell him that my life being his mom is my dream come true. That he is more than enough.

As a matter of fact, he is everything.

Then he starts crying, tears brimming in his eyes before he brushes them away. It haunts me that I never made time to tell him these things when he was alive.

"This is maybe my best day ever," he says softly.

As I place my hand over his, a new thought emerges. If Aeon Expeditions doesn't bring me back—if I'm somehow able to stay here a little longer—can I experience what life is like if he doesn't die?

Chapter Six

Andy

∽

The liquor store clerk thinks I'm shady. He has the permanent frown of someone who's seen it all and I'm yet another troublemaker. I don't think he believes my story that I'm buying three chilled bottles of Dom Perignon champagne at $230 each for a friend who's proposing to his girlfriend. He thinks I'm scamming him.

The total cost is over seven hundred dollars, and I pay with cash. I've always had a habit of carrying a chunk of cash to help me keep a handle on my spending habits, but this much cash seems suspicious to him. I grow impatient as he inspects every bill like he's a counterfeit money expert. There's so little time.

After he's checked them all beneath a bright light and compared the fifty-dollar bill to one he has in the register, he reluctantly hands me a receipt. I drop it on the counter and make a beeline to the door.

This champagne idea is crazy. It probably won't work. But it's my best chance.

I race next door to her apartment building and stand in front of the callbox. She's in apartment 218, but there's no way she'll let a stranger in. Especially not one who calls from the street at this hour.

My confidence sputters. Is this the "huge waste of money" my parents said it was? My friend Jonathan was certain that I'd regret this trip and that I'd quickly see that Kate wasn't as into me as I'd thought. Am I about to have my heart crushed all over again?

I suck in a deep breath and press the button for unit 224.

"Hello?" a man answers.

"I'm from Junipero's Liquor and have a delivery of a bottle of Dom Perignon champagne for you," I improvise. "Would you come down to get it?"

"What kind of bullshit is this?"

"It's completely legit." I hold up the bottle to the camera. "I'm told to deliver it to 224 in this building."

"What the hell for?"

"New owners at Junipero's want to thank you for your . . . loyalty," I stammer. "You want it or not?"

"New owners?"

"If you want it, please hurry," I say. "Or I've been instructed to give it to others."

There's a long pause, then, "I'll be right down."

The guy who shows up at the door is short and bald, wearing a gray T-shirt that's two sizes too small. From the deep lines around his mouth, he looks about forty, but he's probably younger.

"I have to deliver the rest of these in the building," I say, handing him the bottle. "Okay if I run up?"

"Sure," he says, distracted by the silver shield logo on the bottle.

Then my reptilian brain kicks into overdrive and hijacks my nervous system. My heart races, my muscles tense, and I can feel circles of sweat under each arm. I brush past him and zip up the stairs. Piano music drifts down the hallway.

Kate is playing the piano.

I knock on her door. Surprisingly, it's a courteous knock, even though my heart is thudding a million times a minute. I wonder if this is what a stroke feels like.

I hear someone shuffle on the other side of the door. I have the sense that she is looking at me through the peephole, so I try my best not to look wild or freaked out.

Then her voice. "Who is it?"

"I'm delivering champagne to a friend, and I can't figure out what apartment he's in. Can you help?"

Silence.

My palms are sweaty as I try to anticipate her answer. If she won't open the door, everything is ruined. All the money I spent on the jump will have been a total waste.

"Who're you looking for?"

"David Harrison," I say, invoking a name of a kid I knew back in third grade. Random.

I hear a lock turning and then a second one. The door opens a little and a sliver of her peeks past the door chain and straight at me. "I don't know him or where he lives. I'm sorry, I can't help."

She begins to close the door. My heart stutters, as if bracing itself to be broken all over again.

"Wait," I say. "My phone died. And I have no way to get in touch with David to find him. I'm wondering if I could get a quick charge?"

"I don't—"

"Look. I swear to you I'm not some kind of creep or scammer. I'm really delivering Dom Perignon to my friend. He needs it to propose to his girlfriend."

The whole ruse isn't fair, really. I've chosen a champagne that Kate has always desperately wanted to try.

"I know you," she says quietly.

My eyes widen. "You do?"

"You're that writer. Andy Schapiro. *Here to Stay*, right?"

I nod. I sell a lot of books, but few people know my face. But on our first date, Kate had professed to loving *Here to Stay* then too.

She unhooks the chain. When she opens the door, my heart scatters. She is stunning. Her thick dark hair falls to her shoulders in effortless waves. I can't see a stitch of makeup, but her skin is luminous in the soft light.

"I'm Kate Montano," she says, reaching out to shake my hand.

I stare at her hand touching mine and it all feels impossible.

"Well, are you coming in or not?" she asks.

I take a deep breath to calm my racing heart, then step into her apartment.

* * *

How do you hide your feelings?

The only thought that comes to me in my nervous state is to minimize eye contact. Everything lies. Except the eyes. Didn't Van Gogh—or maybe it was Tupac—say that? And if my eyes meet hers, she will know how I feel. And she'll think it's strange.

I don't know how I'll talk with her without giving away my feelings, without mentioning the details we know about each other or sharing one of our inside jokes. How do I pretend to be meeting her for the first time?

She points me to a charger next to the couch in her living room, and I plug in my phone, switching it off so she can't see that it has a full battery. Engineers have made huge leaps with travel to the past, but our phone batteries still take good old-fashioned electricity and time to recharge.

I've never been more nervous in my entire life. My heart races and I feel butterflies in my stomach, a sensation that I'd always thought was something we writers made up.

"Would you like to have a seat for a minute?" she asks.

I'm fixated on her lips. I have a sudden urge to stop this charade and to lean in and kiss her. I draw a deep, steadying breath instead. "Could I interest you in sharing a bottle while I wait?"

She looks at me in surprise. "You want to open a bottle of Dom Perignon with a stranger? It's so expensive—are you sure?"

"My friend only needs one bottle to propose to his girlfriend. I bought a second bottle because . . . well, because I'm curious what all the fuss is about."

I notice her lips curve slightly. "Me too," she says. "Ever since I saw Bill Pullman order it in—"

"*Sleepless in Seattle*," I say. "But he called it Dom DeLuise."

She laughs. Few people love that movie as much as Kate. It came out before she was born, and I'm pretty sure she has memorized every line.

"That's another reason why she dumped him for Tom Hanks," I add.

She smiles, probably surprised that anyone remembers such an obscure scene in that movie. But I have snuggled with her in this very room and watched her laugh and cry through *Sleepless*, and I think I know every scene that she loves.

Kate heads to the kitchen to get some glasses. While she's gone, I breathe in the warm floral perfume that lingers all around. Jasmine.

Sometimes my body has these sensations that I can't put into words. Even though she is in the next room, I feel the memories of my life with her like sparks on my skin. A fingerprint on my heart.

Her living room is exactly as I remember it. Vibrant paintings and cold gray photographs grace the walls, over the fireplace, and above shelves sagging with books. A baby grand piano is covered with sheet music even though she has the same scores on her iPad. She would rather turn the pages than swipe a screen.

I peek into the kitchen and see her illuminated by the open fridge. She is perfect in this light, all alabaster skin and soft angles.

I can't let her see my expression or she'll wonder why a stranger is gazing at her with such familiarity.

I pinch myself again. Hard. I'm *actually* here.

She returns with two champagne flutes, and I can't speak. It's as if the photos of her that I've been gazing at all these years have suddenly come alive.

I swallow the lump in my throat. "Did I hear you playing Bach earlier?"

"Yes," she says. "Do you play?"

I shake my head. "Just a listener. Were you playing one of the Goldberg Variations?"

She snaps her head away from setting the champagne glasses on the coffee table and looks at me in surprise. "How did you know? Most people wouldn't recognize that piece."

I'm no classical music expert. When we knew each other the first time, she'd told me she had practiced her way through most of Bach's thirty Goldberg Variations and played several for me. Then she showed me how she struggled with Variation 23 because of "its wicked hand crossings."

I know so much about her. But I've got to stop saying it aloud.

I pop the cork on the champagne and pour some for her. "Then let's toast to Bach. And to you, for lending me some of your electricity."

We clink our glasses, and I watch her close her eyes and take a sip.

"Delicious," she says. "Better than I'd dreamed."

When she opens her eyes, she catches me gazing at her. "Would you play some more?" I ask.

Listening to her play is one of many things I miss about her. I've always felt as though the stories of her heart were woven into her playing. Wonder, desire, questioning, love—they were always there whether she was playing Scott Joplin or Beethoven.

"Are you sure?" she asks.

She's only being polite. She loves to play. She has a day job at Pottery Barn and plays piano for small private events around the city.

"Positive," I say, then settle into the couch. I've lived this before—listening to her play—but I'm surprised at how new it feels to be with her. And how easily we've slipped into an easy conversation.

She plays a piece so filled with longing that it feels like it was written for me. For the next three minutes the whole room shimmers with the magic she spins with the music.

Tears prick the corners of my eyes. I try to stop them, but that only seems to make it worse. I am tasting life with her twice. That is something surely worth crying over.

"My fingers are a bit rusty," she says, finishing. "I wish it'd been better."

"It sounded amazing to me," I say.

She leaves the piano bench and sits beside me on the couch. Everything about her distracts me.

"What are you working on now?" she asks.

My mind goes blank. The last thing I want to do is talk about my writing. I want to hear her speak. I long to listen to her tell me about her day. Anything, even ordinary stuff. What did she have for breakfast? What are her plans for the evening?

Then my thoughts are hijacked by memories. I remember her standing in this room, her hands encased in blue oven mitts, holding a deflated but still good loaf of bread we'd made together. I remember returning from an art show—a collection of paintings of snow scenes from around the world—and wolfing down crackers, cheese, and a Sauvignon Blanc while she played the piano.

"I hope what you're writing isn't a secret," she continues, bringing me back to the moment.

I suck in a breath. Could this be an opportunity to understand why she left me? "In the story I'm working on now, my main character is a young man whose girlfriend disappears the day after he tells her he loves her. I have all kinds of ideas on how he'll look for her. All the wrong turns he'll take. But I can't come up with any reason his girlfriend would leave him."

"Maybe the boyfriend is dangerous or abusive? Like the protagonist in your book *Night Watch*, who leaves her husband in the middle of the night."

"No, the boyfriend in this story isn't dangerous. If you were the girlfriend in this story, why might you leave?"

Her eyes flash. "Maybe I don't have feelings for him?"

Her words send a sudden chill through me. This has always been my biggest fear. That she didn't feel the same way about me. She'd ghosted me.

"If you didn't feel the same way, would you tell him?"

She eyes me over her glass. "Maybe not. If I'm hiding secrets."

"Secrets?"

She sets her glass down. Gathers her thoughts. "Something I don't want him to know about me. Something he'd find out if we were together longer."

I glance at my watch and realize there's only a few minutes left. I fiddle with my champagne glass, trying to ignore my racing pulse, hoping I look normal.

Any second, Aeon will extract me back to the future where I won't be able to sit with her like this. I'm staring down the last moments with her. And like a kid who feels the roller coaster ride is going to end, I want to eke out the last seconds of this precious ride.

"Can I be honest with you?"

She leans forward, curious. "Haven't you been honest with me all evening?"

My mouth goes dry. She makes me feel guilty, as if those inquisitive eyes of hers can see right through the charade about the champagne and the dead phone.

I want to say that in the future I still think about her so much that I'm unable to fall in love with anyone else. What comes out isn't that at all. "What I want to say is that even though we've just met, it feels as if I've known you longer than that. This has never happened to me before. It's . . . nice."

Nice. I think of myself as pretty good with words, but they utterly fail me here.

Her eyes find mine briefly and her cheeks flush. She doesn't answer.

"Maybe it's the champagne talking. I'm sorry if I made you uncomfortable," I add.

"No, don't be," she says softly. Her eyes meet mine again. "It's strange how the world works. We meet by complete accident, and yet, it seems like, I don't know, like I'm *supposed* to meet you."

I choke up. How can I not? This is why I haven't been able to move on. Because being with Kate has always felt like this. *Meant to be.* If the future has taught me anything, it's that I won't ever feel this way about anyone else.

I sneak a glance at my watch, and my stomach sinks when I realize my sixty minutes are up. As the seconds slip by, Kate is waiting for me to respond. I can't hide my feelings any longer. And I've got nothing to lose. "I think you're the one in a million, Kate."

We'd been warned that the extraction from the past is painful. It will feel like your whole body is being squeezed into a straw. I brace myself to be hurtled back to the present.

Nothing happens.

Kate grows silent and looks at me with curiosity. She opens her mouth and then closes it.

"You hardly know me," she says softly.

I'm ruining things. Now I'm gripped with terror because I've always been most afraid of this possibility. That she wouldn't like me in the same way—that she won't ever fall for me—the second time around. Was it the magical ingredients of our first meeting—a party, piano music, Frank Sinatra—that sparked our relationship? Maybe it would be impossible to recreate the magical, spontaneous connection we shared. Maybe we can't replicate the past.

"I know we just met," I say, and my heart slams into my chest. "But that doesn't change how I feel."

Her cheeks flame red, and the way she's looking at me makes me think—well, I don't know what to think. I'm just a giant sack of emotions right now. Maybe I'm imagining it, but there is something there. A spark of something that would've otherwise been invisible if I didn't already know her so well.

"Maybe," she says lightly, pouring me some more champagne. "You should get to know me a little more. Then you can see if you change your mind about that."

By the time we finish the bottle, we are laughing and sharing stories, many I'd never heard before. Then she brings out another bottle of some wine her friend bought in Paso Robles. We end up talking through the night, drifting off to sleep then waking to talk again. We did not kiss or make love—it was enough to feel her next to me as we collapsed on her bed and fell asleep in the early hours of the morning.

Yet, as I lie awake before dawn, she is beside me in her bed, her breathing slow. Blame it on the champagne. And on me for blurting out my feelings.

She's been in my dreams often these past months. Sometimes we are standing by the ocean together and other times we're snuggled together on the couch watching a movie. Or we might be doing mundane things like cooking dinner together, only somehow they feel bigger and more important. Other times, we're making love, and when I wake up, I can still feel the warmth of her body next to mine in the bed. But she is never there.

Now she is.

As silvery morning light filters through the window, she stirs. Whatever she's dreaming has put a smile on her face. But I'm filled with dread. I've already been here twelve hours. It's only a matter of time before Aeon Expeditions locates my life-signature and takes me away from her.

The Aeon coaches had briefly mentioned what to do if the return jump doesn't begin in sixty minutes. They rushed through it, much like flight attendants briskly mentioning the seat cushion as a flotation device—because it's something that rarely happens. In Aeon Expedition's case, never. Of the tens of thousands who've jumped each year, every single person has returned within the allotted hour. The protocol is simple: Stay calm and wait.

Not that I want to be extracted. I say a silent prayer that they don't fix whatever problem they're having, and they don't find me. Let me be the one jumper they can't retrieve. If that happens, I won't waste a single moment of this gifted time with Kate. I will make each day with her unforgettable.

Then, as it always does, my mind returns to the last day I spent with her. That morning, piles of yellow-tinted clouds spiraled upward and made our walk on the beach feel like we were walking through a Renaissance painting. We were watching a pod of dolphins leap the foamy waves when it seemed so natural to tell her how I felt about her. I got kind of dizzy because I was overwhelmed by how clearly I could feel our future together. It dawned on me that I could marry her someday. It was so easy. Not the least bit scary.

"I hope this doesn't sound too fast, but I think I'm falling for you." There were other words, many of them, that tumbled out as if I'd planned them, though I hadn't.

"I'm falling for you too," she'd said softly.

Our relationship was so new that I hadn't yet met her parents, didn't know many of her friends. I didn't know any of the boring things like whether she had mountains of debt or even important things like whether she wanted to have kids someday. I just knew I wanted to figure it out with her. All of it.

Then her phone dinged in her pocket. She looked at it and said, "I'm sorry. I have to go."

"Everything okay?" I asked.

"I need to take care of something."

"Can I go with you? Maybe I can help."

"I'm fine. Really."

She looked like she was going to cry, then she wrapped her arms around my waist.

"I'll see you tomorrow," she said, kissing me.

Then I watched her run across the sand back to her car.

When she didn't answer my texts or phone calls for weeks, my friend Jonathan pressured me to move on.

"Face it, you've been ghosted," he'd said for the millionth time. "She just wasn't as into you as you thought."

I was in denial. I really believed she was going to return. Then my cousin Justin called. He's a junior at Ventura College and the night manager at the 7-Eleven on Bristol, two blocks from the beach. I'd introduced him to Kate when the two of us raced into his store in a desperate quest for Strawberry Shortcake ice cream bars.

Justin's call was unexpected—we didn't really talk very often—and his voice was nervous and breathy. "I just want to tell you that I saw your girlfriend in here last week."

"At 7-Eleven? When?"

"Thursday. The twenty-fifth."
The last day I was with her.
"She was with someone," he said. "A guy."

I begged him to show me the security camera footage. He'd resisted, telling me he would get in a lot of trouble with his bosses. "Someone just got fired for doing that," he'd said somberly.

I pummeled him with endless questions about the guy—what he looked like, what the two of them said to each other, and if they left in the same car. He didn't remember many details. Eventually he agreed to let me peek at the footage if I came into the store at two in the morning when no one's usually in there.

The security camera perched over the cash register captured Kate at 9:13 PM, four hours after she left me on the beach. The man with her was tall and clean-cut with dark, wavy hair. Although it kills me to say it, he was good looking in a boy-next-door way.

He paid for some things at the cash register—six bottles of water, salted nuts, crackers—then presented them to her. She accepted them like she was receiving a wonderful gift and placed them into a backpack slung over her shoulder. Then she hugged him for an eternity of five seconds—yes, I counted—and they disappeared together into the night.

Jonathan was right. I'd been ghosted.

Chapter Seven

Logan

～

After inhaling three tacos apiece at Castro's Taco Stand on the way from Mount Whitney, Haley and I catch the train back to Ventura. The altitude and ten hours of hiking have taken a toll on us, and we settle in a comfortable silence.

While I'm grateful to have the use of my feet, they hurt. Bad. So do my knees. We nap in fits and starts most of the way, exhausted from the ninety-nine switchbacks and the half-mile vertical chute, but also blown away that we'd climbed to the top of the one of the tallest mountains in America.

We're five minutes from our exit when I wake her up and ask to her to go kayaking with me the next day. I'm desperately hoping that Aeon can't find me, and I'll still be here tomorrow. She resists at first, saying she needs more than a day to recover from the hike, but it doesn't take much to convince her to say yes. Maybe I'm reading too much into it, but if she's willing to get into a kayak with me even when her legs and feet are aching, that's a good sign.

After I let her go, I stumble back to my apartment where I fall heavy into my bed like I'd been drugged with sleep. When I wake up, I feel the soft sheets beneath me and a cool breeze against my skin. The sun is warm, and music from the apartment next-door floats over me.

I yawn, letting the haze of sleep pass over me. Then an unsettling jolt hits me.

When is this?

I'm dizzy as I glance at the pale curtains hanging in the windows. The ceiling fan rotates slowly above my head. My backpack from the hike is slumped on the floor where I'd left it.

I'm still in the past!

I cup my hand over my mouth. I'd once thought I had to go to extremes—heliskiing, a zero-gravity flight, an expedition to the Arctic—to experience euphoria, but here I am feeling the same thing while sitting in my apartment that's the size of some people's closets.

Then a thought races in: *Maybe I'll never have to return.* Maybe I won't have to go back to a future where I'm just a wobbly head and torso on legs that won't move.

"Easy," I whisper. *Don't get your hopes up.*

I touch my legs, feel the weight of my hands against them, a sensation that still stuns me. And then ideas of all the things I can do with this unbroken body start buzzing in my brain. In this instant, I see the possibilities. All the thousands of choices I can make right now and in every moment that I get to live and breathe. I could raft the Zambezi River, swim with the turtles in Ningaloo, rappel into a volcano in Iceland, summit Kilimanjaro, and sky dive in Interlaken. I don't need to fear altitude sickness, storms, snow, raking winds, heat and dehydration, sprained ankles, or broken bones. These are the smallest price to pay for the freedom, danger, and poetry of using my unbroken body for every challenge and pleasure it can possibly experience.

My phone dings and a text swoops across my screen. My friend Marco writes: *You coming? Or are you still on Mount Whitney?*

Most Sunday mornings, I'd already be in the YMCA pool knocking out a couple hours of high-intensity practice with him. At this point in time, we're both competing in U.S. Masters swim competitions for adults, and I'm trying to slash my time on the thousand-yard freestyle to under ten minutes, which would keep me in the top ten in California. Marco's specialty is the backstroke, but he's had a rough go of it during the last two competitions, so he's been doubling up on practices and prodding me to join him. Not that I need the reminder.

Working out is the only way I stay sober.

A few years ago, I made a living selling pills and spending my free time at tailgate parties and bars. I got canned for drinking on the job and blacked out from mixing pills with tequila at my friend's wedding, but still convinced myself I didn't have a problem. When I drank too much, I'd blame other people for getting me in that situation. When I did drugs, I'd say it was because everyone else was doing it. Those were just excuses.

On the eve of my twenty-second birthday, police caught me selling pills outside a food truck in L.A. That kind of arrest carries with it a minimum three-year prison sentence, and that thought alone gave me full-blown panic attacks. I couldn't sleep. I stopped eating. When I found out the cop misplaced the evidence and the charges were dropped, something inside me woke up.

His mistake had to be a sign. A second chance.

I packed my stuff and moved far away from that L.A. life to Ventura, a hundred miles up the coast. I couch-surfed with some friends from high school and worked as a dishwasher at a barbecue joint until I saved up enough for a studio apartment.

"Don't be afraid to dream big," I'd written on the first Post-it for my bathroom mirror. "Show the world nothing is impossible."

Bullshit.

I was a walking carcass, sweating through the sheets, my skin turning gray, and my body trembling for more of all that I gave up. When the shaking finally stopped, I'd wake up every morning at three and run five miles in nearby Alamo Mountain, carrying fifty pounds on my back. I was out of my mind. After a few weeks I morphed my dread into biking twenty miles a day and swimming at night. The fear that I'd go back to the way things were was always in me. And when that anxiety crept up on me, I'd head back into the mountains and lift five or ten pound boulders and fling them around until my shoulders burned and the panic subsided. Then I'd pedal my bike until my heart thudded and I tasted blood in the back of my throat. When I got back home, I'd shower, apply for better jobs at places that wouldn't hire me, and then I'd repeat the whole thing all over again the next day.

Even though I was getting clean, I felt like a dope fiend for exercise. If it rained and I couldn't run in the mountains, I'd go into withdrawal. I'd pace my apartment, twitching and pissed off. I wasn't training for a healthier lifestyle. Or for some big marathon or trek. I was training to rid myself of the demons that had control of my life.

If I'm getting extra time with a body that works, I'm going to use it every second I still have it. I text back to Marco: *On my way*

I slide out of bed, throw on some clothes with an ease that I don't think I'll ever take for granted, and head into the bathroom. I splash cool water on my face and glance at the current Post-it taped to my bathroom mirror, scribbled with black Sharpie to make it feel permanent. I remember scrawling this one in the middle of the night when the world was crypt quiet. It's a reminder of who I wanted to be before the accident:

I want to be:
Financially independent
The Guy with the Great Dane
Someone who speaks German
Top 10 swimmer
A better person

The learning German thing was because I wanted to ski the Alps and thought it would be cool to sound European. The Great Dane idea landed on the list because I'd been on a back trail in Yosemite when up came this dude with a gray and white Great Dane. The dog didn't do much except stand there, looking like the gentle giant he was at three feet tall. Still, everyone just stopped. Even the grizzliest hardcore hikers were taking selfies with him. And yeah, the girls couldn't get enough of him, laughing when he was bouncing around happy and cooing "aww" when he slumped with disappointment because he wasn't getting enough attention.

These ambitions feel crazy-innocent. After I was paralyzed, my goals were colossal and impossible: Push through the pain. Survive. Live.

Mist still hangs over the road and clings to the trees when I get on my bicycle. Its carbon fork is bent from a collision I had with a tree in Yosemite. That makes the steering heavy and slows me down some, but at least it's not a wheelchair.

On my earbuds, I've got "Highway Star" by Deep Purple cranked high and it makes me pedal faster. When I was a kid, my dad would put "Highway Star" on an old Walkman, blasting it as he plunked me on the back of the motorcycle he'd named The Beast. He'd park a cold Olde English 800 malt liquor between his legs, then he'd launch us into the horizon until we hit what felt like the speed of sound.

The song has always felt like a victory anthem, and this morning it gives me wings to power up the hill. I spin over to Palermo Coffee Shop on Main Street to get some caffeine circulating in my veins before the swim workout. I breeze along the street, park my bike out front under the sycamore tree with the gnarly roots, and tear through the door. I feel invincible.

Last time I was here, I had to wheel in along the narrow metal ramp and yank the door open from a wretched angle. Waiting in line meant blocking the entrance with my wheelchair so everyone had to step around me. Like I was in their way. No longer a person. Time in a wheelchair also meant traveling at crotch level on the subway or getting a face full of someone's backside in line. Busy places were perilous. It's ridiculous how many times I've been smacked in the head with shopping bags or purses.

Now with my six-foot height, my eyes can sweep the room and take in everything. While I'm standing in line, I notice a woman staring at me. She's got an Angelina Jolie thing going on with high cheekbones, but she's too old for me. Maybe fifty?

And she's being way too obvious about looking at me. The kind of stare I might get in a bar from a girl who's had too many drinks at one in the morning.

I ignore her and order. In the future, I mostly drink the office coffee, which tastes like brown water with a dash of bleach. Today, I'm going for a dark roast. Black.

After I pay, I have the feeling the woman is still watching me. I glance over and get a good look at her. And then I realize, that's not lust in her eyes.

It's tears.

And I know exactly who she is.

Chapter Eight

Brooke

August 21, 2025

What I'm seeing can't be real.

He's wearing a dark blue sweatshirt and jeans, hair askew as if he's recently woken up. He smiles at the cashier, his eyes scanning the board behind her, deciding. The coffee machine hisses behind the counter.

I can't stop staring. He is moving through space. Flesh and blood.

"Dark roast," I hear him say.

He turns his head and notices me looking at him. He seems to recognize me. That's impossible.

Everything in front of me blurs. And the fear that whispered to me every day in the future is now roaring in my ears:

You might think you're a good person, but when it comes down to it . . .

It seems like cruel fate to meet him now when I've come to the past to escape reminders of that tragic night.

After my hour had passed and I hadn't been extracted, I'd wrung pleasure out of everything, certain that at any moment Aeon would return me to the present. I'd fought against sleep, staying with Olivia while she slumbered, then I padded into my bedroom, where James and I made love. I couldn't get enough of the saturated energy, the charged space between our bodies, and the experience of loving him while he still trusted me.

I'd stayed awake the rest of the night, soaking everything in, impatient at myself when I'd nodded off. I'd been given these bonus minutes, and I wasn't going to waste any of them.

Just before dawn, I'd tiptoed out to the garden, breathed in the scent of night jasmine, picked a few tangerines, and ate them one by one, captivated by their stunning color, their scent, and the explosion of sweetness when I bit into them. Every minute was an intoxicating brew of the sensations of being in this life. *My* life.

Living as if every moment could be my last is exhausting. I can only put so much energy into savoring every sensation and feeling. That's why I came to this coffee shop. The routine of it—something I've done countless times—is exhilarating. There's a quiet joy in picking up a few things I know Olivia and James will love. An Irish cream cold brew for James. A cake pop for Olivia. It's a simple task that feels more meaningful when I know all the pain that's ahead of me.

I've been on edge, worried about being extracted any second, but of all the things I was anxious about, the last thing I'd ever expected was to run into Logan Sandoval.

He strides over to me.

"Mrs. Dalton?" he says. His voice is rough and low.

It is hard to look at him. Strong, with muscled shoulders. Chiseled legs in bike shorts. A firm jawline. He didn't appear in court, and the only photos I ever saw of him were the ones the prosecutor presented at the trial. By that time, his legs had shrunk, he was thin and gaunt, and this warm summer tan I'm seeing had long faded.

I feel dampness on my cheek and whisk away the tears.

"*Brooke* Dalton?" he says, emphasizing my first name. Everyone ignores us. They whirl around us, ordering and getting and drinking coffees as if this impossible meeting isn't happening.

"My name is Logan Sandoval. I've seen your car on the PCH. You drive a Mercedes. Black. E-Class. Right?"

I nod. *How does he know this about me?*

"Slow down on the PCH. Pay attention."

"What're you saying?"

He turns on his heel, pushing through the customers standing in line.

"Logan, please wait," I call out.

I hurry after him, but by the time I reach the entrance, he's already on his bike, maneuvering it into the street with ease and speed, as if the bike is an extension of his body.

I am sick, a sharp pain that feels like my abdomen will burst. It's as if all my mistakes have become finely sharpened knives, cutting into me. There can be no worse agony than meeting one of the people whose life you will ruin forever.

I catch a glimpse of myself in the mirror behind the coffee bar and see the hideous person I am. In the stark light, the reflection staring back at me is mottled and red, as if the ugliness of what I'll do is already written on my face.

The lawyers my husband hired to defend me had forbidden me from reaching out to Logan because the threat of a lawsuit always loomed on the horizon. A lawsuit never transpired, but I never stopped writing "Dear Logan" letters explaining my anguish, even if I wasn't allowed to send them.

Every day I'd have nagging questions. What would've happened if I got on the road ten minutes earlier? Or five minutes later? If I hadn't stopped at the yellow light at Bristol, I wouldn't have put me directly where Logan and Sam were at that very moment. Why were they in the bike lane at that time of night? Had they done that so many times before that they didn't see it as dangerous? I have replayed that night over and over in my mind. Had I known what would happen, I would never have turned onto the PCH.

"Logan, your dark roast is ready," the barista calls out.

My heart rate kicks up a notch. There's only one way Logan could know these things about me. He must also be a time traveler.

How can there be two of us jumpers here?

He can't possibly realize I'm one as well.

I think about the contents of all those "Dear Logan" letters I'd written but never sent. Could this gifted time offer an opportunity to talk with him? Maybe he can tell me why he was in the bike lane that night. Perhaps I might understand why I made my tragic mistake.

I text my friend Lisa, who has the uncanny ability to find almost any information online: *Need a cell phone number for Logan Sandoval in Ventura. ASAP.*

* * *

James is finishing breakfast when I return. He's handsome in the beautiful light blue shirt I'd bought him when we were in Milan years ago.

I hand him the Irish cream cold brew, and his face lights up as if I'd just scoured the four corners of the earth to bring him a rare gem. "For me?"

He looks up at me. A slight wink. And in this simple glance, I feel something I haven't felt in a long time. Love.

I forget about Logan for the moment and take a shortcut to happiness. I know it's not like that for everyone who jumps, but I have never felt more loved, more desired, or more hopeful than I do right now.

People who haven't traveled yet think the travel-to-the-past thing is an induced hallucination. A dream that only feels real. But in dreams, we see things that aren't there, we believe what simply can't be true, we have wild mood swings, and when we wake up, we swiftly forget almost everything we experienced.

This is no dream.

I'm aware of every physical sensation: my racing heart, the rush of blood to my face, and the tingle of my skin as he draws near. I feel the steadiness of my love for him, the sense of wonder when I look at him, and the tender way he looks at me makes me feel . . . extraordinary.

"Did you enjoy the party last night?" he murmurs, threading an arm around my waist. I breathe in the woodsy scent of his aftershave.

"Yes," I say. "And everything else."

"It was all wonderful," he says, gently moving a lock of my hair from my face. "You're wonderful."

I've always loved this about him. His British accent. The easy way he compliments me, yet it never feels like he's just saying what he thinks I want to hear.

He lowers his mouth to mine. His lips are soft and searching, a dreamy intimacy. He pulls away and looks at me. "Are you crying?"

"Am I?" I say, whisking away the tears.

Then his lips are on mine again, soft and warm. I close my eyes and soak in its perfection—the sweet taste of cinnamon, the way his hands hold my face. I want this moment to go on forever. And there's no doubting he does too.

Anyone can see he loves me. It radiates in his blue eyes, liquid and warm. After ten years of marriage, he still looks at me as though we're newlyweds. He pulls me into another kiss and mixed in with growing need, I feel a rush of shame and remorse.

In a few days, I will ruin all this.

Chapter Nine

Logan

August 21, 2025

My stomach aches. Hard, like there's a boulder lurching around in it.

Even an intense swim session with Marco isn't enough to rein in my anger. I pound through lap after lap in the Olympic size pool, at once grateful for my working body and angry at the woman who takes it away from me.

After I knock out twenty-two laps at top speed, Marco says, "You're like a demon out there."

The other swimmers in the pool have stopped to watch me too, including one college kid who outpaces me most mornings. That feels kind of good. The trim young woman who'd been puttering in the lane next to me for the last twenty minutes asks, "Hey, do you think you could train me how to swim like that?"

"Not today," I say. "But sure."

"I'm Kate," she says. "I'm here every Sunday morning. Catch you next week?"

I nod, but who knows where I'll be a week from now?

I hit the lane again, even faster now, channeling my anger with every stroke. Before today, I'd never met Brooke Dalton, but I'd read a lot about her. She owns a restaurant in town, and her husband's some badass lawyer who apparently is the go-to litigator for high-end real estate lawsuits. Badass because he wins more than 95 percent of his cases. And because of that, they own a mansion in town and another down south on the beach in Laguna. Rough life.

Before she slammed into me with her Mercedes, she'd been celebrating some friend's birthday on the beach at a catered party which I heard cost more than I earn in a month. She told the judge she hadn't been drinking, but I'm sure she lied. Police had no way to prove whether her blood alcohol was over the limit or not. Because she didn't stop.

After she sent my body flying fifty feet and hit another man, killing him, she didn't turn back. Instead, she left me to die on that deserted highway.

Here's what gets me. I read that while I lay unconscious on the asphalt, bones and spine broken and kidney crushed, she went home, opened her liquor cabinet, and poured herself a glass of wine. A frickin' Chardonnay. Like she was either channeling Lex Luthor or celebrating what she'd done.

Fuck her.

They made her pay some money for restitution, enough that my medical bills were paid off, but the way justice works she only served time in the county jail and then she went back to her sparkling life. Like nothing ever happened.

I hate every version of Brooke Dalton. Even the one in Palermo who hasn't yet paralyzed me. I hate that she served 900 days in the county jail while I get to spend the rest of my life wearing a diaper in case I can't get out of my wheelchair in time to get to the bathroom.

I remember sitting outside the Ventura County Hall of Justice after the verdict and staring up at the golden letters on the glass that read "Hall of Justice" and thinking: *That's a blatant lie.* They might be upholding the law in there, but what they decided wasn't justice.

The Dalton woman is haunting me here too. Somehow, she's gotten my cell number and texted me: *This is Brooke Dalton. Call me. It's important.*

That isn't going to happen. With my luck that she'll claim I was harassing her in the coffee shop. That's how money like that operates.

Still, I can't make any sense of why she was crying.

* * *

I got it all wrong.

That's what I think as I watch Haley slide into the kayak with me in her striped swimsuit and jean shorts later that afternoon.

I'd been thinking of time in the past as though things only work a certain way. *Use your body, idiot. Your body brings you happiness.* Now I'm seeing there are choices, other ways that things can happen that might bring a different kind of joy.

Strange, but they leap right at me today.

I'd wanted this jump so that I could recover my legs. To live a big athletic life outside of a wheelchair. Hanging out with Haley like this scares me some. Because I like it too much. The solo life of swimming and mountain climbing I'd imagined doesn't seem quite as attractive today.

This is Haley's first time in a kayak on the Pacific Ocean so she's gripping the paddles too tight. She's also working harder than she needs to, not realizing her legs need to get involved. I give her a quick lesson and she adjusts, then smiles at me. And the way she's looking at me makes swimming with the turtles of Ningaloo seem less exciting. Unless she was there.

It's the kind of thing I imagine some old dude saying at his wedding, "Everything in my life is better when I'm with her." Lame. I know guys who say things like that to make their girlfriends or wives feel good. It's just words. I've kayaked this part of the ocean a hundred times in better weather and in more challenging swells, without anyone slowing me down with their sloppy paddling technique, but those days don't really compare to this easy kayak trip with her.

Yeah, I'm going soft. Moments like this I feel like the older version of me is trying to tell the younger version what's going to be important later on. What I'm going to care about. Given all the poor choices I've made up until now, I'm listening.

On the way here, I kept worrying that maybe that hike was some kind of Cinderella thing where she accidentally saw me as some handsome prince, but when she sees me again, she won't recognize me. Now that I think of it, that's not the Cinderella story. I also thought maybe Haley was just acting like she was into me because she was scared to be alone on that hike. We do crazy things when we're afraid. Don't I know it.

"Did you know that the first kayaks were invented four thousand years ago?" she says. "Kayak means *hunter's boat*. What should we go hunt?"

I smile at her chatter. Sometimes she talks about strange facts like she's been preparing to be on *Jeopardy*, but I like hearing her voice. Knowing what she's thinking.

Most things I do don't involve talking. I'd scaled a limestone wall in the Canadian Rockies, and my buddies teased me afterward because I didn't utter a single word, even the couple of times I'd dangled in the air to secure a better foothold only to stare down hundreds of feet at the ground below. There's a fine line between genius and madness, and you can't ride that sharp edge if you're a talker. No, the only way for me to be a force of nature is to get into a flow where my body and mind are perfectly lined up. I can't get into that flow if I'm talking or listening.

I feel like I can talk to her.

"Should we help them?" she asks.

"Help who?"

"Those boys. Looks like they're having a hard time."

I follow her gaze and see two middle-school age boys, their kayak teetering on a wave and close to capsizing.

Heck no. Boys that age are a pain in the ass. They're probably rocking the kayak just to scare each other. Or to play pranks. No good's going to come from getting involved.

"They'll be all right," I say.

We keep moving farther out to sea, me paddling behind her, the water all sparkly from the sunlight. She's getting better at paddling, but I like it best when she turns around to tell me something funny. I just like looking at her. Her long brown hair pulled into a messy ponytail. Her slim shoulders.

"Look at them now," she says with alarm. "They're overboard."

I glance over to the right, and the boys are now bobbing in the ocean, buoyed by their life jackets. Their kayak has capsized.

"I think they meant to do that," I say.

"Should we ask if they need help?"

"They'll figure it out."

"Maybe we should do something," she says, her eyes meeting mine.

She's stubborn, like me, so there's no way I can keep saying no. Her face lights up when I turn the kayak around and head over there.

"You need help?" Haley calls out.

"Nah, we're okay," the one with the freckles says.

They're not okay. I can see it on their faces. Their reflector-white skin tells me they're tourists and all this ocean stuff is new for them. They want us to think they are okay, but the water is deep and cold, and they are tired and have no idea what the hell they're doing. Inside they're freaking out. I remember being that age and always acting like I had it together even though inside I knew I was a poor, pathetic son of a drunk.

"You, with the freckles, here's what you do," I say. "Get toward the middle of that kayak."

The freckled boy shrugs. All attitude. "I know what to do. Don't need your help."

The other boy, who's thirty pounds heavier with long stringy hair hanging in his eyes, locks eyes with me and says to his friend, "He looks like maybe he knows something."

"I know a thing or two," I say, thinking about all the pain I endured trying to claw back some semblance of a life after the accident. "Sometimes the shit that looks hard is actually the easiest. Move over there now."

The freckled kid hears my tone but rolls his eyes anyway. Just to make sure I know he's tough. He swims over to the kayak.

"Now climb over the kayak and pull it toward your body to turn it right side up," I tell him.

He does what I tell him and turns the boat over. The look on his face is priceless. Like he'd convinced himself there was no way to do it. I know that feeling.

"Now put one hand on the far handle and the other one on the handle close to you and boost yourself up until your belly button is over the seat. Don't worry about how it looks. Take your time."

He shades his eyes like there's no way this is going to work. Then the whole move is awkward, all skinny arms and legs flailing around, like he's a fish who's dying a slow, terrible death.

"Now get stable. Take your time, easy now," I say. "When you're ready, twist your body and get your butt in the seat."

He twists and sits, looking like maybe this was the biggest thing he got right all week.

I motion to the other kid. "You're next."

The freckled boy is grinning, like he can't wait for the heavier kid to try so he can snicker or snort or laugh. "Don't you even think about laughing at him," I say, and he wipes that stupid expression off his face.

Five minutes later both kids are settled in the kayak and heading back to shore. I'm kind of glad Haley made me do it. And the way she's looking at me makes the whole thing worth it.

"You're not just a mountain man," she says, with admiration. "You're a water whisperer. Those kids are lucky you were out here."

"Yeah," I say, kind of owning it.

I think back to the first time around, and I didn't notice this about myself at all. All I could see was that I was a fuck-up, making bad decisions, getting myself in losing positions, useless, hanging in the wrong places, and so filled with rage at who I was that I couldn't see straight.

We think all we are is what we see on the surface.

But there's always more.

* * *

After the kayak ride, Haley and I wait in line to order tacos at a food truck down by the beach. She kisses me. Not a peck, like I'm her favorite puppy. And not some over-the-top PDA that is supposed to let everyone around us know that I'm hers. This feels like she did it impulsively. Like she can't help it.

I feel her fingers graze my shirt as she leans in, and that's all it takes for me to feel warm. And wanted. Then she clasps her hand in mine, and her whole face brightens into a soft smile that makes my insides melt. No one has ever looked at me like this before.

"What're you smiling about?" I ask, squeezing her hand.

She's shy about answering, then finally. "Do you believe in fate?"

"Not really. Do you?"

She twists her mouth. "When we met on Mount Whitney, I was supposed to be there with another guy. That's why I was there."

I smile. "I'm supposed to *like* this story you're telling me?"

"Yes, because if he had shown up, I would never have met you."

"Why didn't he show?"

"He got a second interview for a teaching job at some big high school in Los Angeles."

I feel a spike of jealousy. All I have is a high school degree and a crummy job at a courier company. I can't compete with a guy like that.

"Who is this guy?" I say, keeping it light. "Should I be worried about him?"

"We grew up next door to each other. He was this smart kid who got straight As and took all these AP classes, then went off to Northwestern. After he graduated, I ran into him, and he admitted he had this crush on me when we were in high school. He asked me to go on that hike. As a get to know you kind of thing. If I hadn't agreed to go with him, I wouldn't have met you," she says.

"And if I hadn't had a flare-up of mountain sickness, I wouldn't have fallen behind and met you either."

She beams. "See, it's fate."

"Maybe we'd have met somewhere else," I say, although I don't believe it. "Maybe I'd have walked into Celestine and seen you all beautiful behind the counter and gotten over my shyness and asked you out."

"Would you really have done that?" she asks, her eyes glistening.

In my normal life, I'm bad at eye contact, but tonight I gaze into her eyes. "I would've wanted to. And I'd like to think I would." And now it's my turn to land a kiss on her lips, all warm and knowing, even as I wonder if I would have had the courage to talk to someone like her who's out of my league, in a restaurant far outside of my natural habitat.

"I guess I should thank the guy," I say, breaking the kiss. "Because I don't see you going on that hike otherwise."

"Well, now I would." She leans into me and laughs. And there's that feeling again. Her body close to mine, making me think things I don't dare feel.

"Who is this guy?"

I feel her eyes on my mouth, like maybe she's going to kiss me again, to reassure me she doesn't have feelings for this guy.

"You wouldn't know him. His name is Sam Saunders."

I look at her and feel dizzy. The quiet only heightens the sensation. I'd always thought that Sam's and my life only intersected once—the night on the highway when he died and I was paralyzed forever. But things are never that simple. Or separate. If Sam hadn't made plans to go to Mount Whitney with Haley, I would never have met her.

Chapter Ten

Andy

~

August 21, 2025

I've drifted back to sleep when I become vaguely aware that Kate has shifted away from me, taking her warmth with her. She slips out of bed. As she pads into the bathroom, my mind snaps awake. How could I have fallen asleep when I might only have minutes left with her?

As I wait for her to come out of the shower, I wander around her apartment, trying to imprint every detail into my memory. It still feels impossible that I'm here, and I'm determined to remember everything. The curtains are drawn halfway, allowing the warm, golden glow of summer to filter through. The cool ocean breeze drifts through the window. Sheet music is scattered across the piano. I'll remember all of it.

I look around the room for a photo of her and can't find any. No pictures of her with friends or family. Very few personal items. No mementos or souvenirs. It's as if she decorated the whole place with a few clicks on Wayfair.

I glance through the books on her shelf. A memoir by pianist Lang Lang isn't a surprise, nor are books about the history of the Channel Islands, a series of islands off the coast of California, and some bestselling fiction, including one of my own books, *Night Watch*. She clearly has eclectic tastes because alongside a book about self-defense there's a memoir by Matthew McConaughey and a worn copy of *The Lord of the Rings*.

The small closet by the front door is slightly ajar so I move to close it, but before I do, I peek inside. A couple of her jackets hang from the rod. On the floor, I'm surprised to see a lightweight tent, a sleeping bag, a heavy flashlight, and a sturdy navy-blue backpack. Camping gear. Kate never talked about any interest in backpacking or camping, but the serious level of this equipment makes it clear she has some experience with it.

My gaze lands on a brown purse tucked behind the backpack, and it strikes me as an odd place for it—hidden and not easily accessible. I hesitate. Do I dare peek inside? What if she catches me? I can picture the hurt expression on her face if she finds me rifling through her things.

Still, I reach for the purse and slowly unzip it, which sounds like a shout in the silence. Inside are the usual things. Lip balm. Keys. A few crumpled receipts. A twinge of guilt hits me just for looking. Then my eye falls on a card wallet. I flip it over and gaze at her driver's license photo. While most of us look like maniacs in our license pictures, Kate manages to look stunning. Her hair is a lighter shade of brown here and longer than it is now, well past her shoulders. Even in the harsh light she radiates a soft beauty.

My heart stops. The name on the license isn't Kate Montano. It's Sarah Canford. The address is in Grand Junction, Michigan.

I can't process what I'm seeing.

I slip a credit card out of its slot. It's also embossed with the name: Sarah Canford.

I hear the shower cut off, so I scramble to put away the purse, leaving it, I hope, the way I found it.

"I'm going to run out and get us some breakfast," I call out, but my voice sounds strange.

"Okay," she calls back.

I race down the stairs and out the door, and in case she glances out the window, I keep walking until I'm a block away.

Outside the entrance to the bakery, I stop. My fingers tremble as I type *Sarah Canford* into Google on my phone. The last name is unusual enough that there are only a few entries. A LinkedIn for an actress in her forties and a college scholarship named after a schoolteacher in Arizona. None of them are Sarah Canford from Grand Junction, Michigan.

I go through the motions of ordering pastries at the bakery, but my mind is whirring a thousand miles a minute.

Who is the person in that apartment? Is she really Kate Montano and using fake identification for Sarah Canford? Or is her name Sarah Canford?

The cashier hands me my order, and I stare at it for a moment, wondering what I should do next. I have no idea if I have another hour or another ten seconds with her, so I race back to her apartment building.

There's got to be a simple explanation. Maybe Kate is her nickname. My friend Douglas in school was called "T" by all his relatives. That could be all this is.

I press the button to 218. She doesn't answer right away, and then I'm remembering doing this very thing in the days after she ghosted me. How many times had I pressed this button, hoping she'd answer?

Finally, she buzzes me in. When I reach her apartment, I hear the murmur of voices inside. I can make out a word here and there, the rise and fall of laughter. I recognize one voice as hers, but the other belongs to a man. I lean my ear closer to the door, but I can't hear what they're saying.

I knock.

"Oh good, you're back," Kate says, answering the door, her face flushed.

"I brought pastries," I say, but my attempt to sound normal has made my words soft and unformed around the edges.

"I got a surprise visitor while you were out." She motions to the man on the couch whose back is to me. "Andy, this is my friend Sam."

The man turns to greet me, and my body reacts with shock.

He's the 7-Eleven hugger. The guy caught on camera with Kate. Sarah. Whatever her name is.

I freeze in place, fighting to seem normal.

"Hey, great to meet you," he says. "Kate says you're an author."

"I am." I try to look casual, like you do when you're meeting someone for the first time, but I know I'm failing. I'm staring. "How about you? What do you do, Sam?"

"Sam came by to share some amazing news," Kate says, beaming. "He just landed a job teaching astronomy at a high school in Los Angeles."

"I'll be teaching physics too."

I want to understand how he knows her. He looks a few years younger than she is, early twenties. *What's their relationship?*

He glances at his phone and rises. "I got to run. Great to meet you, Andy."

"You too," I say. "What did you say your last name was?"

He smiles, polite, but distant. "I didn't. But it's Saunders."

Kate embraces him in a hug. "Thanks for stopping by. And congrats again."

I watch him go, and when the door shuts behind him, I place the bag on the counter.

It feels like a jealous-guy move to press for more info about their relationship. I try a different approach. "Nice guy. You've known him long?"

"He's the first person I met when I moved here."

"Oh, when was that?"

"Last spring. I didn't have a piano then so every day, I'd stop by the antique store on Main Street to play the old upright there. Turns out, the store belongs to his aunt, and he helps now and again when he's home from college. I played the piano so many times that he ended up loaning me a piano the family had in storage." She motions toward the piano in the living room. "That's how I got that beauty."

"You probably told me last night, but I overdid it on the champagne. Where are you from?"

She looks at me, her expression unreadable. "I'm from San Francisco."

If I didn't know about her driver's license, I'd believe her.

* * *

This is where I met Kate the first time. Jonathan's party. Just like before, I arrive a few minutes past nine and the party is already packed with friends sampling wine and prattling on about their vacations, their promotions, and the latest foodie paradise they've discovered.

I already know who's here. What they'll say. Jonathan's brother, Anthony, will regale a few of us with his harrowing tale about a brush with the cartel on his trip to Colombia. We'll all give him crap about whether it's true or not, but he won't retract his story. Sophie, a childhood friend of ours, will whisper about the affair that breaks her parents apart. Meg will drop a wineglass in the kitchen, and she'll spend ten red-faced minutes shooing everyone out of there so she can sweep and vacuum up every sliver.

Kate doesn't know I'll be here. I'd mentioned that I was going to a friend's party tonight, but she didn't ask for details. It felt like it would've been awkward to drop Jonathan's name in hopes that she'd connect the dots.

Like before, she's in the middle of Sinatra's "Fly Me to the Moon." I walk up beside her and sing softly, in what I hope is a not too terrible voice:

You are all I long for, all I worship and adore.
In other words, please be true.

She laughs, not missing a note. "Andy! What're you doing here?"

I swing around and catch her smile. "You knew it was me?"

"I recognized your voice."

"That bad, huh?"

"I'd keep your day job if I were you," she says, her eyes sparkling. "*How* are you here?"

"Jonathan and I've been friends since fourth grade when his homemade bubble gum rocket crashed into my head at summer camp. What's your excuse?"

"He posted online that he needed a piano player. I got the gig. He's *paying* me to play the piano," she beams. "What would you like me to play next?" she asks, finishing Sinatra.

"Maybe something by Chet Baker?" I ask, anticipating what I already know happens.

Her eyes register surprise. "Amazing that you'd suggest that."

"Maybe 'There'll Never Be Another You'?" I say, settling in the chair beside the piano.

"You're not actually going to sit and listen to me play, are you?"

"Of course."

She laughs. "You realize what you're missing, don't you? Your friend has a fortune teller in the other room and a whole wine tasting thing going on in the kitchen. Everyone's going to wonder why you're hanging out here with the newbie piano player."

"My friends will see that I'm the smartest guy in the whole place."

Her cheeks flush. "I'm not sure I deserve that, but thank you," she whispers.

I lean in to brush a kiss on her cheek and when I do, I notice a thick pink scar, about six inches, just below her hairline. I guess I'd never seen it before because her hair normally covers that part of her forehead.

She notices me staring. "Softball accident," she says softly and pushes her hair back in place. "You've got your homemade bubble gum rocket accident. I've got Brenda Makowsky pitching one straight to my head."

"Brenda must've had one hell of an arm."

"She went on to play for Tennessee State," she says and launches into Chet Baker's "There'll Never Be Another You."

My insides twist as I do the math. High school was at least six or seven years ago for her. I'm not any kind of expert, but that scar looks newer. And there's something else I notice. She seems worried that I'd discovered it.

Chapter Eleven

Logan

August 22, 2025

I'm a ball of nerves as I head to Celestine, the restaurant where Haley works. Scaling a mountain is easy compared to figuring out how to navigate a relationship. Or a flirtation. Or whatever this is.

The bar is set up as a square, and three bartenders in the center take drinks and dinner orders from there. It's not too busy, so maybe she'll have time to talk to me.

I see her right away and my heart twists. Her hair is pulled back in a low ponytail and she's wearing a black apron like the rest of them, but she stands out. Like that deer in the mountains, I can't stop looking at her.

They're playing Flaming Lips' "Do You Realize?" which probably doesn't mean anything to most of the fortysomething patrons here, but the mellow vibe and the words feel like a soundtrack for my life right now:

Do you realize that happiness makes you cry?

"Hey, mountain man," Haley says. "I've been waiting for you to show." The way she says it makes me think she might mean it. She wipes down the counter in front of me and leans over to whisper, "The fish tacos are okay here, but nothing like the ones we had yesterday. Try the fish and chips."

"I'm not really here for the food," I say, giving myself points for being somewhat clever.

She smiles. "You're here for the drinks, then?"

"Not that either." I'm openly flirting with her and she's still smiling. She doesn't suddenly remember she has a boyfriend or mention she's about to move out of town. Since I've been in a wheelchair, I've become a grand champion at being ghosted. "I'll have a ginger ale, so your boss doesn't kick me out."

"You got it."

She fills a glass with fizzy liquid from the soda gun and presents it to me. I've never seen anything more perfect. Sure, the ginger ale looks fine, but it's her I can't stop staring at.

The sharp echo of boots on the tile floor pulls me back to reality. I turn to see a stately woman stepping through the front door, dressed in black pants, sleek designer boots, and a turquoise blazer. *Brooke Dalton.*

"You have your growl face on," Haley says, teasing.

"I have a growl face?" I ask, relaxing my mouth even as my heart is thudding.

"It's that look you got on the mountain when we were heading up the incline. It's like a growl. You don't bite, do you?"

I try to smile at her. Really try. Then I sense Brooke moving near the door, I glance over and she's looking right at me.

Holy hell. I feel the blood drain from my face. For a moment, I imagine myself going over and shoving her. Hard.

Haley looks alarmed. "You okay?"

I whisper. "Sorry. That woman who just came in? She's been stalking me."

She nods toward Brooke, who's talking with the hostess. "You mean Brooke Dalton?"

I can't keep the surprise out of my voice. "You know her?"

"She's the owner."

Oh, hell. Of course she is.

"Are you sure *she's* been stalking you?" Haley asks. "She's like fifty. Married. With an eight-year-old daughter."

Brooke turns away from the hostess, and her eyes lock with mine. She stares at me hard, like she can see right through me. I stare back. We look like a couple of gunfighters in the Old West preparing to draw.

She makes a beeline my way.

"Logan, we really must talk," Brooke says and motions for me to follow her.

* * *

A dark pulse of anger courses through me as I follow her to the back of the restaurant.

How could it be that I've come face to face—twice—with the person I've hated since the moment I learned her name?

"Come in," she says softly, opening the office door.

The place smells of vanilla and other sweet stuff. A shipment of boxes crowds one corner, but otherwise, the room is decorated like something you'd see in an Instagram photo of rich people's homes, all creamy whites and beiges and soft textures. Expensive. Not what I expected from the monster who paralyzed me and killed Sam.

When she closes the door, I whirl around to face her. "What do you want from me?"

She motions for me to sit, and after I do, she drops in the chair across from me. The couch is so soft, it feels like it's going to swallow me whole. She leans forward. "My manager texted me you were here."

"Your manager?"

"I gave him your description and instructions to call me if you came in."

"You were *expecting* me to come here?"

"Haven't you been getting my texts? I've been asking you to stop by or text back."

"What for?"

"You're a jumper, aren't you?"

My mind reels. How does she know I'm from the future when time travel hasn't been invented yet? Then it all clicks in. She's a time traveler too.

"Are you?"

"I've been here almost two days."

Holy heck. What are the chances that two of us would be stranded at the same time and in the same place?

I don't hold back. "Meeting you . . . this is hell."

She looks at her hands. "I understand why you feel that way."

I'm shocked at how normal she seems. I'd imagined her as a privileged drunk, part sociopath, and a singular force of evil. I'd dreamed many times of how I would like to physically hurt her, and the temptation rises.

"I know an apology doesn't mean a whole lot—"

"Save it. You were drunk and you mowed me down."

Her voice is sharp. "That isn't true. I didn't have a drop of alcohol at the party."

"That's always been your story. But if you'd stopped and called the police after you sent me and Sam flying, we'd know for sure if you were drunk or not. But you didn't stop. You left me there to suffer. And all you can say is you're *sorry*?"

A sob escapes her throat. Not the quiet, repressed sounds of sadness, but the anguished cry of a child. I've been waiting for this moment. Wanting desperately to see that she was in pain for what she did.

"I'm really sorry, Logan. If you'd give me a moment—"

My voice trembles. "You *should* be sorry. Do you realize that I'll never walk again? I'll never stand upright on a surfboard. I will never swim. Never stand up in the shower or my wedding or some future kid's soccer games. I'll never forget all you took from me."

Her face turns white. "I want you to know that I'm haunted by it. Every day I live with the terrible knowledge of what I did to you."

"Did you rehearse that? Feels like it."

"I've been writing 'Dear Logan' letters since I realized what I'd done."

I shrug. "I never got anything from you."

"The lawyers wouldn't let me send them."

I scoff. "The lawyers. People like you always have excuses."

Her voice is small. "Do you want to know what the letters said?"

"Not really, no."

She tells me anyway. "They were all different. But they said the same thing. The accident changed me forever. And I think about you every day and will continue to do that for the rest of my life. I am so sorry, Logan."

I feel like I can't breathe. I can feel her regret, but I can't find a way to accept her apology. And never will.

I stand, my heart hammering. "I have to go."

She holds up her hand. "Wait. Please."

I turn to look at her. Her bony hands are clasped so tight together that her knuckles have turned white. She waits before speaking. "Don't you think it's strange that the two of us are stranded here?"

I sigh. "What's your point?"

"Maybe it's an opportunity."

"An opportunity for what?"

"Maybe we can change what happens on August twenty-fifth."

"We can't change the future. We both know that."

She looks down at her hands. "No, but if we're stranded here—as it seems we are—we can live it out differently, can't we? I could stay off the PCH that night. And so could you. And then—"

I raise my voice. "And then what? Eventually, we'll be extracted back to our present lives. Where I'm still paralyzed."

"If we *aren't* extracted, though," she says softly. "We could experience the other possibilities that August twenty-fifth held. I *wouldn't* be a murderer. You *wouldn't* be paralyzed."

My throat feels raw. Her idea intrigues me, honestly. But there is no way I'm going to let Brooke Dalton think I have any respect for her. That I'm even close to forgiving her. Or that I want to be part of any plan she's thinking up.

Chapter Twelve

Elizabeth

~

August 22, 2025

I wake in a panic. I open my eyes and scan the room and whoosh out a breath. I'm still in the past. I know that because I'm wearing the same clothes I had on last night when I dropped exhausted into bed. I know it because the white linen curtains on the windows aren't the blue and white striped drapes I'll install in a few years.

But something is wrong. I can feel it. I have the sense that Sam isn't here.

I pad to his room, my heart thumping, hoping I'm wrong. Overreacting.

I'm not. Sam's bed is a rumpled mess, but he's not in his room.

"Sam?" I call out, my voice raw with fear.

No answer.

I try to remember what happened on this day the first time around, but I don't have the kind of memory that remembers every hour of every day three years in the past.

I text him: *Good morning! Where're you off to?*

A few minutes later, his text swoops across my screen: *With a friend. Back soon.*

I'm relieved, but my hand still hovers over the phone. The urge to call Mark gnaws at me—it's what I always did when he was away on business. Decades of marriage has etched this ritual into our lives. I tell him about the sunset or the dolphins breaching the waves that he's missing at the beach. He tells me what hurdles the company is attempting to overcome. The looming deadlines.

But I'm frozen. Twenty years of marriage and now I'm afraid to speak to my own husband.

Mark has an uncanny ability to decipher my every expression. He'll hear the hollowness in my voice, the slight pause between words, and he'll notice something is wrong. He'll ask about it. How can I hide the fact that I've lived through Sam's death and our divorce?

Even worse, what if he decides to return home? He'd see all of it. There's a look that accompanies devastating loss. I've seen it staring back at me in the mirror—a light that's gone out behind my eyes, leaving them dull and flat.

This Mark, the one from three years ago, doesn't know any of what's ahead. He's still proud of Sam's achievements in college. Looking forward to the future. Is it fair to burden him with a future he's powerless to change?

As my finger hovers over his name on the screen, I'm surprised by how much I long to hear his voice. Not my emotionally distant ex-husband's, but this Mark's. The one who still looks at me with love. This simple realization surprises me. Beneath the layers of grief and resentment, could it be that I still have feelings for him? It's heartbreaking to consider that a part of me still loves the man I'm destined to lose.

I set the phone down on the counter. The only choice is to not call him—to shield him from the pain of our future. Even if it means carrying this heartache alone.

While I wait for Sam to return, I walk through my home, letting my pulse settle. After Sam died, it had been impossible to be alone in this house with all its painful reminders of him. I remember walking through the living room and coming upon his shoes, a low-profile black pair he put on each time he headed out for a hike. I stopped, bent down to pick them up, and started to cry. I'd look at the objects from Sam's life and remember the things Sam said and did with them, as if the things themselves were transmitting the memories.

Now I see the extraordinary in all of it. The random things in life that I once took for granted take on new meaning. The first time I'd lived this life, I'd rushed through it, ignoring the details around me. I'd looked at the things in my life without really seeing them at all. Today, it's the little things I latch on to.

There are a pair of blue parrot candlesticks Mark and I bought, thinking them absolutely ridiculous but finding that they soon became our favorites. How many dinners and special occasions had we placed those candlesticks on the table and shared a laugh about our unexpected love of them?

On a shelf above Sam's desk, long forgotten by him I'm sure, I discover his treasured collection of Lego Minifigures along with a toy car and army man figures. I feel a surge of love as I remember his little voice and the way his eyes would light up with excitement each time he added a Minifigure to his collection. I breathe it all in, experiencing it with fresh eyes.

Then my eye falls on a credit card bill on Sam's desk. Although I don't feel good about it, I snoop. I slide open the envelope and glance at the bill. The first time around, I'd ignored the charges for Dick's Sporting Goods because the cost was under fifty dollars. Seeing it now makes the questions start creeping in. What is this charge? If I knew more about his life, if I'd learned more about what he spent his time doing, could I erase the hollowness in my heart that taunts me every day? *You could have stopped him from dying.*

I head to the safe and open it. The cash that I'd discovered was missing after Sam's death is still there. But the gun is missing.

Suddenly, I hear the front door open and Sam bursts in.

"I got the job, Mom! I can't believe it!" he says, his face flushed with excitement.

I remember this, of course. Sam received an email—on a Saturday, no less—that he'd been offered a teaching position at a prominent high school in Los Angeles. When I found out the first time, I should have been proud. Excited, even. Instead, I'd worried about him living ninety minutes away in a harsh and unforgiving city like L.A. I wanted him to be safe. I never imagined his life would end in the haven of safety and friendliness of Ventura.

I'd skated past this big moment, consumed with worry, and squandered the chance to embrace what surely was one of the happiest moments of his life. I'd assumed, like we all do, that we'd have more time.

I see this moment for what it is. An opportunity to do it differently—to embrace and celebrate his achievements without reservation.

"I'm so proud of you," I say, wrapping him in a hug. "This is an amazing opportunity."

"I can't believe they said yes so quickly after the second interview," he says.

In so many ways Sam reminds me of Mark. It's not just the physical resemblance—the thick mop of wavy dark hair and brown eyes that slope downward—but also in the way that his eyes become sharp and bright—almost as if he can see through things—when things go the way he wants them to.

His smile fades and his eyes focus on the open safe. "Everything okay?"

"Yeah, fine," I say slowly. "Only . . . I noticed the gun is missing."

He looks up at me with big brown eyes. "Oh, I forgot to tell you. I've been practicing at the gun range. I've been storing it there, so I don't have to carry it back and forth."

"Why are you practicing at the gun range?"

He flicks his eyes away, and I know he's lying. "Just something to blow off steam while I waited for job offers."

The answer is plausible enough, but something is off. "Hey, I'm starving," he says. "Want to celebrate over lunch?"

"Of course," I say brightly.

I'm getting my do-over. Although I have pressing questions about what he took from the safe, I'm determined not to miss a chance to revel in this moment with him.

As we walk toward Main Street, a warm breeze blows from the ocean, carrying the scent of salt water and brine. Sam points out the unusual orange tint in the sky. "That's from the fires in Central California. It's kind of like Mars," he says, his eyes lighting up. "The reason Mars looks red is because there are so many dust particles in the atmosphere."

I lay my hand on his shoulder, trying not to cry. I've missed him so. As a boy, Sam was always curious about everything. When he was five, he begged for a telescope, determined to see Saturn's rings and the craters on the moon. Throughout elementary school, our home was a revolving laboratory of volcano kits, bottle rockets, and exploding chemistry sets. In high school, he was devouring science fiction novels and comic books, taking mechanical things apart only to tinker them back together again. It's no wonder to me now that he'd be passionate about teaching science.

The Italian restaurant with the deep-dish pizza that's been his favorite for years has a line out the door, so we stroll down Main Street to find another spot. The next thing I know we're walking up to Celestine, and Sam is checking in with the hostess at a table outside. An icy wave of dread washes over me.

"How about we go somewhere else?" I suggest.

"Why? You always liked this restaurant."

I want to tell him that the woman who owns Celestine will end his life in three days. That it feels perverse to allow her to profit from us now or ever. But I can't make my mouth form the words.

Before I know it, the hostess seats us in a booth. I look around and wonder if I'll see Brooke Dalton here. And if I do, will I be able to control my anger about something she hasn't yet done? I'm not a violent person, but for a moment, I imagine what it might feel like to unleash my anger at her.

"Remember Haley Reinhart who lived next door when I was in middle school?" Sam asks, bringing me back to the moment. He nods in the direction of the bar. "That's her."

I look over at a willowy young woman with blonde hair and deep blue eyes. "That's Haley?" I ask, trying to sound normal but failing. "Last time I saw her, she had a mouthful of braces."

"We were supposed to go hiking together on Mount Whitney," he says. "But I had to bail because of the second interview at Summit Ridge High."

I watch Haley place a beer mug on the counter in front of a young man in a denim shirt. She's smiling at him, flirting. He turns his face slightly and I notice his eyes. And then the tattoo on the back of his neck. With a sick feeling, I realize who he is.

Logan Sandoval. The man who will be with Sam the night he dies.

My chest heaves as I try to get my racing heartbeat under control. I had searched for Logan in the months after Sam's death, desperate to discover why Sam spent his final moments with him, but he'd never responded to my letters or emails. Still, I did uncover details about his troubled past, including a post on the Los Angeles County Sheriff's website. A log entry from two years prior revealed Logan had been arrested for selling fentanyl outside a food truck in Los Angeles, though the charges were later dropped when evidence disappeared.

Locating him proved impossible. And yet, here he is. Twenty feet away from me.

The rest of the world is operating like everything's normal. Except me. "Who's Haley talking to?" I say, my voice quivering. "He looks familiar."

Sam glances at Logan and shakes his head. "No idea."

"I think his name is Logan." My head feels heavy. Dizzy. "His last name is Sandoval . . . I think you know him?"

"No idea who he is."

"Are you sure?"

"Never saw him before."

His words land like a punch in the gut. Why is Sam lying to me?

Chapter Thirteen

Logan

August 22, 2025

I march out of Brooke's office like I'm escaping a fire. I feel the heat leaching through my skin and the sweat breaking out on my back. My legs ache, as if I have a fever.

I'm sitting at the bar now, hoping for Haley's attention. At the same time, I'm trying to come up with some believable story that'll explain to Haley why Brooke wanted to talk to me. I think about saying that Brooke wants me to do some work for her. What kind of work?

Haley notices me and comes over, sliding a fresh ginger ale my way. "So, was my boss stalking you?" she whispers.

"She just wants me to give her daughter swimming lessons," I say, with surprising conviction.

"You teach swimming? That explains why you were so great with the boys who fell off their kayak. You going to do it?"

I shrug. "Could be fun, actually."

Two women nursing a couple of cosmos get Haley's attention and off she goes again. I watch her helping them, smiling at something one of them is saying. Just beyond them, in a booth near the door, I see a face I recognize.

Sam Saunders.

I blink. It feels like I'm being haunted. Everywhere I look is a reminder of the night I lost my legs.

I'm guessing from the gray streaks in her hair that the woman with Sam is his mom. She hunches over the table like she's carrying a heavy burden and then glances over at me with disappointment. The tatts do that to some. Then again, maybe her angry look has nothing to do with me. Could be that the service is crummy, and I just happen to be in her line of sight.

But I know him. Or at least I will meet him. Briefly.

He looks different here. Happy, like he's celebrating something big. I've got blank spots in my memories before the crash, but I can't forget there was terror in his eyes.

Chapter Fourteen

Elizabeth

August 22, 2025

What to do about Logan Sandoval, who's sitting at the bar, fewer than twenty feet away? This is the man who somehow convinced Sam to be on the highway that night. He's the person who will erase motherhood from my life.

The fierce mama bear in me imagines walking over and confronting him. It would feel crazy-good to unleash my anger. I wonder if I could do it.

"You okay, Mom?" Sam asks, bringing me back to the moment. "You look kind of pale."

"I think it's a little hot in here," I say, then make a show of taking a few gulps of water.

My heart is pounding as I turn my attention back to Sam.

What if this is the last time we'll sit together? The last time we'll talk. I live every moment with a sense of impending doom, worried that Aeon Expeditions will solve whatever trouble it's having and this—the hiss of the coffee machine behind the bar, the murmur of people talking, the clatter of dishes, Sam sitting in front of me—will all be over.

I miss being his mom. Even when I think of his childhood and managing the exhausting sleepovers, juggling the endless to-do list of shoes and clothes that needed buying or washing or folding, and the dropping-everything-because-he-has-a-fever days, I know that being his mom always will be the greatest honor of my life.

Logan's presence does, however, give me an idea. I know I cannot change the future that I will return to. Scientists at Aeon have made clear that there's a reset when we return. The future remains unchanged by what we do here.

But what if Aeon can't bring me back to the future? If I'm stranded here for even a few more days—*do I dare hope for that?*—I can make it so that Sam isn't on the PCH with Logan when Brooke Dalton barrels through that curve.

I can prevent the accident from happening.

I'll get to be his mom for as long as I'm stranded here. I can live a different life.

The waitress comes by and asks us if we need anything else, and I answer absently. My mind is elsewhere, developing a plan. Whatever Logan will do to persuade Sam to meet him on that stretch of highway, I will stop it.

* * *

I can't shake the feeling this is a fool's errand, an impossible mission that only a heartbroken mother would undertake. It's irrational and illogical and goes against everything I'd ever done before. I'm following Logan home.

After we finished dinner, I'd spotted him leaving Celestine and told Sam that I'd catch up with him at home because I needed to check on my friend Alba, who'd broken her foot. While it was true that Alba had broken her foot, I have no intention of stopping by her home.

Instead, I've put in my ear buds, pretending to listen to music while following Logan for block after block, first along Main Street past its busy restaurants and home décor and clothing storefronts, then through leafy streets lined with cute beach cottages and cozy bungalows until we get to a neighborhood of two-story apartment buildings that look like they haven't been renovated since the 70s. Luckily, Logan's too busy looking at his phone to notice that I'm a block behind, keeping pace with him.

I think about calling out to him and talking to him right here instead of acting like I'm a gumshoe detective on a stakeout. But I am curious about where he lives. How his life became entwined with Sam's.

Suddenly I realize that Logan and I are alone on the street. My pulse pounds, and I weigh the pros and cons of continuing to follow him. The obvious risk is that he could turn around any second, notice that I've been trailing him, and confront me. He might have had too much to drink and be belligerent. Angry. My mouth goes dry and suddenly I'm not sure if I can go through with this. But I'll never know why Sam was with Logan that night unless I talk to him now.

I watch him go into his apartment building, a stucco box painted in a bleak color, every window disfigured by the same yellowed plastic vertical blinds. The barely there landscaping looks like the landlord hasn't visited in years. I head up concrete steps painted bright blue, then find his last name scrawled in black ink on the old-fashioned doorbell panel.

I press the button. A male voice squawks through the speaker. "Can I help you?"

My stomach quakes, but I sound surprisingly calm. "My name is Elizabeth Saunders. I'm looking for Logan Sandoval."

"What for?"

"I'd like to talk to him."

It's a lousy introduction so I'm surprised when, a few seconds later, the door buzzes, letting me in. I grab the handle and step inside the hallway. The hall light is out, giving the place a gloomy feel. Then the apartment door in front of me swings open and Logan stands before me. All the vim and vinegar I'd been summoning suddenly whooshes out of my body. He's much more imposing up close than he seemed in the restaurant, all broad shoulders, thick thighs, and a wide stance. The heavy metal music he's playing on his ear buds is loud enough that I can hear.

"I'm Logan," he says removing an ear bud. His voice is softer than I'd imagined. As if all the sinew and mass is an elaborate cover for a gentle man.

"Elizabeth Saunders," I start, repeating myself. "I think you know my son, Sam?"

He stares at me like I'm a strange bird. "What's this about?"

"Maybe he's one of your friends or . . ." I trail off. His sheer size makes me nervous about accusing him of selling drugs to Sam.

He steps forward, towering over me. "Why are you here?" The way he says it makes me snap to attention. Like he might know me. Yet I'm sure we've never met.

"I want to ask you about Sam."

He stares at me, incredulous. "I saw you at Celestine earlier. Did you follow me home?"

My voice sounds bolder than I feel. "This is going to sound crazy. I know it will. In three days, you'll be in an accident on the PCH. Sam will be there with you. Sam will die. And you . . . you will be paralyzed."

The minute I say it, I regret every word. I've broken every Aeon rule and I sound like a lunatic. I expect him to look at me like I'm raving mad. Surely, he'll close the door. Instead, he pushes it open. "I think you should come in."

"Seriously?"

"I'm pretty sure you're a jumper. Like me."

Chapter Fifteen

Logan

August 22, 2025

My body vibrates with shock. This is impossible. Elizabeth's presence here means there are three of us stranded. Not just me and Brooke. Three of us connected to the night that my life is wrecked forever.

Elizabeth steps into my apartment and looks around the room, and the desperation of the life I'm living is on full display: a cheap coffee table from Ikea and a worn-out couch I'd retrieved from the parkway. Only thing decent in the room is the TV, which I fought for in a Black Friday sale.

Her hair is tied away from her face, making her look frail and tired. Her cheeks are deep red. Side effect of the time travel, I'm guessing.

"How long have you been here?" she asks.

"Thirty hours. Give or take. You?"

"The same."

"Did you follow me home because you already knew I was a jumper?"

"I followed you because I need to know why Sam was with you on that highway on the night of the accident."

I'm surprised by her question. "Sam wasn't *with* me."

Her mouth twists in anger. "Why are you lying? Why are you *both* lying about this?"

"I didn't—I don't—even know Sam."

"But he was . . . they found his body . . . there with you."

"Look, I was at a party my friend Emmett was throwing. I was minding my own business, pacing in the bike lane, my AirPods at full volume when—"

"I'm not buying that. Why would you be pacing in the bike lane at 11:30 at night?"

"I don't owe you any explanations."

"Why were you there?" She sighs. "Help me understand what happened that night."

I draw a deep breath. "A half hour earlier, around eleven, some college kids rolled up in their dad's Lexus. They were high on Molly. Ecstasy. They brought out some other pills and started passing them out. That's when I bailed. I'd been trying to stay clean and when other people are drinking and getting high and I feel the urge to join them, I hightail it outdoors. Sometimes I'll sprint until my lungs hurt and I can't catch my breath. Other times I'll do some ridiculous number of pushups. That's how I burn off the hunger for that stuff."

"The police talked to the guy who hosted the party. Emmett. He told them that Sam wasn't a guest. That he didn't know him. That leaves only one possibility. That Sam was there to meet you. What for? Drugs? Something else?"

The "something else" lingers in the room.

"He wasn't there to meet me."

"Then why was he there?"

"I don't know."

Tears are leaking out of her eyes, and she doesn't bother wiping them away. "Why are you lying to me?"

"I'm not."

"Tell me," she says, real soft. "Tell me why Sam was on the highway with you."

I shake my head. "I turned around and there he was. A split second later I was flying."

I think about telling her that Sam looked horrified. Panicked. But her eyes are flooded with tears. No sound escapes her lips. She buries her face in her hands. I've got no idea what to do. Should I say something? Leave the room? Maybe bring her a tissue. I loosen my grip on the arm of my chair, thinking I should get her a glass of water.

The next thing I know, my hand is on her shoulder. Gentle. We both lost something that night. And we're both here trying to get it back.

Chapter Sixteen

Elizabeth

~

August 22, 2025

"We're not the only ones," Logan says, handing me a glass of ice water.

My heart skips. "There are other jumpers?"

"Brooke Dalton is here too."

The name hits hard, sending a wave of unease through me. Logan's face is pale, his eyes fixed on mine, and the air between us grows impossibly thick with everything we're not saying.

"It can't be a coincidence, can it?" Logan says finally, his voice tight. "Three people sent back to relive the worst day of their lives? That's no accident."

"Aeon doesn't have the technology to send us to a specific date. We heard that in every orientation session," I say, though doubt starts creeping in.

"They lied about the safe zone. Could be lying about this too."

I set the glass down with a shaky hand. "What do you mean?"

"They told us we'd feel pain if we went more than ten miles out of the safe zone. I got on a bus. Did just that. Nothing. No pain."

"That can't be—" The engineers were specific, so sure. But now I wonder . . .

"They didn't tell us everything. Maybe they *can* jump us to specific dates."

My mind spins. "Look, my ex-husband is Mark Saunders and—"

Logan freezes, his eyes widening. "Wait. The founder of Aeon? He's your ex? What does he say about what's happening to us?"

My voice falters. "I haven't talked to him."

His eyebrows shoot up. "Why not?"

I hesitate, weighing how much I should reveal. "If I talk to him, he'll ask about the future. He'll want to know what's coming. And what do I say? That his son dies? That we divorce? All of that would destroy him."

"You could lie," he says, but even he doesn't sound convinced.

I shake my head slowly. "After more than twenty years of marriage? He knows me too well. He'd see straight through the lie."

He stands, running a hand through his hair, clearly frustrated. "Okay. But if they *can* send us to a specific date—and it looks like they do—why would they send us to relive the *worst* day of our lives? Why do that?"

I stare at the floor, my thoughts spinning. "I don't know. Maybe it's some kind of glitch, a mistake."

"A mistake." His voice drops, low and heavy. "So we could be stuck here forever?"

"Would that be so terrible? Do you even want to go back to the future?"

The question hangs in the air. He manages a single word. "No."

For a long moment, neither of says anything. Then his voice cuts through the silence. "But if we're here even for a while... we have a shot at something big. We can change what happens on August twenty-fifth."

The date rings in my ears, the memories crashing down on me. The phone call from the sheriff. Sam's broken body.

"We can talk to Brooke," he says, his voice steady. "Keep her off the PCH."

My stomach twists. "I can't talk to Brooke," I say, my voice barely audible. "I can't talk to the woman who killed my son. I can't do it."

His jaw tightens and a flush creeps up his neck. "If we keep her off the PCH, Sam lives. I get to keep my legs. We get the lives we've always wanted."

The air suddenly feels electric, charged with something I haven't felt in years. I've been trapped in grief for so long I've forgotten what hope feels like. But here it is.

"Okay. Tell her I'll meet with her."

There's a chance. A real chance to stop this.

We can save Sam.

Save ourselves.

Chapter Seventeen

Andy

~

August 23, 2025

I'm trying to cram everything into one day. All the things we did the first time around. I don't have the benefit of knowing how much more time I'll have with her, so I arrange the activities like I'm assembling a giant jigsaw puzzle.

We went paddleboarding on Mondos Beach in the morning, then wolfed down lunch at an Indian restaurant nearby. After that, I took her for a tasting at a local craft winery and, like before, we overdid it and had to dry out in her apartment, putting back strong coffee and listening to Puccini and Verdi operas all afternoon. By evening, neither of us had an ounce of energy to go out for dinner and karaoke, so we decide to do that another time.

I don't know if we'll get another day together. So, the next morning, I arrive early at her apartment and take her to the batting cages where she shows off some of her softball skills from high school. Then we walk Hobson Beach, not under the silvery moonlight like before, but on a sun-drenched summer afternoon with dozens of families and kids and dogs all around us playing in the surf and building sandcastles. As I watch her join in on a game of frisbee, my heart squeezes. I've lived this once before so you might think the novelty would've worn off, but I still feel like I'm in a state of constant discovery.

I keep promising myself I'll ask about the name on her driver's license or quiz her about the scar on her forehead. But falling for someone is like an unchoreographed dance. Things flow, we're drawn together, we share laughs, swap stories, and the joy of discovering each other's quirks takes over any impulse to dig for facts.

By the time the sun sets, we're both slowing down some, so we order Thai food from the restaurant down the street, and when it arrives, we eat it while relaxing on her living room floor.

A slow, mournful orchestral piece comes on her HomePod, and suddenly she jumps up and races to the wall, flicking off the lights and plunging the room into darkness.

"What're you doing?" I ask.

"In the dark is the only way to listen to this," she whispers then settles again beside me.

She turns up the volume and lets the plaintive melody fill our darkened sanctuary. As we listen together, I felt an undeniable pull between us. Time seems to slow, and I realize I'm experiencing a new moment with her that I'll probably remember forever.

"This is a song about Orpheus," she says softly. "He's deeply in love with Eurydice, and when she dies, he can't stop thinking about her. He can't figure out how he'll live without her. He's so desperate that he travels to the underworld and sings this melody to Hades, the god of the underworld, to plead with him to let him take Eurydice back with him."

"Does it work?" I ask, desperate for hope that you can be reunited with someone you've lost.

"Not exactly. Hades makes a bargain that if Orpheus doesn't look back at Eurydice on his walk out of the underworld, he'll let her stay with Orpheus in the land of the living. But Orpheus doubts himself. He doubts Hades. He turns around to look at her and . . ."

"And he loses her forever?"

"He does."

"So his trip to the underworld was pointless."

She turns to me. "Or you could see it another way. Because of Orpheus, the two were reunited, however briefly. That's something."

* * *

An hour later, we're looking at vases in the antique shop on Main Street. This store has been here since I was a kid and hasn't changed any since then. The low hum of an old phonograph playing scratchy jazz records fills the air. The same stark fluorescent lights hang overhead. Dusty shelves are lined with antique clocks and pocket watches, silver tea sets, and advertising memorabilia from decades ago. A not-so-great upright piano stands in the corner, a relic that's been there since I was in middle school.

"This is the piano I played when I came to Ventura," she tells me, running her fingers over the keys.

I don't think Kate has a passion for antiques, but she examines every one of the vases in detail as if she does. China. Porcelain. Glass. She holds one iridescent specimen to the light and examines it closely, but it feels like she's pretending to be interested.

It wasn't my idea to come in here. After dinner, we're walking down Main Street to get some gelato, when she suddenly grabs my arm. "Let's go in here," she said tersely, then we slipped inside the store, and she made a beeline toward the vase collection in the back.

"Can I help you find something?" the bald guy behind the counter asks.

"Just looking," she says.

As she glances through another shelf of vases, I notice things that I didn't before. The first time around I'd been falling for her, and other details just sailed by. For starters, her eyes dart to the door every few minutes. It's a subtle tic and anyone else might think she's just looking around, but there's a nervous energy to it. And she keeps up a steady patter about the vases to keep me from noticing that her hands are trembling slightly.

"Look," she says lightly, showing me a vase with a strange reptilian creature painted on one side. "Who would ever have something like this in their home? There's got to be a story behind this."

I look at the price tag. "Someone who's got eighty dollars to burn."

She smiles and then the bell over the front door dings, and her gaze swings to the door again. A trio of women, their faces tinged with sunburn, walk in seemingly excited about a vintage lamp in the window display. Kate's shoulders relax, but her eyes stay on the door, as if she's expecting someone else to walk in.

"You still have sale stuff on the patio?" she asks the shopkeeper.

He nods. "Yes. Just a reminder, we're closing in ten minutes."

I follow her out the back door and into a tented patio area with a couple of folding tables jammed with vintage computer equipment, old 45s, and boxes filled with vintage mirrors.

She lifts a 45, inspecting it. "Would you mind if we head back to my place?"

"You want to skip gelato?"

She blows out a breath. "Honestly? I'm kind of beat."

She reaches for my hand as we step off the patio, then we head into the narrow alley that meanders behind the bustling chaos of Main Street stores.

"Can I show you a shortcut?" she asks.

"Lead the way."

The route she chooses has us winding around overflowing dumpsters and hurrying past tall mounds of black trash bags. In the fading evening light, she points out the quirky architectural details: a huge plastic flower display dumped into a parking area, the brief place where asphalt becomes cobblestones, the row of potted herbs growing in repurposed Folgers coffee cans.

I set aside the strangeness of the setting and see this for what it is. What I always wanted. More time with Kate. All it really takes to be happy sometimes is being with the one person who really gets you.

Then she glances behind us uneasily and I follow her gaze. No one else is in the alley or nearby. Still, she picks up the pace.

"Let's go this way," she says as we hurry through the side yard of a duplex that leads to the back entrance of her building. She swipes her key card, and once we've climbed the steps and we're inside her apartment, she closes the door and turns the deadbolt. It's subtle, but I can't help but feel that something has spooked her.

I'm quiet for a moment, giving her a chance to catch her breath, not wanting to add pressure.

"It felt like we were running from something—or someone—back there," I say. "Or was I imagining things?"

Her eyes meet mine, wavering until they finally drop. "You're a writer. You *live* in your imagination, don't you?" she says with a laugh.

"We weren't running from anything?"

"No," she says. "I thought you'd have fun alley-hopping. Let me get us some water. Sparkling or flat?"

"Sparkling."

She leaves the room, giving me a moment to think. We are both telling each other a story. I'm pretending to be meeting her for the first time, and she's pretending that everything's normal, that we weren't running from someone or something.

That's when I see a camera near the ceiling. I never noticed it before because it's white and small enough—the size of a golf ball—that it blends into the light trim. Security cameras are common even in sleepy Ventura. But I don't know anyone who has a camera *inside* their apartment. Why does she have it?

She returns with two glasses of sparkling water, and we sit on the couch together. My body is noisy with thoughts and questions. I have no idea how to act. Should I ask about the camera? Should I bring up the subject—again—of why we left the antique store abruptly and ran home through the alley? What is her real name?

She settles beside me, touches her hand to mine and leaves it there, knitting a bubble around us. This feeling—as if the two of us are in our own world—is what it's always felt like being with her. I *know* her. We end up talking about everything under the sun for a long while, and I realize I rarely stop smiling when I'm with her. We make plans to watch *Sleepless in Seattle* the next day. She laughs at a few of my jokes, if you can call them that, and I'm so distracted by her that I forget about all the questions I have and the things I need to understand.

"Tell me about your family," she asks. "Do they all live here in Ventura?"

"My parents do. My dad is a professor of engineering at UC Santa Barbara. Mom is a writer. Scholarly articles about language development in babies and things like that," I tell her. "I have no siblings but two cousins, one who's going to college here. And another who's in pharmaceutical research at Pfizer in Kalamazoo, Michigan."

Michigan. Maybe this is how I can ask her about Michigan.

"I'm visiting him this fall," I continue. "His name is Mitchell. Have you ever been to Michigan?"

She glances out the window. "Not yet. Someday maybe," she says with such conviction that I almost think I'd misread her driver's license.

"Where's the most exotic place you've ever been?" I ask.

She hesitates for a moment, choosing her words carefully, then tells me about the time she visited the French Quarter in New Orleans. Her story about her endless quest for fried green tomatoes is funny, but she leaves out any mention of anyone who was with her or when she was there. I'm beginning to see that much of what she says stays in a safe zone, as if she's uncomfortable revealing too much.

"What ever happened with your friend?" she asks, turning the questions back to me. "David Harrison?"

I shoot her a blank stare and then remember. The champagne. "David Harrison's" bottle is still chilling in her refrigerator.

She laughs. "Isn't he mad that you never brought it to him? Did he propose to his fiancée without the Dom Perignon?"

Busted.

"He thinks I'm a terrible friend. But he'll forgive me when I tell him how I met you."

She turns to look at me, serious now. "Was there really a David Harrison or was that a ruse?"

I stammer through my answer. "There was—is—a David Harrison. Meeting you made me forget all about him."

Her face flushes.

"I just want to say that the other night . . . having too much champagne," she says quietly. "You staying over. That's not something I . . . ever do. I opened the door because—well, this is going to sound strange—but I felt like I already knew you."

I look at her in surprise. "You did?"

"From reading your books."

"What do you think you know about me from reading them?"

"Well," she says, a hint of a smile playing at her lips. "I think you're an optimist, for one."

I laugh. "No one would call me an optimist."

"But you are. Even in the darkest moments of your stories, the characters find their way through. There's a sense . . . like you believe things can always get better."

"I don't always believe that. Life has a way of proving otherwise."

She holds my gaze. "Maybe. But your stories . . . they make me feel hopeful. Like when things fall apart, there's still something worth holding on to. They make me feel safe. And so do you."

I know most guys wouldn't like to be told they're "safe." The term feels like the precursor to being exiled into the friend zone. And the way she says it makes me think that's what she's looking for. Safety. Was I always the safe, but brief, choice for her? Had I mistaken her need for safety as romantic feelings?

"That's why I invited you in, to be honest. I wouldn't have even answered the door if I didn't know you. But because of your books you . . . you felt . . . you *feel* like an old friend—someone I've known for a long time."

Her words make my heart race. I try taking a deep breath to get it to slow, but it's not working. For a brief instant, I consider saying something funny to defuse the tension building between us.

Then I feel a sharp pain in my bones, and then the whole world seems to be slipping away. My skin feels like it's vibrating. Damn.

I'm returning to the future.

I'm staring down the last moments with her. All the muscles in my body tense and I clutch her arm, panicking.

"It will always be you, Kate," I say, my heart beating out of my chest.

I lean in to kiss her, and as quickly as it began, the pain and the rumbling stop. My body is still.

From the look on her face, I've said too much again. I sound too far along in my feelings.

"Do you want me to go?" I ask, my voice catching.

"No," she says. "Why would you?"

"Because of what I said. I don't want you to feel like—"

"No, I thought maybe I was imagining how you felt. That I was misreading what's happening between us."

The memories of us swell around me, drawing me to her. "You're not imagining it."

We stop and gaze at each other for a long moment. Then she leans in, and her mouth grazes my cheek until it settles on my lips.

The kiss is like a thunderbolt. A confession of all my feelings. It's a manifestation of the confusion and upheaval I'd held on to since she ghosts me in the future. When my lips are finished with that narration, I settle, remembering all the ways she likes to be kissed.

Chapter Eighteen
Elizabeth

~

August 24, 2025

My finger hovers over the painted seahorse doorbell button on Brooke Dalton's front door, but I can't make myself press it.

After I left Logan last night, I thought I could do this. Now that the moment is here, I'm sure it's a mistake. Every minute since I committed to meeting her, I've been on edge. I'd hardly slept, and when I did, it was the kind of restless sleep where I woke up in fits and starts. On my way here, I glanced in the rearview mirror and noticed the dark hollows beneath my eyes. They looked like warning signals from my body. *Don't do this.*

I lower my hand from the doorbell and consider walking away. Logan can talk to Brooke without me. It won't take two of us to convince her to stay off the PCH. Unless she's an idiot, which she might be, she's probably come to the same conclusion herself.

At the same time, I can't deny that I'm curious about her. Is she the callous woman they portrayed in the media? The woman who came home and poured herself a Chardonnay after killing my son? Could such a person exist?

Then it occurs to me that I may never have this opportunity to talk to Brooke Dalton again. Every moment is filled with possibility and meaning. Even the painful ones like this one.

I press the doorbell, and seconds later, Brooke opens the door. Her voice is surprisingly warm. Normal. "Hello, Elizabeth. Please come in."

Her home is one of the newer custom-built homes within walking distance of the harbor with soaring views of the ocean. Gigantic living room, stunning chef's kitchen with a built-in wine cellar, and a dining room that looks straight out of *Interior Design* magazine. Knowing that this beauty belongs to her makes it all feel like a tacky façade.

She's dressed differently than I'd expected. Her clothing is kind of slouchy. Sweatpants, a pink flannel shirt despite the warm weather, and scuffed tennis shoes. And she's pale, almost dead white, to the point that she looks nothing like the designer clotheshorse I'd seen in her online photos.

Her voice trembles. "I'm so grateful you're here. I've wanted to talk to you so many times before . . . but the lawyers . . ."

My tone is sharp. "The lawyers? That's the first thing you want to say to me?"

Her face flushes. "Logan isn't here yet. Would you like to have a seat?"

She motions for me to sit on the spotless white couch in her living room.

"Can I get you anything? Tea? Coffee?"

"No." It feels like a betrayal to Sam if I accept anything from her.

She sits across from me looking more like a benign aunt, soft and engaged, instead of the person who murdered my son.

"Nothing I do can bring him back to you," she says softly. "I want to start by telling you how sorry I am for the mistake I made."

"Mistake? Is that what you call it?" I say, struggling to catch my breath. "Do you have any idea the pain you caused my family?"

She turns to me, her brown eyes glistening. "I know that your life can never be the same. I'm ruined by what I did."

I don't answer. What can I possibly say? I see pain reflected on her lined face, but what she's experiencing can't come close to what I've lost.

"The day I drove on the PCH, I wasn't drunk. Or distracted," she says, looking down. "I wasn't looking at my phone or the radio. I wasn't speeding. I hadn't had a bad day. In fact, I'd been having a good day. And then the accident happened and whatever good things I might have done in my entire life were all erased by this single moment. I took your son's life. I paralyzed Logan. No matter how much I want to, I can never change any of that."

"Why didn't you stop after you hit them? Why did you keep going?"

"I don't know how to explain it." She looks away, her face crumpled. "I didn't believe that I could've hit anyone on that deserted highway so late at night. I accepted the only answer that made sense to me: that at worst it was a raccoon or a deer. Not any *people*. Even when I found out that there'd been a hit-and-run accident on the PCH, I couldn't accept that *I* was responsible. It just didn't seem possible that I did that."

I don't buy her story. How can she expect me to believe that she didn't know she'd hit two people? "If I were in the same situation, I'm sure I'd know if I hit someone," I say.

"But you weren't in the same situation," Brooke says. "So you're either saying I'm a liar . . . and I'm not. Or you're saying I should've known something that I simply didn't see in that moment."

"I'm saying that you should have seen what you'd done. Yes. And to add insult to injury, you only served 900 days in jail for what you did. That doesn't seem fair. I hope that made you happy."

"Happy?" she says, her voice rising. "Happy? It's safe to say that that was the *last* day in my life that I was ever happy. Or ever will be happy. To be honest, I'm not sure I want to be happy. Look what happened the last time I was happy."

"It's not fair," I say, my voice rough. "You get 900 days in jail, and I have to live the rest of my life without my son."

"Would it have made a difference to you if I'd served a longer sentence?"

"Of course it would. Because someone must pay for this tragedy. *Someone* does."

Brooke blinks and doesn't respond. Her silence makes me wonder if I've got it wrong. If this was truly an accident, does she—does anyone?—have to pay for this tragedy? And if they do, what is the price?

The doorbell rings and she rises to answer it. When she steps to the door, I'm filled once again with what feels like a never-ending sorrow. The way I felt in the weeks after Sam died. But there is a difference, a glimmer of something else pushing its way in. A feeling that surprises me. Hope? That makes no sense. Nothing this woman has said has given me any reason for hope.

"Sorry I'm late," Logan says. He strides into the living room with Brooke trailing behind him. The three of us stand there a moment, and none of us knows what to say. We're strangers, and even the knowledge that we're time travelers and that we're stranded here and connected to the same horrifying event doesn't make it easier to figure out where to start.

"The reason we're here," Logan says, clearing his throat. "Is that we can stop the accident from happening tomorrow night."

"I'll make sure Sam isn't on the highway," I volunteer.

"I sure as hell won't be there," Logan adds.

Both of us look at Brooke, awaiting her answer. "Of course I'll stay off the PCH. I'll do anything and everything to stop this from happening."

"How *did* it happen?" I ask, turning my eyes to Brooke. My tone is sharp, more accusatory than I'd planned. "If you weren't, as you say, drunk or distracted or having a bad day, why did you hit Sam and Logan?"

She sits across from me. "I've asked myself that question at least a thousand times." She stops then, looking at the wall behind me as if the answer might be written there.

"And?" Logan presses.

"I thought I saw something beyond my headlights. One appeared as a quick flash of white, almost like a ghostly figure at the edge of my sight. The other was a dark blur."

"Ghosts?" I ask, the disbelief clear in my voice.

"Not ghosts exactly," she stammers. "Whatever they were, they sped across the highway, and I swerved to avoid them."

"But you'd been drinking," Logan interrupts.

"I had not been drinking. And then my wheels veered into the bike lane . . ." She lets the answer trail, waiting. "And I hit Logan and Sam."

"You swerved to miss *what* then?" I ask incredulously.

Her shoulders slump. "I don't know what I saw. It happened so fast."

"The police said no one else was at the scene. Just Logan," I say. "And Sam."

She sighs. "I know. And when I looked in my rearview mirror afterward, I didn't see anything or anyone either."

I turn to Logan. "You were there. Did you see these *things* she's talking about?"

"I have broken memories of the accident. My head injury messed things up. But if what you say is true, Brooke . . . if you saw something . . . then maybe I didn't imagine what I think I saw—"

"What're you saying?" I ask, cutting him off. "You saw something too?"

He sighs. "Look, my memory of that night is filled with blank spots. I can't be sure . . ."

Brooke stares at him. "What do you *think* you saw?"

"Two blurs . . . Moving fast. Maybe one was *wearing* white?"

"They?" I press.

"Maybe it was real or could be that it was a trick of the headlights on Brooke's car."

"Are you *both* saying someone else was on the highway with Sam and Logan?" I demand, my pulse racing.

"I'm not sure," Logan says, shaking his head.

I turn to Brooke. "If you saw something, why didn't you tell the police? Why wasn't this in the police report?"

Her eyes flicker with doubt. "I don't know if what I saw was real."

"If there was something—or someone—there, why didn't the police find them after the accident? And if it was people—humans—who ran across the highway, why didn't *they* stop when they heard the accident?"

"Elizabeth's right. Maybe light was playing tricks on our eyes," Logan says. "It's dark on that highway. Why would anyone be running across that highway at 11:30 at night?"

My voice is small. "Maybe for the same reason Sam was there."

Chapter Nineteen

Andy

August 24, 2025

I'm a terrible spy. For one thing, I can't sit still for very long without feeling antsy. For another, I'm not good at figuring out how to stay hidden. Plus, I'm wracked with guilt. I've never spied on anyone, and yet here I'm sitting at a café across the street from the Pottery Barn on Main Street where Kate works. If she sees me here, there's no way she's going to think it's a coincidence, even though I've brought my laptop and have all the props—notebooks, coffee, pens—that make it look like I'm deep into my writing.

My reasons for following her are, well, crummy. And proof, possibly, that I'm overreacting. Now that I'm paying attention to everything she says and not just heart-struck, I'm seeing how many excuses she makes. When I asked her to have Sunday brunch with me, she turned me down, saying she swims at the Y every Sunday for ninety minutes. Ninety minutes of actual laps, not water aerobics or water jogging. Laps. When I joked about her training to be an Olympic hopeful, she didn't laugh. And she didn't invite me to join her. Probably a good thing because I would've dropped out after five minutes.

Then, when I asked her to go to dinner with me tonight, she'd told she had some things to do after her shift at work and wouldn't be able to meet me until nine. The math didn't make sense. Her shift ends at five, so what was she planning to do during the four hours after that?

My mind raced with the possibilities. Maybe she wants some time to practice the piano. Or she really does have some errands to run. Then the darker ideas slip in. Maybe whatever she's doing is why she's using a different name. Why she has a security camera in her apartment.

About 5:15, she steps out of Pottery Barn. Gone are the black business casual clothes the employees wear and instead she's wearing Nikes, leggings, and a gray T-shirt. Although she does a quick scan of her surroundings, she doesn't seem to notice me.

Instead, she heads down the street. I'm not brave enough to follow her, but from my vantage point, I can see her stop about a block away. She heads into the Training Hall gym.

That can't be right.

Training Hall isn't a gym where average people go to work out. There are no weight machines or treadmills. This is a gym where you go for Olympic weightlifting, Strongman classes, and a form of wrestling called mas-wrestling involving pulling a wooden stick from your opponent's hands. With her petite frame, I can't imagine Kate fitting in with the crowd there.

I toss a twenty on the café table, quickly pack up my stuff, then head to Training Hall, my heart pounding a million times a minute. I open the glass door, and the woman behind the counter immediately says, "I'm sorry, the class has already started. We're not allowed to let anyone join late."

The door to the gym space is to her right, and it's firmly closed. "What class is it?" I ask.

She pushes a pamphlet across the counter. "Self-defense. It's techniques you can use in the real world," she says, her pitch rising into sales mode. "You can sign up beginning next week. We recommend classes twice per week to get the best results."

"Could I take a look at the class in session?"

She shakes her head. "The instructor doesn't allow observers. Privacy and all."

"Twenty seconds wouldn't hurt, would it?" I ask. "I mean, that way I'd know if it's something I want to sign up for."

My interest in signing up seems to sway her. "Okay. Just peek in. Don't do anything to distract anyone or the instructor will kick you out. And you'll get me fired."

I step toward the doorway, turn the knob slowly and quietly, and when I have it open a few inches, I look inside. Two students are sparring in the center of the gymnasium while a small group of others look on from the sidelines. The sparring is intense—fist punches, headlocks, kicks to the groin. It all happens in a flurry of fast, aggressive movements. Then suddenly one of the sparring students is pushed to the floor.

It's Kate.

The instructor's voice booms, "Get up. Quickly now. You must keep fighting, even if you're exhausted. Don't give in. Don't give up."

Kate pulls herself back to a standing position, but her sparring partner is quick and knocks her back down.

"Never stop attacking, Kate," the instructor continues. "Never let your guard down. No matter what happens, you've got to find your mojo to keep fighting."

The instructor steps forward from the group on the sidelines and offers Kate a hand so she can stand up. "Try it again. And again. It has to become as natural as breathing."

"You see enough?" The receptionist whispers, bringing me back to the moment.

I close the door, my hands tingly. My heart is pounding so hard I can feel it throbbing in my ears.

"We're running a 20 percent discount this month if you want to sign up." she says.

* * *

Kate has walls up. When I see her at nine that night she doesn't mention the class. She's showered and changed, with no sign of the exhaustion that should come from a grueling self-defense session. Even when I ask about her day, she deflects, talking instead about her twice per week swimming sessions at the Y and how she can push through thirty laps without stopping. Still, nothing about the class. Why is she avoiding it? From what I saw, this wasn't her first time.

Her answers often skim the surface. She dives into the frustrations of her day job at Pottery Barn, the ridiculous complaints from customers, and the litter of kittens she discovered behind the store. But when it comes to her past—or even much of her present—she subtly shifts the conversation.

I kick myself for not seeing this the first time around. Back then, I'd been so caught up in trying to be perfect for her, molding myself into whatever I thought she wanted me to be, instead of being the guy who moped around his apartment agonizing over his writing career. I didn't see how much of herself she was hiding.

Chapter Twenty

Brooke

∼

August 24, 2025

I tell James that I'm not going to Lisa's party tomorrow night, and he doesn't have any reaction to my decision. Of course, he wouldn't. He has no idea that my attendance at the party will be the catalyst to losing everything we have together and will shatter all that we're taking for granted in this easy moment. In his mind, this is just another party. I envy him for not knowing what is to come.

We stand on our front porch looking out at the purple crepe myrtle trees lining the walkways of the neighborhood we've lived in since before Olivia was born. We've had had ten years of tables lined up down the middle of the street for our block parties the first weekend in October, a decade of Nick and Clay's New Year's Day parties where we all eagerly waited for them to bring out their heavenly ham and homemade fudge, and countless Fourth of July get-togethers where we'd roll a firepit into the street and roast marshmallows while a group of neighbors played guitar and sang classic rock songs from the 80s.

James sees my decision as an opportunity.

"Let's go out then," he suggests. "Olivia will be at a sleepover, right?"

I turn down the idea of going out—no way am I going anywhere on August 25—but I promise to cook him something amazing at home. What he doesn't know yet is that he won't be here for that dinner. In a few hours, he'll find out that he needs to fly to San Francisco for a client meeting in the morning, returning the next day.

Now that I know I can prevent the accident, I'm immersing myself in the ordinary, mundane moments of life I'd once breezed past without appreciating their beauty.

James tells me about the settlement he's reached on a case he's been working on for over a year. It's not an extraordinary story—just a rundown of the tactics the opposing counsel tried and failed. I probably look silly, laughing at his corny puns and smiling throughout. I can't help it. I love everything about him: the way he looks after a long day, his hair slightly mussed, his crisp white shirt unbuttoned at the top, sleeves rolled to his elbows.

I think of days that I once wished would go on forever. My wedding day. Christmas morning when Olivia was little. Opening day at Celestine. An ordinary moment like this one wouldn't make the list before. Now it would.

He moves closer. "You seem really happy tonight," he says.

"I am."

His hands cradle my face, and he kisses me tenderly, then roughly, as if he can't get enough of me. How much I love these long moments with him, his arms wrapped around me. When it's just the two of us and the rest of the world fades away. Time stretches and slows. There is only him, and for long moments I let myself to believe it will always be this way.

For the first time in a long while, I feel truly happy.

Everything is under control. I won't be on the PCH tomorrow night. I won't cause Sam's death or Logan's injury. And if I'm stranded here, whether it's for an extra hour or a decade, I'll get to live out what it feels like to keep this life.

That night, I drift off to sleep like I did when I was young. I dream and sleep without pauses or restarts. I don't startle awake with a pit in my stomach, wondering how I'll slog through the years ahead of me with the shame of knowing I took someone's life and permanently injured another.

That won't happen. I'm free.

Part Two

August 25, 2025

Chapter Twenty-One

Brooke

5:32 PM

Every time I see the date—August 25, 2025—I feel that familiar, sickening twist in my stomach. I find it hard to breathe, constantly thinking about the tragedy looming at the end of the day.

Or at least it *would* happen, if I allowed it to unfold. But I won't.

The first time, I was powerless—helpless, as everything unraveled in seconds. But now I know what's coming. And I will stop it.

Just like the first time around, James's high-profile clients called and asked him to fly to San Francisco for an in-person meeting in the morning. He's in an AutoDriver now, slogging his way to the airport for a seven o'clock flight. And like before, Olivia is at her best friend's house, thrilled for one last sleepover before school starts.

I'm home alone, staying away from the PCH as I promised. But like the first time around, there are potato peels jammed in the floor sink at the restaurant, and the crew that's serving the dinner crowd can't unclog them. My manager, Eduardo, who's a MacGyver with things like this, is home sick with a 102-degree fever so the call comes to me.

Some bosses would just delegate the chore to someone else. But as shitty as the work is at times like this, anyone who does it year after year like I have really loves it.

It's the hardest job in the world. It's like the Super Bowl all day long. I know people think owning a restaurant is sexy and consists of shaking hands and buying drinks for loyal customers. The truth is, for every Gordon Ramsay who screams on TV and bosses around a terrified legion of employees, there are thousands of owners like me who work grueling hours at their restaurants, haven't screamed at anyone, and know how to clear the potatoes from the floor sink.

I decide to go in and solve the problem, with a firm plan to be back within the hour. The thought of being anywhere outside of my home on this date makes my heart race. I take a route down some side streets that adds fifteen minutes to the commute.

The potato peel problem takes a little longer than I expect, but I used some kitchen wizardry—pouring a bunch of baking soda followed by white vinegar—to finally get the drain unclogged. But my hands are trembling, and my left foot feels numb. This has been happening all day. Something is wrong, but I have no idea what to do about it. Thinking it's low blood sugar, I snack on a chocolate chip cookie fresh from the oven. Still, the trembling continues.

I step out of the kitchen, removing my apron, when I spot Sam Saunders at the entrance talking with the hostess, Emma.

I can't help but stare.

Why is he here?

Perhaps he'd been in the restaurant the first time around too, but I hadn't noticed him? Maybe I'd seen him, but he'd blended in with the blur of customers who come and go all day long and I'd had no idea then that my future would be consumed by him. That he would mean something to me someday.

How many *"Dear Sam"* letters had I written? Fifty? One hundred? All of them totally useless because they could never be sent. What will I say to him now that he's here?

I intercept Emma and ask if I can take care of the customer out front. She looks at me with worry. "Why? Am I doing something wrong?"

"No, I know his family. What's he here for?"

"It's his mom's birthday and he wants to surprise her with one of our cheesecakes."

"Would you get one ready and I'll go out to talk to him?"

"Okay," she says nervously. I have the feeling she still thinks she's going to get fired because I'm doing her job for a rare moment.

My knees shake as I walk over to greet him. "I'm Brooke, the owner."

"Sam," he replies, his voice full of youth and promise.

"We're preparing your cheesecake for your mom's birthday," I say, trying to disguise the tremble in my voice. "Is it today?"

He nods. "Yes."

An awkward silence falls between us because I can't think of what else to say. I'm on the edge between anger at putting myself in this situation and staggering grief.

"You're a great son," I say, finding my words again. "To get this for her."

Now what? What can I possibly say that will have any meaning or make any difference to him? My mind flickers to sliding through the curve on the PCH and hitting Sam with my car. Taking his life.

You will never have this chance again.

"Elizabeth will love what you're doing."

He narrows his eyes. "You're friends with my mom?"

"I'd like to be," I say softly. "But do you know what she'd like more than cheesecake?"

He tilts his head. I'll bet he's thinking I'm trying to upsell him on some other dessert.

Think, Brooke. Nothing comes. I am exposed. Standing before him, I'm shattered into a thousand pieces. And suddenly the walls that had been separating me from him come crashing down. Tears slip from my eyes.

"Are you okay?" he asks.

"Yes," I say, brushing the wetness from my cheeks. "I'm sorry for a terrible mistake I made. Something that I can't erase."

He looks at me with big brown eyes and although he has no idea what I'm talking about—and isn't capable of forgiving me for something I haven't yet done—it's freeing to say these words aloud to him.

"I know that my words cannot take away what I did. But I wasn't being careless. I wasn't uncaring. I did the best I could in that moment."

He looks at me with confusion. As painful as this moment is, I'm grateful that I get to say these words.

"Okay," he says, then Emma arrives with a cheesecake in our signature red box and hands it to him.

"It's on the house," I say. "But promise me you'll stay home tonight. Be with your mom on her birthday. Spend time with her. That's what your mom wants more than anything."

He gazes at me in surprise. His phone buzzes, and he glances at the screen with alarm.

"I will," he says, distracted. "I will."

Chapter Twenty-Two

Andy

5:32 PM

We're on the beach, standing in the exact place where we were the first time around. The sun warms the sand, as it did before, but this time I notice some things I hadn't before. There are dark circles under her eyes, which she conceals with makeup, and her cheeks look drawn. Tired. Like before, the piles of yellow-tinted clouds spiral upward and make our walk on the beach feel like we have wandered into the heart of a Titian masterpiece.

"Look!" she calls out, pointing to a tide pool filled with dozens of starfish.

I'd forgotten about this moment. This discovery.

"The storms last week must have carried these little fellows in from deeper waters," she says, crouching down to get a better look.

I squat beside her and reach for one of them. "Maybe we should throw them back into the ocean, so they have a better chance of surviving."

She grabs my wrist. "Don't. Starfish are extremely fragile. They have tiny structures all over their bodies that are easily injured." She blinks, as if she's close to tears.

I look at her, seeing her worry for these creatures and sensing something more—pain. As if she identifies with these lost starfish in a way that's still a mystery to me.

"What should we do then?" I ask. "They might not survive these shallow tide pools."

She shakes her head, determined. "Starfish can protect themselves by regrowing their limbs when they're attacked," she says softly. "They take steps to protect themselves. And they're resilient in the face of danger. We can't interfere. We have to let nature take its course."

We stay there a moment, watching the starfish in the clear water. I sense there's something more she wants to say. I wait, my breath high in my throat, hoping I'm right. When the silence stretches, I ask, "Is there something you want to tell me?"

She looks at me with watery eyes. "I don't know what you mean."

Just then, a pod of dolphins jumps through the foamy waves, maybe twenty feet away, distracting us. Like the first time around.

"Will you look at that!" she shouts, jumping to her feet, changing the subject.

As we stand inches apart, captivated by the dolphins, the space between us is charged with a quiet but unmistakable energy. She leans in, her breath warm against my skin, and presses a tender kiss to my lips. The dolphins—and the world—seem to fade away, leaving just the two of us on the beach.

My heart racing, it seems natural to tell her how I feel about her. "This thing between us," I whisper, wondering if she can feel my heartbeat pounding through my shirt. "It's *real* for me."

Her eyes meet mine. "Are *you* even real?"

"What do you mean?"

"The first time we meet, I've already read two of your books. So I feel like I know you. Then you come in with a bottle of champagne that I've always wanted to try. You even quoted the Bill Pullman character in *Sleepless in Seattle*, one of my favorite movies. Then you recognized that I played Bach's Goldberg Variations—no one ever does that. Sometimes it feels like you already know me. As if I'm imagining you and everything about you."

I consider telling her that I'm from the future. Then settle on another truth. "I want to see you tomorrow. And the next day. And the day after that," I say, pulling her closer. "Promise you won't disappear on me."

She blinks at me in confusion. "Why would I disappear?"

"Sometimes I get the feeling that there are things you're not telling me."

A rush of blood stains her cheeks red. "You're right," she says softly. I look at her, letting my silence do the job of my racing heart. She takes a deep, steadying breath. "I'm not from San Francisco like I said I was. I'm from Michigan and moved here nine months ago."

"I don't understand. Why'd you say you were from San Francisco?"

She sighs. "I guess I wasn't ready for questions about why I left Michigan."

"Why did you leave?"

She hesitates before answering. "I didn't belong there anymore. The people I knew were either settling down and having kids or running to all-night parties in the woods."

Her phone dings in her pocket and she pulls it out. I can't see what's on the screen, only that it seems to be a video with movement, but her expression shifts suddenly.

"I have to go," she says briskly, shoving the phone back into her pocket.

"Would you finish your story first?"

She looks like she's going to cry. "Sorry, I need to go."

"Let me go with you," I offer, reaching for her hand.

She places a hand on my shoulder and drops a brief kiss on my lips, whispering. "Stay here. Keep an eye on the starfish for me."

Then she races across the sand to her car.

* * *

5:42 PM

My eyes are locked on her taillights as I trail her through the city streets. She slips through a red light and barely taps her brakes at a four-way stop, her driving a reckless ballet that keeps me fifty yards behind. After a few blocks, she pulls into a gas station, jumps out, and opens the trunk with a quick, practiced motion. Before she peers inside, her gaze sweeps around as if she senses someone watching. A leafy shrub is blocking her view of me—or so I hope.

From my limited vantage point, I can't make out what's in the trunk, but it looks like she's rummaging through a duffle bag. She grabs a few items, slips on a red flannel shirt, a pair of sunglasses, and a navy-blue baseball cap before snapping the trunk shut. She returns to her car, now transformed into someone unrecognizable.

She accelerates out of the gas station with the skill of a race car driver, weaving through traffic. I follow her, but I get trapped behind a slow-moving pickup truck, unable to pass. My heart races as I watch her white Kia make a left turn, but by the time I get to make the same turn, a dad and his young son amble into the crosswalk. Her car has disappeared from my view. *Where did she go?* I tear down street after street, scanning for her vehicle, and instruct Siri to call her phone. The voicemail picks up: "Hi, it's Kate. Leave me a message."

After ten minutes of frantic searching, I'm almost ready to give up. Then a thought strikes me—she might have gone to her apartment building. I head there, but since the building has an underground garage, finding her car on the street seems unlikely. I search the area anyway.

That's when I spot it—a black pickup truck idling across the street from her building. The sun's glare on the windows hides the driver's face, but I see movement inside. A chill runs down my spine.

I park and leap out, glancing back at the truck. A guy with dirty-blond hair slouches in the driver's seat, his face obscured, staring at his phone. Maybe I'm being paranoid, but something about him feels off.

I press the buzzer and force a smile at the camera by the door, hoping she's there. Silence.

I dial her cell again. Voicemail: "Hi, you've reached Kate. Leave a message."

I text: *I'm outside.*

No response.

A tall woman in a gray hoodie exits the building, and I quickly slip through the door before it clicks shut. I sprint up the stairs two at a time. At Kate's apartment, I stop short—the door shows signs of a struggle—scratch marks, dents, and splintered wood around the lock. Something's very wrong.

I try the handle. Locked. I knock, my heart pounding.

"Kate?" I knock harder. "It's Andy. Are you in there?"

Silence. Or is it?

I hold my breath, convinced I hear a faint movement inside. A swish—maybe my own breathing? I strain to listen.

Why won't she answer?

I knock harder. "Kate, it's Andy." My voice cracks with desperation, and I hate how scared I sound.

I call her number again. Voicemail.

I rush back down the stairs and to the front steps, glancing up at the camera and pressing the buzzer one last time, hoping she's been in the shower and only now hearing the doorbell. No answer.

The black pickup truck roars to life and speeds off, leaving a cloud of dust and leaves in its wake.

* * *

6:30 PM

I suck at Internet searches. I've looked up the name *Sam Saunders* on LinkedIn and there's no trace of the Sam I'm looking for. Maybe some college grads don't bother with that app? I move on to TikTok and Instagram, but there are dozens of people with his name, and none of them look like him.

I'm running out of options. And time. Today—August 25, 2025—is the day she disappears from my life forever. But I've got to believe that, armed with what I know now, there's still a chance that I can stop that from happening.

My apartment is freezing cold, so I turn on the heat. It's seventy-five degrees outside, but I feel bitter cold in my bones.

I'm grasping at straws. But Sam might know where Kate is. If nothing else, if everything happens as before, he'll meet her later tonight at the 7-Eleven on Bristol.

But I cannot find *him*. In this city of a hundred thousand souls, there is no way to find a twentysomething guy named Sam Saunders with dark hair. There isn't.

I rise from the table, and my entire foot goes numb, like it's in an ice block. Pain shoots into my big toe. *Damn.* The pain throbs. I collapse back in the chair.

Wait. Wait. Wait.

I'm remembering one of the Aeon Expeditions orientation sessions. The first one. The one that was essentially a big party celebrating how fortunate we all were for being accepted. The one where we got faux but beautiful gold coins commemorating our upcoming experiences, where we signed seventy-two digital pages of liability waivers, and where we made our final deposits with a complex crypto-lock procedure that ensures the payment can never be disputed or rescinded.

The splashy opening video, produced by a big-name Hollywood director, played on a massive screen in an auditorium that holds two hundred. Aeon Expeditions founder Mark Saunders talked about living in Ventura, California, and how his experiences living in the small town steeped in California history shaped his desire to create a way for people to experience the past. I remember thinking how cool it was that this guy lived in my same hometown.

Mark wanted to name the machine after the HAL 9000 from his favorite movie, which was, not surprisingly, *2001: A*

Space Odyssey. The choice of name was not because the technology Saunders had developed was artificial intelligence like HAL, but because HAL 9000 was seemingly omniscient. Exactly what we jumpers would be during our sixty minutes in the past.

The problem was, HAL 9000 was associated in customers' minds as an antagonist and a murderer. The brand experts didn't think that was a good association, especially given how much money people pay for the experience and how fearful of the technology everyone was in the beginning.

Saunders decided to soften the name of the behemoth machines to SAM 5000 and publicize that it was inspired by his young son, Sam Saunders. The video showed a photo of Sam, a young boy with thick black hair.

Could Sam Saunders be Mark Saunders's son, only grown up?

I type in *Mark Saunders + son*, and there's a photo of the two of them at a fundraiser for a local charity. *It's him*.

A little sleuthing helps me uncover that Mark's wife's name is Elizabeth. And then some hunting on the real estate sites shows that Elizabeth and Mark Saunders are the owners of a house on the beach here in Ventura.

I scribble down the address, stamp my left foot trying unsuccessfully to stop the buzzing and tingling, then hobble out the door.

* * *

There is power in secrets. Elizabeth answers the door and has no idea I'm a jumper from the future. She can't fathom that my very presence on her doorstep is because of her husband's future invention.

My first thought after that is that she's been crying. Her eyes are puffy, sure, but there's a slackness to her skin that makes me think she's exhausted herself with tears.

She's wearing a gray sweater, and she wraps her arms around her chest like she's bitter cold too. Maybe it's not just me who feels like I've walked into a refrigerator even as the sun blazes and the temperature outside registers seventy-eight degrees.

"My name is Andy Schapiro. I'm looking for Sam?"

She peers at me. "He's on his way back. Would you like to wait for him?"

"Sure." I expect she'll suggest that I sit here on the steps, but instead she ushers me inside the house, then through the living room and onto a sun-drenched deck with a stunning view of the beach and the Channel Islands in the distance. I'm surprised she's so trusting with a stranger.

She motions to two beach-facing lounge chairs with thick cushions. "I'm Elizabeth," she says, shaking my hand. "Have a seat. Can I offer you some water?"

"I'm good," I say, settling in. I could get used to this view and the sunshine sparkling on the waves. And the warmth.

"I'll text him to let him know you're here."

I think she's going to head inside and let me wait out here by myself. But no. "How do you know Sam?" she asks, producing an ice-cold bottle of water from a small refrigerator and handing it to me, even though I'd declined earlier.

"I met him through my girlfriend, Kate."

"I haven't met Kate." She says it solemnly, like knowing Kate is somehow important to her. "They went to school together?"

I shake my head. "I don't think so."

"What's her last name?"

The intense way she's looking at me makes me realize that she's brought me inside because she's snooping on her son's life.

Trying to figure out who his friends are. The questions make me think she isn't just an overanxious helicopter mom. She's worried about her son.

"Montano," I say.

"You spend a lot of time with Sam?"

"Actually, I've only met him once."

Damn. My hand trembles again, and I hide it under my thigh, hoping she doesn't notice.

Inside the house, a door slams. Then a man's voice calls out, "I'm home!"

"Outside," Elizabeth answers. "Your friend Andy is here."

"Andy?" He steps out onto the deck and blinks at me in the bright light. The look on his face is one of pure shock. "What're you doing here?"

"I texted you that he was here," Elizabeth says.

Sam withdraws his phone from his pocket, glances at it. "Just seeing it now."

"What's this?" Elizabeth says, pointing to the box he's carrying.

"For you. Happy birthday."

She lifts the flaps, and I can smell what it is before I even lay eyes on it. Cheesecake.

Tears spring to her eyes. "You remembered . . ."

"It was on the house. The owner of Celestine gave it to me. Brooke, I think her name is? She says she knows you."

Elizabeth expression falters and big, glassy tears fall from her eyes. Sam seems as confused as I am.

"You okay, Mom?"

"I'm fine," she whispers, wiping her eyes. She presses a kiss to his cheek. "I'm just a little emotional today."

He places a hand on her shoulder and turns to me. "What brings *you* here, Andy?"

"Kate's missing. She's not answering her calls or texts. Or the door."

"For how long?" Sam asks.

"About two hours."

Elizabeth gives me a patronizing smile, the kind you give someone who you think is having an emotional crisis. "Two hours isn't long. I'm sure your girlfriend is fine."

Sam ignores his mom. "You've known her for what, a few days?" Sam asks suspiciously. "And when she doesn't answer you for a couple of hours, you hunt down one of her friends—someone you only met once—and come looking for her here?"

"It does seem strange, Andy," Elizabeth says warily. "What's going on?"

I realize I must look like a crazy man in their eyes. They don't know the future. They don't know that Kate disappears from my life—and from all of ours—never to be seen again.

I lower my voice, trying to sound calm. "I just . . . know something is *wrong*."

"Sam, how do you know Andy's girlfriend anyway?" Elizabeth asks. "Did you go to high school with her? College?"

"She came into the antique store during one of my shifts. She was playing the creaky old upright, yet somehow she made it sound amazing. We're friends."

"She's the one you loaned the baby grand we had in storage?" Elizabeth asks.

Sam nods then something on his phone captures his attention. He glances at it, then quickly back at us. "Sorry. I gotta run."

"You just got here," Elizabeth says. "And you promised to—"

"I'll be back in time for your birthday dinner," he says and heads back inside.

"Wait," I call out, following him inside. "If you hear from Kate, have her call me."

"Sure," he says, then rushes out the front door, letting it slam behind him.

I'm about to run after him when Elizabeth calls out, "Are we having an earthquake?"

I turn to look at her. Her skin has turned white, and she sways unsteadily.

"No," I say. "No earthquake."

"Everything is spinning."

Her eyes close, and she crumples to the ground. Motionless.

"Hey, are you okay?"

I rush over to her and push on her arm a few times. Her chest rises and falls, but she doesn't respond.

"Elizabeth?"

I dig my phone from my pocket and press 911. Moments later, the operator answers, "911. What's your emergency?" I quickly recite the address and then shout, "A woman has fallen. I can see she's breathing, but I think she's unconscious."

Elizabeth lifts her hand. "Hang up," I think she says.

"She's talking. Wait a second," I tell the dispatcher.

"Hang up," Elizabeth repeats.

"You need an ambulance. Paramedics."

"Hang up," she says, waving her hands if she's trying to grab for my cell phone. "Please."

Chapter Twenty-Three

Elizabeth

~

6:52 PM

My eyes are closed, but I swear I can see the back of my head resting on the wooden deck. *Impossible.* I move my fingers and I see the blue sky above, despite my eyes being shut. I wait for the surge of pain that's surely coming. In my first extraction, searing cramps thrashed through my body like a herd of scorpions had been unleashed under my skin. Now, my body shivers and trembles in a horrifying cycle that seems to have no end.

The body's pain and violent reaction to the extraction is normal. Temporary. *Don't panic*, Aeon reminded us again and again.

I'm failing at that.

Suddenly, it stops.

I open my eyes. Everything is still. The sun is shining, its warm rays caressing my skin. Andy is still here, crouched beside me, his face tight with concern.

"Are you okay?" he asks.

I turn my head, and everything spins for a moment, then stops. "I think so."

For the first time, I take him in. He is several years older than Sam, handsome with soft eyes and thick lips that make me think of a young Tom Hanks.

"What just happened?" he asks, his eyes narrowing as he studies me.

"I'm probably just dehydrated," I say, trying to sound untroubled. I push myself into a sitting position and reach for my water bottle on the table. I take a long, deliberate swig, trying to regain my composure.

His gaze remains fixed on me so I try to break the tension by asking, "So, what do you do for a living, Andy?"

"I'm an author."

"Oh, have I read anything of yours?" I head to the outdoor fridge, needing the distraction, and grab more water.

"My biggest hit is a book called *He's Gone*."

"I've read that one. That's the one based on the true story of that dead body that washed up on the pier here?"

"Inspired by," he says. "No one knew who the dead body was, so, I made up a story about who he might have been."

I swallow some water and my pulse begins to settle. "One of my favorites. I loved that the detective was jealous of the victim."

His eyes latch onto mine, unblinking. "You're from the future," he says, half question and half shocked statement. "You must be."

Caught off guard, I laugh. How could he possibly know I'm from the future? "Don't be silly."

"The book you're talking about hasn't been published yet," he says. "It comes out next year."

My jaw drops. "I must be mistaken then," I say softly. "About the book."

The look in his eyes tells me he doesn't believe me. "I'm from the future too."

My head starts spinning. I shouldn't be surprised. Not after meeting Logan and hearing that Brooke Dalton is also here. Still, I feel a flash of anxiety. *What kind of catastrophe has happened at Aeon Expeditions that's stranded so many of us?* And not just those of us involved in the August 25 accident, but this man too?

"I've been here five days. How about you?" I ask.

He stares at me with a look of intense surprise. "The same."

"We're not the only ones. There are at least four of us stranded here in Ventura. All of us were jumped here five days ago."

He rises, threading his fingers through his hair and pacing the deck. "Okay. So, what happened back there? Was Aeon extracting you?"

"Trying, I think. It's their third attempt. It hasn't worked yet. Has it happened to you too?"

"Twice. Today I'm having numbness in my hands and feet. Sometimes my body shakes for no reason. And I've got chills, even when it's hot."

My heart thunders. "Are our bodies in danger because we've stayed here too long?"

"What does your husband say?" he asks. "Are we okay?"

"I haven't talked to him."

He looks at me as though I've grown two heads. "What? Why?"

"He's working in Ojai and can't be disturbed—"

"We need his help." His eyes bore into mine. He's scared. "Look at us, our bodies are breaking down."

My throat is dry. Andy's right. We're running out of time. But telling Mark . . . I don't know how I'll look him in the eye and lie about our future. How do you hide the knowledge of what's going to happen? Everything we're going to lose.

"You don't understand. I don't want him to know about our future. He can't know."

His voice trembles. "We're falling apart. Minute by minute. If you don't talk to him, we may not survive this."

A light rain begins to fall, cold drops dotting my skin as my hands start to shake again. Is it just anxiety or something worse? The air feels like it's closing in on me from all sides. In the distance, a seagull cries—a sound I usually find calming—but right now it's sharp and ominous.

"Fine," I say, but my feet stay planted where they are. My phone sits on the table, just inches away, but it might as well be on another continent.

"What're you waiting for?" he asks, his voice laced with impatience.

A knot tightens in my chest. If I don't call, I'm not sure we'll get through this. But if I do . . . I'll break Mark's heart.

Chapter Twenty-Four

Brooke

~

7:02 PM

My wipers are on full blast to keep pace with the sudden rain as I return home from the restaurant. I've switched off the radio to avoid distractions, and, to the frustration of the drivers behind me, I've reduced my speed to fifteen miles an hour. My hands grip the steering wheel as I navigate the starbursts of oncoming headlights and the rain-slicked road.

Avoiding the PCH is crucial. A glimpse of the entrance ramp makes a cold sweat break out on the back of my neck. I roll past the ramp, veering down the side streets again.

The rain intensifies, turning the empty streets into a maze of blurred lights and shadows. In the hazy light from the shops that line the street, I spot a girl in a red shirt running down the sidewalk, her face stricken with panic. Even with my windows rolled up, I can hear her shout, "Help me!"

I'm the last person who should get involved in whatever's going on, but I slide to a stop and roll down my window. "You need help?"

She looks in my direction with fiery eyes and bolts toward the car. For a split second, I think I'm making a mistake letting her in. Her eyes are unusually bright, intense. She looks like she could be strung out on drugs.

It's too late to reconsider. She yanks open the door and slides into the front seat, her face taut with terror.

"Floor it. Please," she says, visibly trembling. She slouches down in the seat so anyone looking from the outside can't see her.

Her chest is heaving, and I'm so flustered by the terror on her face that I can't organize my thoughts enough to do the sequence of things to get going. *Check the mirrors. Lock the doors.*

Finally, I ram the accelerator against the floorboards, and the car roars out into the night. We fly through a stop sign. "You need me to call the police?"

Her breath is ragged. "I already did. They won't come in time. They never do."

I glance in the rearview mirror to see if someone is following us, but as far as I can see there are no cars behind us. No one on the sidewalk either.

"Who're we trying to get away from?"

"He's good at hiding," she whispers, fixing me with a fearful gaze. "Turn left here now."

The light is already yellow, but I do as she says, gripping the steering wheel as the car slides into the turn with a tortured squeal. Her eyes never leave the passenger-side mirror.

"What happened back there?" I try.

"I was walking away from the ATM," she says, her voice barely above a whisper. "He was there. Standing by my car." She breaks down crying then, her shoulders shuddering.

"*Who* was there?"

She doesn't answer. She looks out the window, and I can see her jaw is trembling.

"Where am I taking you?"

She pushes wet hair from her face and wipes her eyes. "The 7-Eleven on Bristol. You know where it is?"

"Wouldn't the police station be safer?"

"He's expecting me to go to the police. I've done that once before and it didn't turn out the way I needed it to."

Ice floods my veins. I'm in way over my head, but I'm suddenly overcome with a fierce sense of protection and survival. "Let's warm things up in here," I say, cranking up the heat. "I'm Brooke, by the way."

She doesn't answer. I glance over at her, and in the pale yellow glow of the dashboard I realize I recognize her. She played the piano at my party a few days ago. I feel bad for not remembering her name.

"You played piano at my party the other night, didn't you?"

She turns to look at me, her voice solemn. "We've never met. And if anyone ever asks about me, promise me that's what you'll say."

My voice is soft. "Who might ask about you?"

"Anyone who saw me get in the car with you."

I slide through a yellow light that turns red while I'm still in the intersection. *Focus.*

I swallow hard. "Are you sure you'll be safe at the 7-Eleven? I could take you to my home or—"

"My friend is meeting me there," she says with some confidence.

"I can call the police. I know one of the senior lead officers. Or I can take you someplace safer."

Her voice catches. "My friend is bringing me something that will keep me safe."

Chapter Twenty-Five

Elizabeth

7:04 PM

The accident will not happen. Sam will live.

Everything is set. I've made sure of it. After Andy left, I called Sam. He said he was helping a friend for a quick moment and confirmed he'd be back before eight for dinner and cheesecake. The pastas and salads from Mama's Osteria will arrive just before that, and after dinner, we'll settle in to watch my favorite movie, *Groundhog Day*, which Sam loves too. He's promised he'll stay home tonight.

With Sam's plans locked in, I turn to the task of calling Mark. Or at least that's what I know I must do. But I still have no idea how I'll answer the questions he's sure to ask about our future.

I dial his number and not surprisingly the call goes straight to voicemail. His familiar voice, warm and low, flows through the speaker. "This is Mark Saunders. Please leave a message."

The voicemail beeps. "It's me," I say, trying to keep my voice steady. "It's urgent. I need to talk with you about Aeon. Would you call me right away?"

Knowing it'll probably be hours before Mark checks his phone, I call his assistant, Paul. I get kicked to voicemail there too, so I leave a message asking him to have Mark return my call.

As I hang up, tears sting my eyes, catching me off guard. I was over Mark a long time ago. Or so I thought. But hearing his voice and standing in our home surrounded by all the signs of our life together, I'm suddenly not so sure.

This house—this life—is filled with all that once was. A photo of us at a party, framed with our smiles frozen in a moment of happiness. The Adirondack chair on the deck that Mark had always claimed as his own. All of it draws me back into the life I'd once shared with him. A life I'd closed the door on.

I've stood in this kitchen dancing with him after Sam was born. We've played hundreds of rounds of Monopoly here. And there was the night the power went out and the three of us sat around the table here doing Mad Libs and reading aloud silly jokes by candlelight.

My gaze shifts to the bookshelf, crammed with books the two of us have bought over the years. There's a small oil painting we'd found during a trip to Spain on one of our wedding anniversaries. A few framed photos tell more of our story—vacations, holidays, the first day of school. In the corner is a vase that had held countless bouquets of apology roses when Mark was traveling and missed important dates.

I had always imagined that moving on meant erasing the past, but here, in this home filled with echoes of our life together,

I'm confronted with a new truth. Maybe my feelings for Mark aren't as gone as I thought they were.

A half hour later, I hear a car door slam, then the soft creak of the front door opening. Sam is back!

"Sam?" I call out.

"Elizabeth?"

It's Mark.

I race to the door and stare at him as though I'm seeing him for the first time. With his thick hair tousled and a three-day beard, he's handsome. Then again, he's always been. There's a bright look in his eyes that I'm not sure how to describe. Is it confidence? Happiness?

"Why're you here?" I ask, finally.

He leans in, dropping a soft kiss on my lips. "I live here, remember? How long have you been here?"

I shrug, caught off guard by the question. "All day, of course. Why are you here, though? Shouldn't you be in Ojai?"

"You called me. And said it was urgent."

"You could've just called back."

He shakes his head, his expression serious. "I had to come. You mentioned Aeon. And I haven't told anyone that's my final choice for the name."

I've messed up. "I said Aeon?"

"At first I thought maybe someone on the team had told you," he says. "They've been pressuring me to decide because we're planning to announce the company launch next week."

"I'm sure *you* told me."

"Then I realized, I hadn't told anyone. And that made me think . . ."

My words are barely audible. "It made you think what?"

"That I needed get here right away. Because . . ." He trails off. "I think you know about Aeon Expeditions because you've used its services."

I let a silent moment go by, wondering how I'm going to word this. "How could I use its services when it's not yet operational?"

"At some time in the future." He looks at me, utterly mystified, as if I'm a rare and wonderful creature he's never seen before. "And something has gone wrong."

My lips flatten. "What makes you think something has gone wrong?"

"Because you say you've been here all day. But an hour is the longest trip that we can take. Safely."

He knows.

"Either you think I'm a raving lunatic," he says. "Or you know what I'm talking about."

"I know what you're talking about," I say softly.

The worried lines on his face ease a little. Then he covers his face with his hands for a long moment without speaking. When he finally lowers them, he gazes at me. "Does Sam know?"

I shake my head.

"How long has your jump been?"

"Five days."

His expression is full of bewilderment. "That's impossible. *When* are you from?"

"Three years from now."

"Three years." There's confusion and uncertainty in his voice now. "But something is wrong there too. Isn't it?"

"What makes you think that?"

"I don't know. Something about the way you're—"

"Mark . . ." My chest heaves as I try to get my racing heart under control. "I don't think we should—"

"They must be okay because you're here," he says with some confidence. His eyes dart as he thinks this through. "You're standing here, so that means I get Aeon Expeditions to work. But the way you're looking at me . . . something is different."

"How am I looking at you?"

"Like I'm a stranger." He pauses a second, thinking things over. "Maybe I'm overthinking. Is everything okay between us?"

I exhale slowly. "Everything is not okay."

I've never seen such pain etched on his face before. His voice shakes. "What happens? Can it be undone?"

"The things that have happened can't be undone."

"It's that bad? Are we . . . fighting? Is that what has become of us?"

I breathe out the answer. "Divorced."

He stares at me in shock, disbelief clouding his features. "Then future-me is an idiot. Why aren't we together? I would never let you go."

"It wasn't your choice."

He walks over to the window and looks out at the beach for a long while, his jaw clenched. His voice is barely above a whisper. "It's because of Aeon, isn't it?"

"Some."

"What, because I'm becoming a walking cliché of a highly functional but compulsive engineer?"

Although what he says is true, I shake my head.

He lets out a slow audible breath. "I don't mean for it to get out of hand."

"But it does."

"And I lose you?" His shoulders slump and he sinks onto a kitchen chair.

"Why has this invention always been so important to you? More than everything else in your life. What is it? The challenge? The money? The fame?"

"Is that really what it looks like to you?"

My words land hard. "That's how it looks to anyone who falls into your orbit."

He meets my gaze, then rubs his eyes, retreating into himself. A deep sigh. "The summer I turned eight, my brother Eli and I, we built a time machine," he begins, his voice softening. "Not a real one, of course. We made this one out of cardboard, duct tape, and some extra lumber our dad had lying around. We'd step inside and pretend that we'd gone back to the time of the dinosaurs—his idea—or to the future where we drove flying cars—mine."

He pauses, lost in the memory. "By the Fourth of July, they'd discovered a tumor in his brain. By Christmas, Eli was gone. After that, our time machine sat in my bedroom for months. Untouched. I'd go to bed imagining that if I could invent a real one someday—even though I knew that was impossible—I'd want to travel back to those times when the two of us sat in that box, dreaming about other worlds we could visit, playing like there'd always be more tomorrows."

Twenty-four years of marriage and I knew that his brother had died, but I never heard about the pretend time machine. Yes, he was a genius and a workaholic. But there was something far deeper, driving his desire to create Aeon.

The sun slants through the window, hitting his eyes so hard he squints. "If I lose you in the process of making this thing, I have to change that. Here and now."

My heart aches for him. He's trying to hold on to something he will lose. To stop it from happening. "You can't. That's not how anything works. We can't change the future."

"I don't know how much time I have with you, but I need you to hear me," he says. "No matter what happens to us in the future, no matter what thing I do or don't do, you'll never stop being the love of my life."

Tears well up in my eyes. It's been a long time since Mark talked this way about us.

"Even if I'm distracted or distant or, I don't know, don't say the right things when I should, you'll always be the most important person in my life," he continues. "I've loved you since our very first date."

"Now you're exaggerating," I say, letting out a soft laugh.

"Not exaggerating. I remember every detail of that night."

I look at him with skepticism, and he goes on. "You had on a blue knit dress and a silver necklace with your initial. Creed's 'With Arms Wide Open' was playing on the radio. You talked about the sea lion you'd seen on Hobson Beach that morning."

I meet his gaze, surprised at the details he remembers from that night so many years ago.

"The restaurant where we planned to eat had lost our reservation," he continues, then snaps his fingers. "It was called the Bellwether. Remember?"

"That's when I asked you if you wanted to come to my place for dinner instead," I say.

"And like an idiot, I said, 'Maybe.'"

I laugh. "Which made me think you *didn't* want to come over."

"Oh, I wanted to. That's for sure. But I was so nervous. I remember thinking: *She's amazing. Don't blow this.* That was proof that all good things begin with a maybe."

The world around me stills. After we got married, this became our catchphrase. Each time we faced a tough decision or one of us wasn't sure what to do, we'd look at each other and say, "All good things begin with a maybe" then jump in to see what "maybe" would bring us.

"After my 'maybe' mishap," he continues, "I came to your apartment, and we made a chicken dish together with all the leftovers you had in your fridge."

"An onion and an open—and very flat—bottle of Chardonnay."

"Over-ripe tomatoes too. I remember we talked until four in the morning. And even then, we didn't want the evening to end, so we went for a walk."

"In the middle of a downpour. The thunder was so loud it was rattling the windows. And you asked me to go outside with you."

"That's when I realized I wanted to marry you." His retelling of a memory reawakens feelings I'd long buried. And the way he's looking at me makes me see myself—and us—in a different light. *How did I give up on us?*

His voice is thick and low. "Then we kissed in the entryway to your crummy apartment building. The one with the stained ceiling tiles and the fluorescent lights that always flickered. I'll never forget that. Can you?"

I fall back to our youth, remembering his tentative touch on my face and the blaze of our first kiss that took us both by surprise.

"I can't imagine my life without you, Elizabeth," he continues. "So, this is me asking you to marry me again. In the future."

For a moment, all the world is right. I gaze into his dark brown eyes, framed by wavy hair, and I feel a jolt of lightness. Like kids on Christmas morning. But we are hardly kids. And there's so much pain ahead of us. I wish I didn't know the way it all would go. The way it would end.

"You've always been and always will be everything to me," he says. "I'm asking you to give us another chance. This is me asking you to *choose us* in the future. I want this to be the memory you carry into the future."

My breath hitches as he pulls me into his embrace, and I feel his heart pounding next to mine. "Promise me you'll give us a second chance."

My vision is hazy with tears as he leans in to kiss me. Making promises about the future isn't easy. But here with him now, I remember what it feels like to be hopeful again.

I give the answer only he would understand. "Maybe."

Everything good begins with a maybe.

* * *

7:58 PM

We have so little time. Every second matters.

I don't tell Mark about Sam's death. Most of us really don't want to know all the pain and loss we'll suffer. I won't crush his joy in this moment by telling him about the grief ahead.

Instead, I tell him about the symptoms Andy and I've been experiencing, and he immediately gets on the phone with his chief health and medical officer to find answers. As he talks, he moves around the room with purpose, the phone pressed to his ear, concern etched on his face.

Meanwhile, I text Sam. *Your dad is here. Come home as soon as you can.*

No reply. A few minutes later, I try again. *Don't forget you promised to be home for my birthday dinner.*

Brooke promised to stay off the PCH, so the rational part of my brain reminds me that Sam is safe tonight. But love does not always accept rational thought.

As Mark talks on the phone, I can't take my eyes off him. The soft intensity in his gaze, the reassuring cadence of his voice—it all draws me in. This is the man I once loved—and perhaps still do, even if we're not together anymore.

"She's experiencing numbness and tingling," he says into the phone, then gently takes my hand in his. "Her hands have a normal temperature," In this crystalline moment, his focus is entirely on me, and while the contact is brief, it sends a jolt of awareness through me, reminding me of the tenderness we once shared.

He listens to the medical officer again, then whispers to me, "He thinks this is a side effect of the failed extractions. He's looking into what we should do."

I focus on his face, the concern in his eyes grounding me. But it also stirs up feelings I thought I'd buried in my grief.

As I stand here, hand in hand with the man I once planned to spend my life with, I realize that this moment, this feeling, and this memory will stay with me forever. What happens here won't change the future, but I am changed by reliving these soft moments with him in the hours before our lives were shattered.

The front door slams, breaking the spell.

"Sam?" I call out.

No answer.

While Mark continues with the medical officer, I rush into the living room see Sam standing at the safe, punching in the combination. I freeze. A backpack hangs off his shoulder and his hair is a windblown mess. A knot of dread twists in my stomach.

"What's going on?" I ask, my heart pounding.

"Where's Dad?"

"He's on the phone. What're you doing?"

His face flushes. "I just need to borrow some cash."

"For what? Tell me what's going on, Sam."

He sighs and stuffs a small stack of bills into his backpack. "I'm sorry, I don't want you to worry. I'll pay you back, promise."

My voice hardens. "Put it back, Sam. Put it all back until you tell me what it's for."

He inhales sharply, avoiding my gaze. "I have a good reason. There's nothing to worry about."

"But I *am* worried. The gun is still missing too. Is it really at the range?"

His face pales. "I'm just trying to keep everyone safe, Mom. That's all I want to do. I've got this under control."

His phone buzzes. He glances at the screen, his expression tightening. "I have to go."

"Sam, you promised. Eight o'clock. My birthday."

He squeezes his eyes shut. "I'm sorry. I'll be back by nine," he says, his voice taut.

My voice shakes. "Sam. Don't leave. *You can't leave.*"

He turns toward me in surprise, and I swear I can see the four-year-old there. The one with the soft cheeks and big brown eyes who needed help with his Transformers. The tears fall.

His eyes soften. "Everything's going to be okay, Mom. Really."

In my bones, I know that isn't true. I have the unsettling feeling that I'm experiencing my last moments with him.

My heart blooms with love for him. I look at him and try to hold time in my hands. "I won't let you go."

"I'll be fine," he says softly. "Love you."

I close my eyes and will myself to see the absolute wonder in this moment, instead of the loss that's ahead. I fill myself with the joy of being with him. And I miss him even while he's standing right in front of me.

He leans in to hug me, and we stay in it long enough that my heart, which is directly over his, can speak to his. The world changes between heartbeats. Not everything is under my control. Even when I want it to be.

Even when I need it to be.

I grip his hands tightly. "You don't understand, Sam. Something terrible will happen to you tonight. I can't let you leave."

My words hover in front of me, as if I can see them instead of just hearing them. My mouth feels like I've been sucking on cotton. I draw in a deep breath, and I have the feeling I'm being pulled upward. The air turns to glue.

I'm being extracted.

"I love you." When your heart is breaking, what else is there to say?

I hear a music box and a man's voice. His words are garbled, like he's speaking a foreign language. A doorknob appears in front of my face, and I reach out to touch it. My body pulses with electric shock.

Then everything is black.

Chapter Twenty-Six

Logan

8:05 PM

Oh, hell. I wake up from a nap and my mouth feels pasty. The same nightmare again and again: I'm standing in the bike lane on the PCH, then realize I shouldn't be there just seconds before the car barrels at me. In another, I see the speeding car, but my feet are anchored to the ground, and I can't move.

I gulp down some water and brush my teeth, trying to shake off the dreamlike haze that clings to everything around me.

I've been a mess today. Not surprising considering the date. My stomach is still tense after my hands went numb this morning. I soaked them in hot water for ten minutes to bring the feeling back. After that, my whole body felt heavy and sluggish, and I fell onto the couch for what turned out to be a two-hour nap, even though I rarely sleep during the day. Even as I brush my teeth, I feel disconnected from the world around me.

A text swoops across my phone.

You coming to do the Double or not?

Just like the first time around, my friend Emmett texts me, reminding about plans to do a double metric century—a 130-mile hardcore bike trip tomorrow that would take us up the coast north of Santa Barbara. With its challenging 6,500-foot climb, it's the equivalent of running a marathon, pushing my body and mind to the limit. Doing 130 miles in a day is a rite of passage for any athlete and one that commands respect. My movements are slow and labored right now, but I know the trip will make me feel strong and unconquerable. And there's always a good chance of a coastal tailwind to make the ride back home super sweet.

The first time around I'd committed to this ride but never made it, instead spending the next weeks in the ICU on my way to being in a wheelchair for the rest of my life. But that accident isn't going to happen. Because Brooke won't be on the PCH, and Sam and I won't be there either. We're making that happen.

The phone chimes with a second text from Emmett. I've been expecting this one too: *See you at the party tonight. You can crash here. We head out at six in the morning.*

I throw together a backpack, get on my bike, and head over to the beach.

Chapter Twenty-Seven

Andy

9:12 PM

I'm waiting in my car, a few yards down the street from the 7-Eleven. If things go as they did the first time around, in a few minutes, sometime before 9:13, Kate will be in the 7-Eleven with Sam. Only this time I'm here too.

A gray sedan races up and slides into one of the parking spots out front. I watch for what seems like forever until I see a figure in a black jacket slide out of the driver's seat carrying a backpack.

Sam.

He stops a moment, scans the area, and when he's satisfied with whatever he's seeing or not seeing, he rushes inside.

He's alone. Where is Kate?

I look down at my hands and see they're clasped so tightly on the steering wheel that my knuckles are white. I loosen my grip, get out of the car, and head to the entrance, gathering my courage along the way. Through the glass doors, I see my cousin Justin, the night manager, behind the register, helping Sam.

Kate is standing right beside him. I can't figure out how she got there. I never saw her come in. Maybe she came in before I arrived? Or arrived through another entrance?

Kate looks like a disheveled version of herself; her hair is twisted into a messy topknot, and she speaks quickly to Sam, gesturing with her hands. The navy-blue backpack I'd seen Sam carry in is now slung over one of her shoulders.

She leans in for a hug. Exactly as she did the first time around. And in those five seconds, my heart goes from fluttering to banging so hard against my ribs I think they will break.

My breath comes in fast, shallow gasps as I step inside.

"Kate?" I ask.

She turns in my direction, and I almost don't recognize her. Her eyes are wide, and in the harsh glare of the fluorescent lights, her skin is almost gray.

"Andy. What're you doing here?" she asks.

I force myself to sound normal, but my heart is pounding so fast I can hear it in my ears. "I came in for . . . water."

We stand there looking at each other, two people who were falling in love a few hours ago, and the air is heavy with unanswered questions. Justin has no other customers, so he pretends he's doing some straightening.

"Are you going somewhere?" I manage to ask casually, even though I know that wherever she goes after this means I'll never see her again. "Wherever it is, I'll go with you."

She glances at Sam and then at me. "You shouldn't be here. I won't put you in the middle of this."

"If I let you go, I'll regret it for the rest of my life."

"You have no idea what he's capable of."

Fear wraps itself around my chest like steel bands. "What *who's* capable of?"

She doesn't answer, instead moving past me to the door.

"I'm coming with you," I say, stepping into her path.

She whirls around to face me. "You're not safe with me, Andy."

"I'm going with you."

She exhales loudly. "Fine. Get in Sam's car."

* * *

"He's here," she says breathlessly as we slide into the back seat. Sam puts the car in gear, and we peel out of the parking lot and into the darkness. "He knows where I am. I have to go."

"Slow down," I say. "*Who* is here?"

"My ex," she says. "Dane Reynolds. I left—escaped—from him last January."

"Your . . . husband?"

"Boyfriend. I want . . . I want to tell you everything about me. But you're not going to like . . ." Her voice trails off.

"You think I'm going to be, what, disappointed in you?" I say. "I won't be."

She looks down. "It's more than that. You'll know that I've lied to you."

I place my hand on hers. "Kate, I want to be with you no matter what you tell me."

She shakes her head. "Why are you so nice to me when I've given you no reason to be?"

If Sam wasn't in the car, I would've told her that I've come to the past searching for her. And in my heightened state, I probably would've overshared. But we're flying at top speed down the

PCH toward some unknown destination and I need to understand why. "Tell me about Dane."

She tucks the food and supplies they've just brought into her backpack. "We were living together for about a year. At first, he was normal. Then he had an injury at work—he works at a paper mill—and hurt his back real bad and started taking pills for the pain. Other things too. The first time he hurt me, he was joking around. He pulled on my hair and laughed. But something felt mean. And the meanness got darker.

"Soon he was coming home most nights drunk or high or both and . . . he'd hit me. Because the refrigerator had a smell. Or he'd tripped over the rug. Or because I talked to the neighbor for too long. Because I slept too late. Or woke him too early. I'd spend my days strategizing how to avoid his anger. How to do everything he wants so I don't get hit. Then he'd surprise me by saying he loves me and then be sweet again. I'd seen movies about abusive relationships, and it didn't look like what was happening to me. Until, one day it did. He got mad about something I said, and he started breaking my piano, an old upright I'd found by a dumpster and restored so I could play every day. He took a hammer and smashed every one of its keys. Wood was flying everywhere. He destroyed the only thing I had that meant anything to me. I tried to make him stop, but he shoved me into the wall so hard that I passed out." Tears slide down her cheeks.

"That's why you have the scar on your forehead," I say softly. "Not a softball accident."

Her voice rises. "Why aren't you angry with me when you know I've been telling you lie after lie?"

"Because I have the benefit of knowing that in the future, I'll miss you. That nothing makes sense without you."

She looks at me like she can't process what I'm saying. "What do you mean you'll *miss* me?"

I've said too much. "Tell me how you got here. To Ventura."

She draws a shaky breath. "After Dane shoved me, I was so scared that even thinking about what happened made me panic. I started putting together a backpack with things I would need to escape. At night, I'd lie beside him while he slept, and I'd planned out every step. I was working at a grocery store and started saving money. But it wasn't enough, so I sold my mother's jewelry. Hid the money away in my shoes until I had enough to buy a bus ticket and start a life someplace new. But Dane had installed software that spied on everything I did on my computer. He saw what I was planning. I got as far as the bus station and there he was, standing at the entrance and mad as hell. He dragged me home and slapped me until my face was red and bloody. Then he put a gun to my head and threatened to kill me if I didn't promise—swear on my mother's bible—that I'd never leave him again. 'I can kill you,' he said. I believed him.

"Of course, he said he was sorry," she continues. "He always did. But then he said I deserved it. And warned me that if I told anyone, he would make me 'sorrier than you ever thought possible.' I was so scared—and angry—that as soon as he went into the bathroom, I grabbed that backpack and ran two miles in a thunderstorm. He came after me, of course. I hid in the bushes and trees and saw his car racing down the road looking for me. Then I ran to the only restaurant in our small town and begged a stranger to drive me forty-five minutes to the Kalamazoo airport.

"I waited outside in the freezing rain for hours until they opened and paid cash to get on the first flight out. I flew to Detroit, and when I got there, I jumped on the next flight out and went to Chicago. Then I got the last ticket on a cheap airline flying to Los Angeles. There was no reason for my choices; that way Dane couldn't guess where I was going because I had no plan. When I got to L.A., I took a train up north and got off at the eleventh stop, another random choice, which turned out to be here in Ventura. But I didn't really escape because ever since then I keep waiting for him to find me."

I release a breath, fighting my anger at Dane and everything he put her through. "What about your parents? Friends? Couldn't anyone help you?"

She looks out the window. "My mom died two years ago. I never met my dad. I didn't tell my friends what was happening. Dane preyed on that. Me being alone."

The anger at Dane comes at me like a wave. "It's not your fault," I say softly. "It's not your fault. What he did to you."

Tears spill out of her eyes, rolling down her cheeks. She swipes them away, but they seem to have a will of their own and keep coming. I reach across the seat and place my hand on hers.

"What makes you think he's here?" I ask.

"I thought I saw him sitting behind the wheel of a black pickup truck on Main Street a few days ago. That's why I wanted to skip gelato and go into the antique shop instead. I didn't see him after that. But I could feel his presence. Watching me. When we were on the beach this afternoon, the camera in my living room recorded him breaking into my apartment."

"That's why you left—"

"I ran to the bank to withdraw cash so I could begin my escape. But when I got there, he was waiting for me in his truck. It's like he already knew my every move. Like he always has. I took off running and, lucky for me, a woman in a car picked me up and drove me to the 7-Eleven."

"How do you think he found you?"

"I really don't know. I'm super careful—I always pay with cash, stay off social media, and try to avoid cameras. Maybe I messed up somewhere? He has a cousin who works in law enforcement who helped him find me the first time I escaped. I'll bet he's helping Dane now."

The three of us are silent then as we hurtle through the darkness. All I hear is the high-pitched whistle of the winds as they kick up and swirl around the car, in tempo with my thundering heartbeat.

"Is your real name Kate?"

"It's the name I use now. My real name is Sarah. Sarah Canford. But I'm no longer that person who put up with Dane. Who was afraid to leave. I've filed the paperwork to legally change my name, but the process takes time."

"We've got to call the police. The sheriff."

"Already did," she says. "They won't come in time. And they won't believe me. The last time I went to them when I was in Michigan, one officer told me I was lying. The other kept saying I was somehow complicit. They didn't take it seriously. Hurting a loved one is somehow different than hurting a stranger."

She wipes her eyes and in even in the dim light of the back seat, I can see her body is rigid with fear.

"What if I called the police for you?"

She holds up a small phone. "Don't. I called them from this burner phone. I lied and said I would wait for them outside city hall. Dane always monitors the police scanner, so he'll head straight there. That'll give me a head start."

"A head start to where?"

"Dane's seen my car already. Sam's too. For sure yours. If I try to drive away, he'll track me. I won't get away."

"Where're we going then?"

"My family owns a boat that Kate is taking to Anacapa Island tonight," Sam pipes up from the front seat.

"Sam taught me to drive it."

"Anacapa Island? In the Channel Islands? It's like three hours away."

She nods. "The boat has GPS."

"Dane could rent a boat and follow you."

"The last boat from the harbor has already left," she says. "And even if he manages to find a boat, he won't be able to track me on the water."

My geography of the Channel Islands is limited, but clearly hers isn't. "After Anacapa, I'll head to Catalina Island. The whole trip is about eighty-five nautical miles, so I'll have plenty of gas," she continues.

"Stay with me instead. You'll be safer."

"Your apartment is the first place he'll go. He's seen me with you. He'll be crazy with jealousy."

"You make him sound . . . unstoppable."

"Because he is," she says, her voice shaking. "He's already proven that. He'll never give up looking for me."

"But Anacapa Island is rocky with steep cliffs. And if you run into any trouble, there's no one there to help."

"Exactly why he won't look for me there," Kate says with confidence.

"But arriving there at night is dangerous. You may not be able to dock the boat easily and you'd have to swim."

"I've been training for that too. Twice a week at the Y."

The realization hits me. "That's why you swim on Sunday mornings."

She nods. "And if Dane *does* follow me to Anacapa, Sam has loaned me some protection." She pats the side of her backpack.

My mouth goes dry. "A gun? Do you know how to use it?"

Her voice shakes. "Sam's taken me to the gun range a few times. I'm not great. But I know what to do."

* * *

"We only have about thirty minutes until high tide when we won't be able to walk on the beach," Sam says a few minutes later. He accelerates. "We have to hurry."

"Where's your boat moored?" I ask. "At the harbor?"

"It was. But the harbor's crowded with people, which would make it easier for Dane to spot her," he says. "And the escape routes are limited. So I pulled the boat out of the marina and parked it in front of one of the houses on Solimar Beach."

"Why didn't you tell me this when I came to your house earlier?" I ask.

"My mom was there, and I didn't want to worry her," Sam says calmly.

"She doesn't know what you're doing?"

He shakes his head. "I've got this under control."

He slides the car to a hard stop and parks it beneath one of the few streetlights on the PCH. He opens the car door. "You ready, Kate?"

"Wait. We shouldn't park *here*." I press. "It'd be easy for Dane to spot us."

Kate sighs. "We need to park Sam's car someplace highly visible. When he sees it, he'll stop. He'll look for me around here. He'll waste time checking to see if I went inside one of the houses. Or he'll check to see if I went up into the hillsides. And if he thinks to look for me on the beach, he won't know which way I went."

"It's at least a half mile from here to the boat on Solimar Beach," I say. "We'd be closer if we parked at your house, Sam."

Sam's face reddens. "I don't want Dane to think for even one second that Kate is at my house. That puts my parents in danger. On the beach, we also have the advantage of a new moon," he says confidently, nodding toward the skies. "The night is totally dark. And I know this beach better than anyone."

It's a smart plan, but my heart knocks hard with fear. And not just about Dane. I'm not prepared for any of this. I'm not in great shape. I've never run from anyone or anything. I'm afraid that I'll let Kate down.

"Let's go," Sam says, getting out the car. Kate and I follow suit and run across the highway, avoiding approaching cars, then head down a narrow access road. My eyes dart and shift at every shadow. The swish of the sand beneath our feet sounds impossibly loud.

Then the sandy road opens to the beach, and my breath whooshes from my lungs at the beautiful distraction the skies and the ocean offer. The sea ripples peacefully, at odds with my racing heart, as the tide rolls to the shore. For a moment, the harsh reality of our situation is in sharp contrast with the breathtaking view.

I linger for a moment, but Sam waves at me with shaky hands. *Keep going.* We walk at a swift pace beneath a starry sky on a moonless night, the waves lapping at our feet. In a low whisper, Sam points out a few constellations and reminds Kate how she can use the North Star for navigation if the GPS stops working. They've thought of everything. In the darkness, Kate slips her hand into mine, and then Sam's voice fades into the surf. I'm only aware of Kate and the sensation of walking by the ocean through the night with her.

The beach at least gives us the illusion of safety. On the right is the vast ocean and endless horizon, and on the left is a smattering of quiet beach houses, their lights from within spilling only the faintest glow. Some of the homes have steel sea walls to protect them from the surf, while others have piles of rocks. Every one of them has a set of stairs that lead from the beach below up to the house, offering possible escape routes if we need them.

The first time around, I'd returned home after our time together on the beach and gone to sleep thinking how happy I was, assuming Kate and I were becoming a couple. I'd slept peacefully, oblivious that Kate was in danger and that her friend, not me, would be giving her a boat and a gun as protection. Why hadn't she confided in me? Why hadn't she let me help?

It feels unfair to ask her anything when we're making her escape. But the question will otherwise haunt me forever. "Why didn't you tell me about Dane?"

"I like you, Andy. A lot." Her gaze drops to her hands, as she gathers her thoughts. "I have this feeling that I could fall for you. In time. I want to be someone you could fall for too. Someone without an ugly past. Or an uncertain future."

How much of the first days of dating is convincing the other person that you're precisely the someone who's missing in their life? How much effort we put into telling them how idyllic and comfortable our lives are so that we don't scare them with the truth of who we really are. In the same way Kate has kept this secret, I'd hidden my depressing self, the person whose emotions hinged on whether my writing was going well or how book sales were going. I'd pretended that I didn't drink too much or spend too much time lying around my apartment in a pathetic spin. Instead, I'd spent the week selling her on a brighter, happier, better version of me. Is it any surprise that she would do the same with the truths in her past?

As we walk toward the boat, the uncertainty of what lies ahead for us weighs heavily on me. A faint rustling sound—like someone stepping lightly on the sand behind us—makes me spin around, heart racing. But in the endless stretch of beach, I don't see anything. I tell myself that it's just the wind or the sand shifting in the breeze. My imagination running wild. But no matter how hard I try, I can't shake the feeling that we're not alone.

The boat feels miles away.

I pull Kate closer, every nerve on high alert.

There it is again. A flicker of movement, just out of the corner of my eye, behind one of the giant rocks that shield the homes from the surf.

I stop. Staring, my heart hammering. I step forward to get a closer look. But there's nothing there. Just shadows. A trick of the light—or lack of light.

"You okay?" Kate asks.

"Fine," I lie, my voice tight.

I know she's on edge too. Her grip on my hand is tighter now.

I listen now. Every sound. Every whisper of wind, every rush of surf, trying to hear anything that doesn't belong.

But the waves are too loud. They swallow every sound.

The boat's not far. Just a little farther. That's what I tell myself to try to steady the pounding in my chest. Kate's breathing matches mine, quick and shallow, her eyes darting around like she's expecting something to step out from the shadows.

We round a rugged bend in the beach, a spot known as Pitus Point. The water rises, and the waves grow higher, more violent. Ahead, I see a crackling bonfire on the beach. A small group, their faces bathed by the gentle glow, gathers around it on chairs and blankets. Their laughter and singing carry on the wind. A momentary relief from the panic.

"We'll want to stay away from that," Sam says quietly. "Walk in the surf, not on the sand, far enough away that they don't notice us."

Everyone is a possible threat. The people by that bonfire could later mention they saw Kate walking down the beach, innocently leading Dane right to us.

We step into the surf, and the chill bites at my ankles. The tide is rolling in, and the waves surge forward, slamming us with brutal force. The cold Pacific Ocean crashes around us, threatening to suck us under. I steady myself, grasping Kate's hand tightly, to keep us from falling in, pulling her back as another wave hits. The ground beneath my feet vibrates with each thunderous crash of the waves that pummel us again and again. Then Kate's hand slips out of mine.

I turn, my heart stopping cold.

She's gone.

I whirl around and there he is. Shadowed in the gray light, maybe six feet away. One thick hand clamps over Kate's mouth, the other grips her neck. She struggles, eyes wide with terror.

I can't move. He fixes a baleful stare on me. "Unless you want to end up dead, keep going."

My heart hammers. I can't breathe. I finally suck in a breath, and a thought strikes terror in my chest. *This is why I never see her again.* She dies because of him.

I step out of the surf and take a few steps forward, close enough that I can see his stringy blond hair, his glassy eyes. My pulse pounds. I'm not a fighter. I haven't thrown a punch or a kick since a fight I'd lost on the middle school playground. But when I see the fear in Kate's eyes, I know I must do something.

I lunge at him. At the moment of impact, Kate tears herself from Dane's grasp, then swiftly whirls around. She throws a kick at his groin and hits it square on. Dane staggers back in shock.

"Bitch," Dane says sloppily, then regains his balance. "You won't get away with this."

He tears at her like a wild animal, a snarl escaping his lips. She's faster though. She hits him with a punch and kick that surprise him, allowing her to escape.

She scrambles up the sandy slope toward the concrete steps to a beachfront home.

I chase after her and then my body is jolted by an intense pressure in my skull. Sharp pain shoots down my spine to my toes. The ocean scent is gone and in its place is the smell of a foul sewer. I hear voices. Before I can make out what they're saying, I ascend into darkness. I'm returning to the future.

Chapter Twenty-Eight

Brooke

~

11:08 PM

The ping of my phone startles me from a deep sleep.

"Can you come get me?"

My skin tingles with alarm when I realize it's Olivia's voice on the other end.

I sit up. As soon as Olivia was picked up for her sleepover at her friend Layla's house, I'd been overcome with a spell of vertigo and sudden exhaustion. My shoulders felt impossibly heavy, and I felt fuzzy as I ambled to my bedroom to lie down a moment, hoping it would pass. I'd fallen asleep on top of the covers, fully dressed.

I glance at my phone. 11:08. I've been asleep for two hours.

If I stay off the PCH, I won't hit Sam and Logan with my car. I won't be a murderer. But any excitement I feel about that possibility is pushed aside by worry for Olivia.

"What's going on?" I ask.

"I'm scared," she says, crying. "I want to come home. Here's Mrs. Phillips."

I hear the shuffle of the phone changing hands, and Layla's mom comes on. "Hello, Brooke?"

"Rina, what's going on?"

"We had a scare. The police came. But it's all clear now. I've been trying to get Olivia and Layla back to sleep, but it's not working. I wanted her to talk to you."

"The police came? For what?"

She tries to sound calm, but I hear the tremor in her voice. "Someone came onto the property. The dogs started barking like crazy, which woke all of us up. We looked out the window and saw a woman hiding on the deck, behind the hot tub. Then all of a sudden a man came up the stairs from the beach, found the woman, and they were fighting. That's when the girls started screaming. I took them away from the window and called 911. When police got here, the two were gone."

"Are the girls okay?"

"They're shaken up, but safe. They were never in any danger. I'd bring her home for you, but Jacob is finally back to sleep . . ."

"Oh no, I understand." Jacob is an infant, maybe six months old, at this point. Rina's a divorced mom and she's told me about his sleep problems, so there's no way she'll be able to drive Olivia home.

"Olivia wants to talk with you again," Rina says. "Here she is."

I hear fumbling again, then Olivia's voice comes back on. "Mommy, can you come now?" She sobs. "My tummy doesn't feel good."

I'm terrified. Rina's home is at Pitus Point on Faria Beach, and the only way to get there is via the PCH. Unless I had a helicopter, there's no other route. The ocean is on one side. The PCH is the other.

"Did you hear me?" she says, sniffling. "I'm really scared."

"Give me a minute to pull my things together and I'll be there. Don't worry. Everything's going to be okay."

Chapter Twenty-Nine

Logan

∽

11:12 PM

I'm at the bonfire on the beach. Not in the bike lane. I'm pounding back water and staying away from the PCH. As before, I'm stone cold sober at a party where everyone else has been doing shots of tequila or bourbon. And everything else.

I'd been indoors earlier and was getting agitated, wanting to get away from all the temptations that were everywhere, so I headed out to the bonfire. It was fine until two drunk guys plopped onto the sand across from me and began irritating the hell out of me. Both trying to remember the words to a Kodak Black song:

We could be superstars
But I'm pretty sure time is up

That's the actual words, but they keep messing up, tangling the words, laughing, then stumbling through more attempts. No matter how bad their singing gets, I'm not moving from this spot.

I glance at my phone and smile. 11:12.

If I stay off the PCH, I get to live a life with my body intact. In a few hours, I'll begin my double metric century ride. I'll return home in time to see Haley after she gets off work. This is the life I want.

Then out of the corner of my eye, I spot someone running along the beach. He's shouting something but with the roar of the waves, I can't hear what it is.

"What the heck?" one of the drunk guys says.

The man races through the sand, toward the bonfire, a blur in the inky darkness. The flashlight on his smartphone is on, but its dim rays are pointless on the dark beachfront. He races toward us. "Kate!" he shouts.

Sam.

My heart thuds to a stop.

"Have you seen a girl?" he asks us, his voice frantic. "Dark hair."

What is going on? Elizabeth had promised me she'd keep Sam away from the PCH tonight.

"You shouldn't be here," I shout.

The Kodak Black singer with his hat cocked to the side answers. "I saw a girl. A few minutes ago. She came down from that house," he points down the beach a little. "And ran into this one." He gestures to Emmett's beach house.

Sam races toward Emmett's house, and my heart starts beating a million times a minute.

"Wait!" I shout. "Want me to check the beach again with you?"

His voice shakes. "She's got to be up here," he says, then bounds up the wooden staircase.

I sprint up the stairs behind him. His eyes frantically scan the crowded deck, searching for someone amidst the pulsing music and laughter. Then he weaves through the party, dodging groups of chatting guests and pivoting around scattered beach towels and chairs.

Sam stops. Whoever he's looking for isn't here. He locks eyes with me. "Are you following me?"

"I'm trying to help. Who're you looking for?"

"She's not here." He points toward the side of the house. "Where's that go?"

My blood freezes. "To the PCH. Don't go there."

"She must have gone that way."

Sam charges toward the side of the house. Ahead of him there's a wooden gate at the end of the narrow passageway that creates a barrier from the Pacific Coast Highway. I know Emmett's family always keeps it locked from the highway side, not the inside.

"Stop!" I shout at him, but that only seems to make him run faster. My hands are clammy with fear, but I manage to push in front of him, blocking his way.

"What the hell is your problem?" He shoves me hard, his strength surprising me.

"Don't go out there. It's not safe."

Sam's face gets super red. Fast. Then with what seems like impossible strength, he pushes me again. "Get out of my way. I'm trying to help someone."

He yanks open the gate and races toward the highway. I think I can grab him. That's what my panicked brain believes. I'm strong and quick enough to tackle him. I can pin him on the ground.

Chapter Thirty

Brooke

⤳

11:23 PM

When I end the call with Olivia, numbness creeps into my fingers and a sudden wave of dizziness makes the room spin. I steady myself by the kitchen sink and gulp down a glass of water.

When the room finally stops spinning, I grab my keys and head to the car. I tell myself the accident won't happen if I get on the PCH. For one thing, Sam won't be anywhere near there. I have no doubt Elizabeth has made sure of that. Logan won't be on the highway either. Besides, it's later in the night. The first time around, the accident was around 11:13. By the time I get to that stretch of highway, it'll be nearly twenty minutes later.

I manage to drive normally until I pull onto the entrance ramp to the PCH. Then my head pounds and my throat closes. No one is behind me, so I slow the car and remind myself that Logan and Sam are not on the PCH.

The highway follows the natural coastline and since straight lines are rarely found in nature, there are only brief stretches which aren't twists and turns. Because of the new moon, the sky is shrouded in darkness, devoid of any comforting light, and its absence casts deep shadows everywhere. The landscape that's familiar in daylight now blends seamlessly into the backdrop of the night.

I drive slowly, gripping the wheel tight, eyes locked on the stretch of asphalt ahead. Occasionally, a soft glow spills through the windows of the houses I pass, momentarily illuminating the darkness.

My imagination plays tricks on my mind, conjuring ghosts and phantoms lurking beyond the reaches of my headlights. Every curve and bend in the road seems to conceal lurking dangers.

It's okay.

Logan and Sam are not on the highway.

A clock begins ticking in my head. Counting down the seconds until I reach the place where it happened—where Sam's and Logan's and my life ended.

Pay attention.

My eyes grow hot, tears threatening. I take my foot off the gas and scan the dark highway, feeling restless and dizzy. Everything is happening too fast.

Chapter Thirty-One

Logan

11:30 PM

One push through the wooden gate to the highway and I see her. A girl in a gauzy white blouse and jeans. The figure I thought I'd imagined. She's standing by the highway, her hair blowing in the furious wind, her chest heaving. A bright red stain blooms at her neckline, and a wound slashes across her left cheek. The whole image has the fading texture of a dream.

Then I hear the sharp crack of a twig. A furious rustle of leaves. Like an apparition living in the trees beside the highway, a man appears out of the gloom. He lunges for the girl and grabs her in a choke hold.

His voice is like a drill, sharp and menacing. "You should never have run away."

Seconds later, Sam's on him, yanking on the man's arms, prying them off her. He kicks the shadow man, and the girl tears out of the man's grasp, kneeing him in the stomach, and breaks free. She races across the highway but the man from the shadows is fast and thuds behind her. Sam takes off after them.

Then I see the car lights surfacing on the horizon, rounding the curve, blinding everything in its path.

"Stop, Sam!" I shout, my breath coming in jagged spurts.

I grab for him, using every fiber of my strength to stop him from entering the highway. My fingers pull at his clothing, but I only end up grazing the back of his shirt. I'm not fast enough. I'm too late.

Then everything goes silent. My head feels like it's splitting in two. Suddenly the highway becomes dark as hell. It's impossible to breathe in all that darkness.

I'm returning to the future.

Then I'm covered in every scent imaginable—oranges, lemons, sardines—as everything I know fades away.

Chapter Thirty-Two

Brooke

◞

11:32 PM

A shift in the darkness draws my focus. A swish of movement. Is something there?

I slam on the brakes, and for the first time I see two figures—two *human* figures—dart across the highway. I yank the steering wheel hard and swerve to avoid them, and the car lurches and swings, narrowly missing them. It feels like the car has taken on a life of its own, unpredictable. Out of control. The next moment, I hear the *thump thump* as I hit something in the bike lane. I slam on the brakes and skid for what seems like an eternity. When I finally stop, my heart is pounding so hard I start to cry.

I try it all differently this time. I slam on the hazard lights, grab my phone, then leap out of the car. Everything around me feels liquid. Unreal. The silence is deafening—the only sound is the fevered crunch of my feet on the gravel and the sounds of the surf in the distance.

In the dim light, I scan for the people who'd raced across the highway, but there's no sign of them. Are they lurking in the shadows? An eerie stillness hangs heavy in the air. I hear the rustle of movement in the trees, but there's no time to investigate.

Sam and Logan are lying in the bike lane. I know it's them even from this distance. In my whirling terror, I call out their names softly, and when they don't move, I shout for help.

I stumble awkwardly to Sam first, summoning a desperate prayer that he's still alive. Hot shame constricts my chest. I press 911 on my phone and drop it on the asphalt with the speaker on. I hear my panicked voice telling the dispatcher to send help. I can still make this outcome different. I can.

I drop to my knees, place a finger on his wrist, feeling for a pulse. Nothing.

I want to believe there will be a pulse. I try again, placing my fingers on his neck, but feel nothing. I check if he's breathing, but his chest is not rising or falling.

I get into position for CPR, determined to revive him. I'd taken a course once, but in my panicked state it's taking too long to remember the sequence of steps. As I lean over his body to begin the compressions, an icy chill rips through my body. Then another. Suddenly I can't hear anything except my own breathing. My sight disappears and in its place is a hallucination: James is waving a paper at me and speaking to me with my mother's voice. Then I see purple bursts of color with thousands of interconnected threads, like I'm watching my neural pathways at work. My thoughts drift and ramble. I feel the pathways connect to galaxies and see that we're all just one with each other.

Part Three

The Return

Chapter Thirty-Three

Logan

～

When I first come to, all kinds of alarms are shrieking and blaring, and the small room I'm in, lined with white curtains, is jammed with people in blue scrubs racing around.

"Don't panic, Logan. We've got everything under control," a nurse says touching my hand. "You're back."

In the present.

Within a minute, the monitors begin beeping a steady rhythm, and the same nurse with hazel eyes asks me a few easy questions: my name, birthdate, and address. When I answer them she says, "You're probably feeling a bit groggy, but give it time and you'll feel like yourself again."

After she and the others scurry out, I succumb to magical thinking. I'm completely still, allowing myself final moments to believe that the return has reset my body and that I'm the way I was in the past. Strong and unbroken.

I instruct my legs to move and when they don't, I'm struck with terror so intense that my arms tremble. I'm unable to move from the waist down. There's no feeling in my legs. I can't wiggle my toes. Instead, my feet are covered in bright orange hospital socks, an ugly reminder of all I've lost.

A wave of helplessness washes over me. Everything I had in the past is gone. The Aeon scientists had told us that our trip to the past cannot change the future, but I'd hoped that it'd be different for me somehow.

My eyes fill with tears. Damn. My fear is greater than it was three years ago when I first realized I was paralyzed. At least then there was still the possibility, slim as it was, that I'd recover and walk again.

Now I have nothing.

I'd have been better off never taking this jump. I could've used the money to relax on the white sand beaches of Hawaii or gazed at the northern lights in Finland or gaped in awe at the Grand Canyon. Instead, I'm a hell of a lot more broke and with nothing to show for it. Except memories.

I push aside the memories and focus on my breathing, trying to slow it down. Then the nurse returns, and I spend the next half hour trying to suck down a liter of blue hydrating gel she insists will make me feel better.

What's wrong with me can't be cured with a gel.

A few minutes later, two nursing assistants come in and transfer me out of bed and into a wheelchair. I roll over to the window. The view is the bleak side of a hulking black hangar, but it beats being stuck dead bug–style on the hospital bed.

Then the memories slide in. No surprise that they start with Haley. Her soft smile. Her lips on mine. I've lost that too.

All too soon that memory fades and in its place is the heat of the bonfire on the beach during those last minutes. Two guys singing.
We could be superstars
But I'm pretty sure time is up
Then I remember my first glimpse of Sam. The gripping terror of realizing that we share a destiny he never knew. And yet, even armed with the knowledge of what our future held, I was powerless to stop it.

I've gained nothing from my jump. I'm exactly where I was before. Nothing more.

The sun sets and darkness settles outside my window until the hangar across from me fades into the black. I remember something Marco always said when we both had hit the "wall" and our swim times stopped improving. "It's not what you look at that matters," he'd said. "It's what you *see*."

Maybe I'm looking at this all wrong. I know things now. Stuff I didn't understand before the jump. I know why Sam ran onto the highway that night. Well, some of it. I know he was trying to help that girl, Kate, escape from the man with bloodshot eyes. I don't know much about what happened before that. Or after. But it's something.

Elizabeth has spent years wondering why Sam was there, what drove him to step onto the dark highway in front of a speeding car at the same moment I was there. She'll need to hear that Sam didn't die because of any cruel words she said to him before he left that night. His last minutes were spent trying to save someone.

She'll want to know.

I wheel over to the corner of the small room—if you can call it that—and push back the white curtain that serves as a door to whatever is outside.

I'm not in a real hospital. At least it doesn't look like one. Instead, it's a cavernous hangar with sections cordoned off by tall white hospital curtains. The facility is filled with the sound of beeps and tones and the hum of people—doctors, nurses, technicians—rushing around or in conversation. There are phones ringing—several of them—which no one seems to answer.

"Where do you think you're going?" a voice says.

I turn to look, and a nurse with bright red lipstick and a coffee stain on her blue scrubs glares back at me.

"I'm looking for Elizabeth Saunders," I say.

"What for?"

"Has she been extracted too?"

She moves to block my way. "You need to stay in your room until you're discharged." She softens as she grabs hold of the push handles on my chair. "Here, let me help you."

"You don't understand. I need to tell her something."

"We need you to stay where you are," she says. And the way she looks at me makes me worried. Did Elizabeth make it back safely?

"Let's get you back to your room," she says, pushing me back where I came from.

Chapter Thirty-Four

Andy

No! Don't go! I hear someone shouting, then realize it's my own voice.

The world spins around me in a hazy dream; then I wake hours later and realize I'm in a hospital bed being shuttled around—down hallways, I think?—under fluorescent lights. There are a battery of tests and scans. What seems like minutes later but probably has been hours, I finally awaken in a space drenched in artificial light and surrounded by white curtains. A doctor with a husky voice and a Tom Selleck moustache asks, "Do you know what day it is?" I don't.

"Do you know where you are?" I assume I'm at Aeon Expeditions, but this makeshift room beeping with monitors looks more like a hospital than the massive hangar I'd departed from.

"Are you in any pain?"

My head hurts, but a deeper pain tears at my heart. "I want to go back."

"We hear that a lot," he says, without looking up from his laptop.

"You don't understand, I *have* to go back—"

To what though? To the beachfront where Dane was racing after Kate?

"The most important thing you can do right now is rest."

After the doctor is satisfied with my test results, he steps out, and I catch my reflection in the mirror on the table beside the bed. Deep circles around my eyes. Pale skin. Crazy hair. The beginnings of a scraggly beard.

A dark storm of dread engulfs me. *Kate's dead.* That's the only explanation that makes sense. She didn't survive Dane's assault. She didn't make it. That's why she never responded to my emails or calls. Why I never heard from her again.

The grief is suffocating, but it's the anger that threatens to consume me. Anger not just directed at Dane but also at myself for not seeing the truth sooner. I roll on my side and fold over in pain.

The memories flood back—sharp and clear. The beach at night, holding Kate's hand as we walked to the boat. The nightmare unfolding before my eyes—a surreal scene as Dane rose from the shadows, tearing Kate away from me before I could even comprehend what was happening.

The memory is shattered by a faint ringing from somewhere nearby. It's not the bedside monitor, a silent sentry monitoring my vital signs. It seems to be chiming from a drawer in the nightstand.

I remove the pulse oximeter from my finger, slip out of bed, and open the drawer. Inside in a plastic bag are all the personal items I'd brought with me when I arrived for the jump a week ago: car keys, wallet, phone, hoodie. The phone is ringing. Jonathan's name flashes on the screen. I answer.

"Hey, Jonathan."

"I'm betting you look like shit," he says, with a laugh. "And probably feel like it too."

"Both," I say, brightening at the sound of his voice.

"At least they're letting this call go through."

"Why wouldn't they?"

"The story's been all over the news. Did you know there were four of you stranded in the past? They're calling you the Memory Collectors. Reporters are gonna fight to get your story. Luckily for you, none of them have your cell phone number."

"Wait. Slow down. How'd *reporters* find out we were stranded?"

"The husband of one of the Memory Collectors—Brooke—is some big shot lawyer. When she didn't return after the usual hour and Aeon didn't have any answers for him, he went to the media. When they discovered that *four* of you were stranded, the story exploded. Overnight, the jump experience most of us could only dream about became extremely dangerous. The good news," he says, his tone lifting. "Is that your book *He's Gone* is blowing up. Top of the bestseller lists again."

I steady myself on the edge of the bed. "What?"

"Y'all are household names now. We've been hearing about the Memory Collectors nonstop every day for the past week. For a while there, all we heard was constant chatter that they *wouldn't* ever be able to get you back. Good thing they did. How're you feeling?"

I pause, trying to figure out where to start. I huff out a shaky breath. "Jonathan, I found her."

He sighs. "Kate?"

My voice catches. "She's dead now. That's why I never heard from her again."

"Back up. Explain."

My throat tightens. "She'd fled to Ventura to escape her ex—he'd tried to kill her. The guy had insane tracking skills and followed her all the way from Michigan. There was no escaping by car; he'd hunt her down. So we planned for her to take a boat to Anacapa Island. But just as we reached the boat, he came out of nowhere and ripped her away from me."

The line crackles with tension. "Holy hell. What'd you do?"

"Then I was extracted."

I hear him blow out a long breath. "You think he . . ." He trails off. Even he doesn't want to say the words aloud.

My voice trembles. "Every moment I thought she'd just ghosted me and walked away, the reality is she was dead."

His response is barely above a whisper. "Oh, man. I'm sorry."

My anger gives way to grim focus. "That means *he's* still out there. Living his life like nothing happened. I'm not gonna let him get away with it."

Chapter Thirty-Five

Elizabeth

My body is connected to a jumble of machines, each of them tracking and blinking and beeping out vital information about me. But as I resurface, those sounds are muted by a man's voice close to my ear. I can't make out what he's saying. Then the words slowly come into focus.

"Elizabeth," he says. "Can you hear me?"

My eyes are heavy, as if my lashes have been glued together. It takes some effort to pry them open and when I do, I see my ex, Mark, standing beside the bed between two men in white lab coats.

"You're safe now," Mark says, reassuring me. Even his comforting tone, a voice that I'd once loved, cannot soothe me. I'm safe, that's true. But in the present.

A waterfall of pain and grief washes over me. I feel Sam's absence as if a physical part of me has been ripped away. The room seems to spin as I grapple with the cold reality of this moment.

Sam is gone.

I knew that I couldn't stay in the past forever. Still, it doesn't make it easier to accept. I blink away hot tears and when I look up I see them mirrored in Mark's eyes.

"Would you give us a minute?" Mark asks the men.

The taller one takes note of whatever is on the monitors by my bedside. "We'll wait outside."

In the silence as the doctors exit, Mark reaches out, his hand hovering briefly before it rests gently on mine. It's a simple gesture, but it somehow grounds me.

Once the door closes, I notice a softness in his gaze, a tenderness I don't remember. Has he changed? Or is it me who's seeing things differently?

"We had problems getting you back. But you're okay. Stable now." His hands have a slight tremble to them. "When you're feeling better, I want to hear everything about Sam."

How does he know I saw Sam? If our jumps are to random dates, as we've been told, I could've easily jumped into a time when Sam wasn't born yet. Or jumped to a time when Sam was already gone. But Mark seems to *know* that I was with Sam.

"How do you know I saw Sam?"

He scans the monitor beside me. "We should have you out of here as early as tomorrow morning."

"What went wrong, Mark? Why were we stranded?"

He hesitates. "Every time we tried to extract any of you, the system malfunctioned. Eventually, we realized it was because your paths kept crossing."

"What do you mean? I didn't meet any of the others until days *after* we were stranded."

"Our monitors showed that you and Andy Schapiro crossed paths in the first hour."

I shake my head. "I was on a walk with Sam during the first hour. I never saw Andy."

"He was there."

I search my memories of that first night with Sam and remember the man carrying champagne who complimented Sting. I was so focused on Sam I didn't notice what he looked like. That must have been Andy.

"Our failure to extract you brought the company to a grinding halt. I put rotating crews working around the clock and across the globe to reconfigure the machines. We suspended thousands of trips."

It sounds like a Herculean task that only someone as smart and resourceful as Mark could overcome. As he tells me about the countless hours devoted to bringing us back and the technical hurdles they overcame, all I can think is that this crisis gave me more time with Sam.

"When you get back home," he says. His eyes are steady, as if he's trying to make them say something that his words can't. "I need to tell you something important."

I shift in the bed. "What is it?"

"Could I . . . come by with dinner tomorrow?"

Chapter Thirty-Six

Brooke

When I step out of the Aeon hangar into the bright sunlight the next morning, the harsh reality hits me hard. I'm back in the present with all the same problems I had before. A husband and daughter who barely speak to me. Friends who avoid me.

It's not their fault, of course. I can barely look any of them in the eye. After I was released from jail, I'd avoided meaningful conversations and sought out solitude, the guilt at what I'd done eating at me every day. Facing them means grappling with the enormity of what I'd done.

I spot James and Olivia across the parking lot waiting by our car. He's leaning against the hood, hands shoved in his pockets, staring at the ground. When he sees me, he straightens and waves, offering a tentative smile. My heart aches at the sight of him. He looks older. Tired. Olivia's eyes are wide, filled with a mix of uncertainty and curiosity. I've only been away a week, but I swear she's grown.

As I make my way to the car beneath a bright, blazing sun, the asphalt feels hot beneath my feet. I take a deep breath, steadying my shaking hands. I'm going home, but "home" feels empty and uncertain.

"Hey," James says, his tone soft but guarded. "Are you okay?"

"Not a scratch on me," I say, a little too brightly.

He opens the passenger door for me, and I slip into the seat. Inside the car, the AC blasts away the August heat. James's hands flex on the steering wheel, and in the rearview mirror, I catch Olivia leaning forward slightly, like she's wanting to ask questions but holding herself back.

"The news said—" Olivia starts, then stops. She's been watching the coverage, of course.

"I'm okay," I say quickly, turning to look at her directly. "Really okay. They've taken good care of us."

James nods, swallowing hard. "When Aeon said they couldn't bring you back . . ." His voice trails off, and I see him grip the wheel tighter. "Well, we've been worried."

"What did you do there?" Olivia asks. "With all that time?"

I glance at her in the rearview mirror, catch a glimpse of the little girl who used to tell me everything. Now her eyes hold something harder—caution. I want to tell them everything—about meeting Logan and talking with Sam, about reliving the accident—but where do I begin? The words tangle in my throat.

"I'm not entirely ready to talk about it." My voice comes out hoarse. I clear my throat, try again. "I learned things I didn't expect. I'm still trying to process . . ."

"We'll give you time to adjust," James says, and I hear the effort in his voice, the attempt to bridge this canyon between us. When I dare to look at him, his expression surprises me. The guardedness is still there, but underneath it is something gentler. Something that reminds me of before. "You've been through a lot."

What he doesn't say hangs between us: we've all been through a lot, long before this past week. But for now, maybe it's enough that I made it home.

The rest of the drive home is quiet, except for the hum of the engine. I notice James avoids the PCH, taking the backroads instead. Perhaps he remembers my fear of that highway ever since the accident, or maybe he just thinks this way is faster.

Every few minutes I feel Olivia's eyes on me, checking, making sure I'm still here. I want to tell her I'm not going anywhere, but those are words I've said before, promises I've broken before.

When we arrive home, the place is the same, yet different—like a memory that's faded at the edges. James leads the way to the front door, and our neighbor Mrs. Chen waves from her garden, trying not to stare. I wonder how many reporters have been by.

"Welcome home," James says, stepping aside to let me enter first. I catch the slight crack in his voice. He busies himself with putting away his keys and sunglasses, a familiar ritual.

I stand in the entryway, not quite sure what to do. On the side table, I spot a stack of newspapers—all with headlines about the Memory Collectors. How many mornings did they sit here, scrolling through news about us, wondering?

"I've missed you both," I say.

"Me too," Olivia says. but she's already drifting toward her room, her backpack clutched like a shield. Five days of worry don't erase years of learned caution.

"Are you hungry?" James asks, moving toward the kitchen. I recognize this—his need to do something practical, something normal, when everything else feels uncertain.

"They gave us lunch at Aeon."

"I have some homework to do," Olivia says, heading to her room.

Homework. Of course. School started while I was gone. Yet more one thing in her life that I'd missed.

"And I have a trial starting tomorrow morning, so I'm going to put in a few hours . . ." James's voice trails off as he gestures vaguely toward his office. "I'll be in here if you need me." They peel away to their separate corners of the house, leaving me standing in our living room. I click on the TV, and a story about the Memory Collectors splashes across the screen. The headline on the news ticker at the bottom reads: **Memory Collectors Return Home.**

Aeon attempted to organize a press conference where the Memory Collectors would reassure the public about the safety of the travel process. A ballroom full of reporters wanted proof that we've returned healthy and unharmed, eager to talk to the four who've become household names this past week.

We all said no.

We were exhausted and wanted to go home. We didn't want our lives inspected and picked apart by the public. Especially me. I know the questions everyone will ask: *You've served time in prison for vehicular manslaughter and vehicular assault. How were you qualified to take this trip?* I don't want reporters to scrutinize and rehash every detail of my worst moments.

Without interviews with any of us, reporters can only guess what our experiences were like. But that doesn't stop them from endless coverage. The screen flashes to images of the four of us. They show Logan in what appears to be a mugshot from when he was several years younger. Is that all they could find for him? The photo of Elizabeth shows her standing by her then-husband Mark Saunders, founder of Aeon, holding hands and walking through a park ablaze with fall colors. Andy's photo is from a book signing of his novel *He's Gone*. Mine is an older headshot from years ago when I opened Celestine. My smile radiates joy at the promise of my life ahead. Before my mistake.

Then my worst nightmare unfolds. Video from the scene of the accident fills the screen. Flashing lights of ambulances and police cars in a surreal mosaic of red and blue. The somber faces of the first responders. The stark outline of Sam's covered body on the stretcher. I click off the TV.

Even when I tried to prevent the accident that killed Sam and paralyzed Logan, I couldn't stop it from happening. My car still hit them. *I* still hit them.

Is it impossible to escape fate? No matter what I did, the accident happened anyway. Could it be that some things in life are simply beyond our control?

There was one difference though. The first time around, I kept driving down the highway. I didn't stop and assess the situation or try to help. I continued on without looking back.

The second time, I made the choice to change how I responded. I stopped. I tried to fix it.

That single choice has given me the closest thing to clarity I've felt in a long time. Instead of running in shame, as I did the first time, I focused on what I *could* control.

I wonder. Could I apply this in the present too?

I flick the TV back on. As I listen to the reporter go on about the Memory Collectors, an idea forms. A crazy one, perhaps. I scroll on my phone to find an email from Aeon

Expeditions, the one pleading with the four of us to do the press conference. All our email addresses are in it.

I send a message to the other three Memory Collectors, inviting them to come to Celestine for a dinner together on Wednesday. I tell them that we'll start with a delicate amuse-bouche of seared scallops, drizzled with a citrus-infused sauce I'd been experimenting with. A rack of lamb. And finishing with chocolate lava cake. But it's not really about the meal.

There's so much we all need to understand about August 25, I write. *There are things I want to express that I should've said long ago.*

As soon as I press Send, doubts creep in. It *is* a crazy idea. Maybe even pointless. Would they even accept an invitation from the person who destroyed their lives? Even if they do, what will I say to them?

Chapter Thirty-Seven

Andy

I'm on the hunt for Dane Reynolds. And when I find him, I'll bring him to justice.

He must pay for what he did to Kate. To Sam. To all of us.

But I'm an author, not an investigator or detective or police officer. Still, I have a million plans. Call the sheriff's office. Scour social media. Research Dane online. I also consider hiring a private investigator, but my entire knowledge of PIs comes from reading Philip Marlowe and Michael Kelly novels. Problem is, in books people find PIs through referrals—friends who know them—and I can't think of anyone in sleepy Ventura who's either a PI or likely to be friends with one.

My newfound notoriety has my phone chiming all day long. Hundreds of people have used the contact form on my author website to send me messages. Thousands of other complete strangers DM me on social media, acting as if we're friends.

"Congrats on your return," a woman writes. She claims she was a couple of years behind me in college, but I don't remember knowing her. She goes on for a paragraph to update me on what she's doing and where she's living, which happens to be about an hour away in Santa Barbara. She wonders if I'd like to meet up for drinks and attaches a photo; she's pretty with kohl-lined eyes and dark brown hair falling loosely to her shoulders.

Others pepper me with questions about my jump, but I don't have answers for them. I'm rigid with grief. I would need paragraphs to explain what it was like to spend a week with someone you loved and later lost. I'd need an entire novel to share the ache of knowing that a love I felt just yesterday is now a long-ago memory.

Sometimes, the flood of emails and DMs feels so overwhelming that the only escape is to write—to capture every moment from the past in words before the details slip away. I'm in the middle of a brief writing session when a text swoops across my phone. From Lauren. Smart, beautiful Lauren who once wanted to share an apartment and a dog with me.

How're you holding up? Hope all is okay!

Guilt gnaws at me. My breakup with her was awkward at best. I'd never meant to hurt her, but I'd stumbled through vague explanations of our incompatibility and murky words of uncertainty. I pushed her away because I believed Kate was still alive and I wanted a past and a future with her.

Now what do I have? Nothing. Kate is dead. I'm sure of it. And after the clumsy way I handled our breakup, Lauren probably wouldn't trust a friendship with me. I type:

It's good to be back.

That's a lie. Delete.

I'm doing great. Thanks for asking.
Another lie. Delete. I finally settle on:
It's been tough but working through it. How're you?
I flop on my bed and wait for her to answer. She never does.

A neighbor starts playing some classical music piece, and then I forget about Lauren and memories of my time with Kate float in. I remember when the Orpheus and Eurydice music came on the smart speaker and Kate shared the story of how Orpheus made the perilous journey into the underworld to beg for his love's return. But anxiety overcomes him, and he fails to bring her back.

"And he loses her forever?" I'd asked.

"He does."

"So his trip to the underworld was pointless."

"Or you could see it another way. Because of Orpheus, the two were reunited, however briefly. That's something."

Was it enough that I got to spend nearly a week with Kate?

That single thought makes the veil of grief lift for a moment. Somehow the bed I'm lying in feels like the most luxurious bed ever made. I glance over at the crap on my desk—the note pads scrawled with ideas, a pack of gum, the dog-eared paperback I'd started reading months ago—and I can't help but see it as a time capsule of my present life. I think about the future and know that even this ordinary moment longing for Kate will be charged with new meaning once it becomes a memory.

That is something.

Later that afternoon, I manage to schedule a meeting with Eric Ingram, commander of the Major Crimes Bureau in the Ventura County Sheriff's office. I tell the deputy who answers the phone that I'm one of the Memory Collectors and that seems to pique his curiosity enough to put me on Eric's calendar for Thursday.

I go online and make reservations for two separate boat trips to Anacapa Island and Catalina Island in the hopes that I can find any evidence Kate or Dane made it there. I know it's impossible that I'll discover anything so many years later, but I'm grasping at any possibility, no matter how unlikely.

After that, I head to the library and search public records for Dane Reynolds, but the only matches I find are a retired seventh grade teacher and a twenty-two-year-old manager of a cannabis dispensary in Portland, Oregon.

I return home exhausted, but sleep is impossible. The white numbers on my phone glare at me throughout the early hours of the morning: 2:12 AM. 3:17 AM. 4:32 AM. My thoughts tumble and roll. I think about turning my apartment into a command center. Posting papers, maps, and photos on the walls connected by red threads, just like detectives do in TV shows. I consider joining some true crime forums—maybe they can crowdsource information or help me analyze evidence if I find any. I have to do something.

Bleary eyed, at 5:02 AM, I post on Instagram to my eleven thousand loyal followers:

I am looking for a guy named Dane Reynolds. 30s. Blond hair. It's for my next novel. He worked at a paper mill in Michigan and was in Ventura, California, three years ago. DM me if you know anything.

I toss the phone on my nightstand, proud of myself for taking action. But inevitably, darker thoughts emerge, and I know all of this is futile.

Chapter Thirty-Eight

Brooke

Today marks my first full day back with James and Olivia, and I'm taking small steps to reconnect. I cook an elaborate breakfast for them, recreating their favorites and experimenting with a blueberry and ricotta pancake that I'm relieved to see they enjoy. I tuck a note into Olivia's lunch, careful to keep it light: *Just wanted you to know that I'm thinking of you. Love, Mom.*

After breakfast, I join James on the porch. Our conversation drifts; he's kind but distant. He shifts in his seat, the space between us heavy with uncertainty.

The only place I feel truly alive is Celestine. Today, I'm revising the menu, planning changes to the décor, and ordering new plates—all to signal the fresh start I desperately crave.

But it's only window dressing. I'm defined by what happened that one night in August, reliving it in my every thought and action. *I may think I'm a good person, but when it comes down to it . . .*

I stand behind the bar, wiping down glasses, trying to help the waitstaff keep up with the constant stream of new customers. I can feel the weight of the customers' gazes. Some look my way, recognition sparking in their eyes. Others exchange glances, nodding discreetly in my direction. Despite my attempts to blend in by wearing the same uniform as the waitstaff—black pants and blouse—I seem to be a magnet for customers' attention, a figure they think they know from the stories and headlines about the Memory Collectors that have turned Celestine into a bustling hot spot.

The dinner I've planned for the Memory Collectors is just moments away, and a knot of anxiety has taken up permanent residence in my stomach. A young man approaches me. He's handsome and familiar, but how do I know him? Then I realize he's the only Memory Collector I've never met.

"I'm Andy Schapiro."

"Brooke," I say, shaking his hand. "I've set aside a booth for us. Let me show you."

As I guide him to the table, Elizabeth strides in, an elegant scarf draped casually over her shoulders, a stark contrast to the tension roiling within me. The glass I've been holding slips from my fingers and crashes to the floor.

"You okay?" Andy asks.

"Fine," I reply, but the way I sweep up the shards of glass in a panicked frenzy is proof that I'm not.

Heat rises to my cheeks as I straighten my blouse, forcing a confident expression even as my stomach is a twisted mess. This is it. The moment I've been dreading and anticipating. How do I even begin to face her?

Moments later, Logan wheels in, spots Elizabeth, and heads over to talk with her. I watch them all introduce themselves to Andy. The din of conversations whirling around them rises as the customers realize all four of the Memory Collectors have gathered here. A few snap photos with their phones.

I consider the logistics of moving us to a private dining room, but the others don't seem to notice or mind the attention. Logan waves me over, and I join them at the table, nervousness tightening in my chest. I'd orchestrated every detail of the table and the menu myself, each place setting meticulously arranged because it's the one thing that I can control.

As we settle into our seats, a rush of excitement takes over. Everyone starts talking at the same time, and our conversation soon becomes a jumble of laughter, questions, and stories all tumbling out at once. It's as if we're all trying to make sense of our time in the past in a single breath.

Suddenly, we all stop talking, like an unseen conductor has waved her baton. I struggle to find the words of apology I'd rehearsed in my head a hundred times. I'm unsure where to begin.

Elizabeth beats me to it. "Thank you for bringing us together," she says, nodding at me. "If I'm honest, I came here tonight for many reasons but mostly to understand what happened the night of August twenty-fifth."

"I think all of us have the same questions," Andy adds.

Her gaze shifts between the three of us. "My son, Sam, left the house that night. He wouldn't say where he was going or why. I said some things I regret. Words I can't take back. But even after a week in the past, I still don't know why he was on that highway in the middle of the night."

"I do," Andy says to Elizabeth. "Sam was helping my girlfriend, Kate. She'd fled to Ventura to escape her abusive ex, Dane Reynolds. But Dane tracked her down. Sam offered her your boat so she could escape to the Channel Islands. We were on the beach, at Pitus Point, heading to the mooring when Dane ambushed us. He grabbed Kate, but Sam and I fought him. Last I saw before I was extracted, Kate running toward a house on the beach."

"Wait." I interject, heart pounding. "Describe the house."

He hesitates. "It was dark. Hard to see much. It had super-wide concrete steps—"

"That's my friend's house," I say, my voice rising. "I'm sure of it. My daughter, Olivia, was at a sleepover at Pitus Point, and the girls heard and saw a couple fighting right outside their window."

"Kate and Dane," Andy says, face pale.

"The police were called. Olivia was terrified and begged me to pick her up." I turn to Logan and Elizabeth, guilt washing over me. "That's why I broke my promise to stay off the PCH. I had to get Olivia."

Andy's eyes bore into mine. "Kate . . . did she escape?"

"I don't know. The couple had vanished by the time the police arrived."

"Wait," Logan says. "She *did* get away from him. Briefly."

"What do you mean?" Andy asks.

A charged silence falls over us as we hang on Logan's every word.

"I was at a bonfire just down from Pitus Point. I looked up and there's Sam sprinting around like a madman shouting for someone named Kate. Some guys at the bonfire yelled that they'd seen a girl run inside the house where the party was going on. Sam searched the party, didn't find her there, so he went to check out by the highway. I tried to stop him, because I already knew how this ends, but he slammed me up against the wall and pushed past me. The girl, she was there by the highway, blood on her shirt."

"Must have been Kate," Andy says breathlessly.

"Just as Sam reached out to her, a man suddenly lunged from the shadows and grabbed her."

"Dane," Andy says.

Logan continues, his voice low and urgent. "Sam was fast and wicked strong. He charged at the guy, but the man—Dane—overpowered him. Still, he gave Kate the opening she needed. She tore away from Dane and bolted across the highway. When Dane realized what was happening, he took off after her. Sam ran in pursuit." He turns to me. "That's when your car hit him."

I stare at him in disbelief, my mind reeling, struggling to reconcile what I'd thought had happened with the events Logan is describing. I blink back tears, trying not to cry.

"You okay?" Logan asks.

"Not really," I say, wiping my eyes. "I don't think I ever will be."

"What you're saying, Logan, is that two people *did* run across the highway in front of Brooke's car," Elizabeth says. "Kate and Dane. You didn't imagine them, Brooke. They were real. That's why you swerved."

"Kate and Dane—where'd they go?" Andy demands of me. "Did you see?"

"I swerved to miss them and—" My voice catches. "I hit Logan and Sam instead."

Andy's face drains of color. His gaze snaps to Logan. "Is that why you're . . ." He can't finish the sentence, just gestures at the wheelchair.

Logan nods.

Andy slumps back, his eyes haunted. "And Sam? What happened to him?"

There's fear in his eyes as he glances from Logan to Elizabeth before finally settling on me. My hands tremble. It's hard to live with the truth about what I did. Even harder to say it aloud. "I hit Sam too. He . . . didn't make it."

A strangled sound escapes Andy's throat, raw and primal. It seems like an eternity before he speaks. "What Sam did for Kate . . . I'll never forget it."

Elizabeth's voice cuts through the heavy silence. "Why didn't Sam tell me he was helping Kate? Why did he hide this from me?"

"He wasn't hiding it. He didn't want you to worry," Andy says, steadying his voice. "He was a capable guy who thought he had it under control. And we all underestimated Dane."

"Did you ever see Kate again?" Brooke asks.

Andy shakes his head. "Dane must have killed her. That's why I never heard from her again."

An uncomfortable silence envelops us. My voice is raw. "I'm so sorry for what I did to Sam." I turn to Logan. "And to you."

Logan looks away for a second before turning back to me. "We're okay," he says finally. "You and me. It was an accident. A mistake. I see that now."

My eyes mist over and I'm close to tears. His words are an unexpected lifeline, cutting through the years of guilt and despair. I look into his eyes, and there's no sign of the anger and resentment I'd seen when we met in the past. I take a shaky breath, but all I can manage is a whisper. "Thank you."

Elizabeth looks down at her hands, then up at me. "I've always thought that if I were you, I'd have done it differently. If I were on that highway, I would've done it *right*. I wouldn't have hit Sam and Logan. We all think we know what other people should do. But I see now that each of us is going on roads only we can see."

Her voices trembles, but her gaze remains steady. "I've been believing that every bad thing that happens has an easily identifiable cause. A perpetrator and a victim. Guilty and innocent. I'd believed the outcome of everything is within our control, and when things don't happen the way we think they should, someone must be to blame. But I see that's not always how it is."

I feel my chest tighten, my breath coming in shallow bursts. "If only I'd gone slower around the curve. Or if I hadn't swerved so sharply. None of this would've happened."

Elizabeth takes a deep breath. "Everything we do, everything that happens to us—good or bad—relies on a million little moments in the past. We fool ourselves if we believe that we control every moment. But we can do something now to change our futures," Elizabeth adds, her tone softening.

"What can we do?" I ask, my voice barely above a whisper.

"I can start by forgiving you."

"I don't deserve that."

Tears pool in her eyes and fall fast, like they're bursting from a dam. She opens her mouth, but no words escape. "Could I give you a hug?" she asks, finally.

She can't mean it. I shake my head.

"It's not just for you," she says. "It would help me too."

She stands and I let her hug me. Her head drops and her shoulders heave. I know she's crying even though I don't hear a sound.

And then I lean into her embrace and my heart cracks open. Something inside me shifts. Relief seeps into my bones. Her arms are whisper thin, but they have the power to heal me.

I'd gone to the past to escape from the pain of my mistake. But I never expected that I'd find healing in the present. Or that these people—Logan and Elizabeth, who I once feared, and Andy, who I'm meeting for the first time—would help me recover from the worst night of my life.

We are powerful. And powerless. There are things I couldn't control that night, and things I could. Things I did. And things I didn't think to do. The outcome wasn't in my control.

As Elizabeth releases me, a thought slips into my mind. If these people can forgive me, maybe I can find a way to forgive myself too.

Chapter Thirty-Nine

Andy

By the time the table full of appetizers arrives, everyone has managed to compose themselves, though our eyes are still puffy. The conversation drifts back to whether we'll all agree to do the press conference that Aeon keeps texting about. We're all debating the merits of that when Logan abruptly stops the conversation.

"Hold a second," he says. "We're not just going to go on like nothing happened, are we?"

We all turn to look at him. His outburst seems to take everyone by surprise.

"We've got to track down Dane," he says. "He's out there somewhere. Thinking he's gotten away with it because no one knows what he's done. Until now, *we* didn't even know."

"What do you have in mind?" Elizabeth asks.

"Bring him to justice, of course," Logan answers.

"I'd like to see that," Brooke says, "But how would we do it?"

"Exactly," Elizabeth adds. "We're not detectives."

"Elizabeth, you could ask the sheriff to investigate," I say. "With all the attention around Aeon Expeditions, he'll listen to you. I've asked him for a meeting, but with your connections, I'll bet you could get him on the phone faster."

She nods. "I'll call him in the morning."

"I've got a friend who's a retired police officer," Brooke offers. "I can ask him to help."

"I'll see what I can find online," Logan says. "I had a brush with the police a few years ago and I got pretty good at searching online public records."

"We can all post on social media," Brooke adds. "And if none of that works, I could help pay for a private investigator."

As everyone starts talking at once, the room buzzes with electric energy. Listening to the whirlwind of ideas, I can't help but feel a wave of gratitude. I'd just met these people—each with their own unique quirks—yet here we are, united by a shared realization. The mystery that's been at the center of all our lives, the source of our collective pain and loss, has a name.

Dane Reynolds.

Some of their suggestions are unconventional, even bordering on far-fetched, but that doesn't dampen my enthusiasm. For the first time, a razor-thin hope slices through my doubt—together, we might actually track down Dane Reynolds and make him pay for what he's done.

Chapter Forty
Logan

"I'm reaching out to you with an offer that combines two things I hope you appreciate: good food and thought-provoking conversation. Enclosed with this note is a tasty sandwich, made with care by the alchemists at Bob's Deli on Main. Consider it a friendly invitation for us to sit down together and have an interview that goes beyond the ordinary."

This was the note a *Ventura County Star* reporter sent with a pastrami sandwich on rye wrapped in butcher paper. He's one of many reporters who text, call, and email day and night ever since we all returned. He's the only one who sent food though. I set the sandwich and note aside. I'm not ready for any interviews.

I'm still struggling with the reality of being here in the present. And yeah, I'm angry at the loss of the simplest of pleasures—the feel of solid ground beneath my feet, the freedom to move without restraint, the ability to live my life on my own terms.

I wheel over to the fridge to get a drink. I open the door and gaze at the contents within. My eye falls on the cans and bottles of IPA and hard seltzers that line the shelves. These have been my steadfast companions, offering comfort in my loneliness.

I pick up one of my favorites, a classic ale, and I'm about to pop it open when memories flood back—countless mornings tinged with regret at the broken promises I made to myself that whatever favorite I was drinking would be my last.

Fear whispers in my ear. *This is who you are now. All you'll ever be. Broken. A victim of circumstances. A drunk. Alone.*

But something inside me is shifting. I feel it. Ever since the dinner at Celestine, I'm beginning to wonder if there's more to me than these bottles can ever bring out.

That idea seems stupid when I'm stuck here in a wheelchair. Again.

But the past is reshaping me. It's not that I've become someone different—it's as if I'm seeing my life with new eyes.

The extended time during the jump forced me to meet Brooke. How many times had I replayed the moment of impact with her car, each time fueling the inferno of my anger at her? As the weeks turned into months, and the months became years, I clung to my rage like a lifeline, unwilling to let go of the one thing that tethered me to the fragments of my former life. Anger.

She turned out not to be the monster I'd imagined. Instead, she was someone who made a horrifying mistake. Someone who saw movement on the highway and swerved to miss it. And hit me instead. I resented her for not stopping, but now I understand that she panicked and, in her weakest moment, didn't do the best thing.

If Brooke is more than the sum of her mistakes, could it be that I am too? Could I be more than my own weakest moments?

I close the fridge door, leaving the bottles undisturbed. A victory for the hour.

The phone rings. I see who it is and sigh with frustration. Gary. My boss. Reluctantly, I answer.

"Hey, Gary."

"Logan? How're you're hanging," he says casually, like we were ever friends. "Man, you've been all over the news. You doing okay?"

"I'm good."

He uses his "earnest" voice now. "Lots of people were worried they couldn't bring you back. But I convinced the higher ups to keep your job open for you."

Sure, he did. There's no way this guy asked the higher ups to do anything for me. And I doubt they were planning to fire me when I'd only been gone for less than a week.

"You coming back tomorrow?" he asks.

A restless spark blazes within me, and the words tumble out of my mouth before I can stop them. "I'm not coming back."

The minute I say it, I regret it. It's not like I've got anything in my bank account that will let me quit. I feel a wave of desperation.

"I don't think I heard you right."

What have I done? Why did I say those words without thinking them through?

Take them back. That's what I'll do. Blame it on time travel fatigue.

Then a feeling of freedom and a sense of clarity I haven't felt in a long time washes over me. Maybe this *is* the right decision?

"I'm quitting," I say.

"That's crazy," he says gruffly. "What other job do you think you're ever gonna get?"

"I don't know."

"Big mistake," he says, like he's the expert on my life. "Did your jump mess with your head or something?"

Or something. I blow out a breath. Everyone knows we can't change the future when we visit the past. But I'm beginning to see that *I've* come back changed. "I'll upload a resignation letter."

After I hang up, I bang out that letter on my laptop. I'm not usually a fast or even a good writer, but fueled by the adrenaline rush of this big decision, the words come easily.

After I upload the document, I find a pen and a Post-it and write:

What should I be doing?

I can't keep drifting through the days, aimless and unanchored, caught in a cycle of monotony and anger. I can't hold on to resentment at the loss of surfing the waves, scaling towering mountains, or biking through the wildness. These activities once defined me. Am I anything more than that?

Meeting Haley changed me. When I was with her, all the things I thought I was—a thrill seeker, an adrenaline junkie—paled in comparison with being with her, talking for hours about nothing and everything all at once.

I write:

Find Haley

The thought of seeking her out fills me with a mixture of excitement and dread. What if she's moved on and found happiness with someone else? What if she wants nothing to do with a guy in a wheelchair?

I cross out *Find Haley*. The practical side of me knows the first thing I need is a job, and the idea of starting over in a new place fills me with fear. What if I'm not cut out for anything but a mundane courier service job?

Still, I write:

Teach what I know

I crumple the note. Everything I have is gone. Feeling in my legs. Haley. And now, thanks to my impulsive words, my job. Writing Post-it notes isn't going to change anything.

But after I toss the note in the trash, I remember all the steps that I've already taken to get to this moment. I think back to the countless doctor's visits, the grueling physical therapy sessions, and the nights spent battling one health problem or another.

Then the memories from the past float in. Trying to stop Sam from running onto that highway revealed a courage I never knew I had. Spending time with Haley helped me realize that the person I want to be is more than just what my body can do.

If I'm going to break free from where I am, I've got to believe that my life is still filled with possibility.

I start a new Post-it:

Find Haley
Teach what I know
Dream big.

Chapter Forty-One

Elizabeth

Mark's made avocado toast, a favorite of mine since the early days of our marriage. Trim and fit in a gray button-down shirt and black jeans, he moves about the kitchen and sets the food on the table on the deck as if it hasn't been three years since we lived together.

Before he'd arrived, I swung through the grocery store, a task I've done hundreds of times before without much thought. Today, I looked up from my cart, at the cashiers, at the shelves that rise to the ceiling, and I realize nothing is the same. It's as though I've been asleep and I'm seeing things as they are for the first time.

The air is softer. Colors seem brighter. Faces are more beautiful.

Everything about Mark seems different too. His voice is more vibrant, full of life. He wears cologne, which he never did before. Something woodsy.

He's not different, of course. It's me that's changed. I'm paying attention to things that once zipped by in a blur.

"Tell me about Sam," he says softly. His expression is the look of grief. Misty eyes. Lips lightly curved up, hiding his sadness. His body rigid and still.

As I speak, the roar of the waves fades away, and I talk about Sam as I remember him from yesterday. His boundless curiosity. His instinct to look out for others. Brimming with life. Happy.

I tell Mark about our time together, and it works like a spoken prayer. Telling our story slows me down, anchors me in the moment, giving light to the pain and grief, and makes me feel connected to Sam even though I can't see or hear him.

The more I speak, the more I feel myself rising above our grief. Moving through space and time. In my memories, Sam is alive.

I tell Mark about the cool ocean breeze during our walk, the warmth of Sam's voice, the way the streetlights cast shadows on the sidewalks. I can feel all the essential, ordinary details of our time together. My memories themselves are a form of time travel that keeps the dark pulse of grief away.

Mark is still as he listens. He too is lost in the world I'm creating with my words and memories. I tell him the things I said to Sam, and it feels as if he's with us. I feel his presence all around.

Mark shares a long-ago memory when we gave baby Sam a bath in the sink so that the warm rays of the sun could whisk away the touch of jaundice he had when he was born. He illustrates his story with his hands, his fingers flying, until he drops them suddenly into his lap. I feel the depth of his sadness. I lay my hand on his, let his grief twist and mingle with my own unbearable ache, and in the setting sun, our pain settles.

It occurs to me then that all we gave Sam—all we did with him—still remains. The baby baths. His first bicycle. The trips to the beach. Camping. Yosemite. They're not lost. They still exist in the ever-enduring past. And in our memories.

The rain starts with a gentle pattering. I glance up, feeling the cool droplets on my skin and see a few dark clouds drifting lazily across the sky. Ventura is usually warm and dry in August, so this is a rare gift.

The shower picks up, a light drizzle that fills the air with a fresh earthy scent mixed with the salty tang of the ocean. Mark gathers the dishes, and we race indoors. The beach house, once our home together, feels suddenly cozy. New. The raindrops patter on the palm tree leaves surrounding our house blend softly with the steady rush of the waves. We settle on the couch together and Mark picks up the light blanket beside me and uses it to gently dry my hair.

"After I was extracted, you said there was something you wanted to tell me," I say, catching my breath.

He hesitates before speaking. "It's still a secret. Only a few of us know. A few months ago, we sent a couple to their wedding night fifty years in the past. We've cracked the code for date-specific travel to the past."

The August 20th date wasn't a coincidence.

I stare at him in disbelief. "You're saying that you sent me back three years ago to August twentieth on *purpose*?"

His voice barely contains his excitement. "That's how I knew you saw Sam."

"Why though?"

"Once I selected the date, we analyzed the millions of essays we receive each year, and we found that thousands of applicants noted that August 25, 2025—the day Sam died—was a day their lives changed forever too."

"What? Like the date had some kind of bad luck?"

He shares a light smile. "If you're talking to a group of scientists and engineers, the idea of bad luck is out of the realm of possibility. What we found is that *every single day* of the year we looked at was the same. No matter what date we chose, there were countless people who told us about loved ones they'd lost, pain they experienced, terrible news they'd been given. It made me see that loss and grief, they're part of the iron law of life.

"And that gave me an idea," he continues. "What if I could change that? Not the grief and loss, of course. *The experience of it.* I knew it would mean everything for you to be with Sam in some of his happiest days."

"That was one of the best weeks of my life."

"Once we knew we could send up to four people to a specific date, we decided to scour the applications to find candidates. We received an application for the man who was paralyzed on August 25, 2025. I realized then that he was the man you and I'd been searching for all this time. The former drug dealer who'd been in the same accident as Sam. Logan Sandoval. The Aeon board had initially disqualified him because of his health issues. But once I saw the application, I convinced them to put him through."

My mouth drops open. "Why would you do that?"

"Maybe it was self-serving, I don't know, but I wanted the opportunity to find out why Sam was on that highway in the middle of nowhere with Logan."

"But you sent Brooke too." My voice is tight. "Why would you grant her a trip when she wrecked our lives??"

"I hated her too." His voice catches. "She was disqualified because of her time in prison. But then I read her essay, and I began to think that giving her this jump was a way I might *try* to understand why she was there that night and why she didn't stop after she hit Sam."

"Then why did you grant a trip to Andy Schapiro? He wasn't involved in the accident."

"I chose him after I read his essay."

"His essay?"

"Well, his essay was actually a short poem. He wrote it for a lost love he was seeking in the past. And I memorized it." he says, then looks away. He's silent for a long moment.

I know Mark so well that when he looks away like this, it's because there's something he wants to say but can't put into words. He's a genius at design and engineering, but words sometimes fail him in moments like this.

"You memorized his poem? Why?"

He looks out at the ocean. "Because it went like this."

In the quiet moments, your presence lingers,
A gentle breeze soothing my tired spirit,
In my dreams, you appear, a fleeting vision,
A specter dancing on the edges of my thoughts.
Left to wander in the shadows of your absence,
I seek hope, finding light only in the memories of you.

We're silent for a long moment, listening to the waves lap against the seawall.

"It's beautiful," I admit. "But that's not your usual good reason to approve a highly coveted time travel spot."

"What he wrote is how I feel about losing you."

A flutter of surprise stirs in my chest. *He misses me.* The idea seems foolish at first. A fantasy born out of nostalgia and memory. And yet, that is what he's saying.

"We both lost Sam. But I also lost you."

I look up at him, and for a long moment, all I can see is Sam. The thought of embracing the feelings that are stirring within me feels like a betrayal, as if letting go of the grief means letting go of Sam.

But I cannot live in the present and the past at the same time. I reach for Mark's hand, and as my fingers close around his, I choose to live in this moment with him and embrace it for all it has to offer.

Chapter Forty-Two

Andy

The Instagram DM had been sitting in my inbox for nearly two hours before I saw it. The other Memory Collectors had promised to help, but I hadn't expected a lead to come this fast.

It's from someone with the handle Reynolds107. And although the message is brief, it still manages to amp my blood pressure.

Why are you looking for Dane Reynolds?

My chest tightens. Could this DM be from Dane? I click on the name and the link takes me to the account: *0 posts. 12 followers. 37 following.* The profile photo of Reynolds107, a red pair of sneakers, tells me nothing.

I type back: *Do you know where I can find him?*

While I wait for a response, I click over to my original Instagram post. Because Logan and Brooke have been sharing it, it's got 1,732 likes, and the comments are mostly glowing: *Here's your chance to help an amazing author on his next novel!* Another reader wrote: *I don't know Dane, but I wish I did just so I could help you finish your next book. Patiently waiting.*

There are a few other DMs as well, but all of them are from people wishing they could help and curious what story I'm writing about a paper mill in Michigan. Was it a mystery or a love story?

A response from Reynolds107 swoops in five minutes later. *Why are you looking for Dane Reynolds?*

My stomach plummets. Why're they repeating their question? If it's Dane, then I need a compelling reason for him to keep communicating with me. He can't possibly imagine that I know he killed Kate. He needs to believe that I'm looking for him because of something that will benefit *him*. But if it isn't Dane and only someone who knows him, then I need to present a compelling reason to help me find him. I write:

I'm a bestselling author writing a novel in which the main character works at a paper mill in Kalamazoo, Michigan. I heard Dane held a similar position. Would love to talk to him to better understand the world of this important character.

To sweeten the pot, I add: *I can compensate him.*

I'm feeling good about how I'm handling this. But I don't want to get ahead of myself. The chances of Dane Reynolds seeing my Instagram post and then DMing me here seem close to zero. This could easily be someone else with the same last name hoping to scam me into paying them for a sham story they'll make up.

Two minutes later:

Are you the Andy Schapiro that writes about World War II?

I take this as a sign that they're researching me online. That probably means they're not a reader, but someone who found the post some other way. The confusion with the *other* Andy Schapiro was common early in my career because there's a man by the same name from Berkshire, UK, who's written seventeen books, most of them about World Wars I and II.

Different guy. I wrote the NYT bestseller He's Gone.

I think about riding on my new notoriety as a Memory Collector, but if they're researching me online, they already know. I click Send.

In the unlikely event I'm communicating with Dane, I'm hoping he feels flattered enough to keep talking to me. Eventually we can forge an online relationship and I can learn where he is. But no matter who's writing me, I'm hoping they'll see I'm a legit writer willing to pay Dane some money to tell his story. That will motivate them to share my post further.

The response surprises me.

What makes you think Dane was ever in Ventura, California?

Shit. What do I say? The only reason Dane came to Ventura was to track down Kate. Probably only a few people in the world knew he was here and two of them are dead: Sam and Kate. How would *I* know he was here?

I consider closing the app and deleting the conversation. But the idea of *not* responding to whoever is messaging me is even more frightening. If it's Dane, I'm already in too deep. If he suspects I know anything about what he did to Kate, he could easily track me down in Ventura. I'm not hard to find.

I make up a story: *I was talking to a boat rental guy at the harbor, telling him about the book I'm writing. He told me he'd met a guy named Dane Reynolds who worked at a paper mill in Kalamazoo. Do you know him?*

No reply.

For a while, I sit at my desk clicking back and forth between Instagram and my novel in progress. Checking to see if Reynolds107 had replied or commented on my post. They hadn't.

I type: *Do you know Dane?*

Then I wait. Hours pass and no response. I think about hiring a professional to figure out who owns this Instagram account. I plan to tell the sheriff, of course, although having the handle with the name "Reynolds" in it wasn't proof that this was Dane's account. He'd probably dismiss it as a social media troll. And he'd probably be right.

Chapter Forty-Three

Logan

All eight lanes of the pool at the YMCA are crowded. Tween boys front-crawl back and forth down the cornflower-blue lanes while their teammates egg them on. Everything here is in motion. And loud. There's the sound of kids jumping into the pool, laughter, and coaches calling out instructions over the din.

I look for my friend Marco, who runs the after-school swim program. When he sees me he turns his head and stares. He's tall, well over six feet, and his long neck, along with his surprised expression, make him look like an odd bird of prey.

"What the heck?" he shouts.

I wheel over to him. It's been three years since I swam this pool with him, but Marco still looks much the same. Black long board shorts that barely skim the top of his knees. Bare chested even as the other coaches wear red T-shirts. A silver whistle on a chain around his neck.

"Seen you all over the TV," he says, leaning over to give me a high-five. The tang of chlorine ripples on a warm breeze. "You're probably too famous to be here."

I've got two cups of black coffee humming in my veins, so my words come out fast. "I'm here to work."

"To work? Aren't you still at the courier service?"

I hold my breath, then release it. "I quit that. I want to do *this*, Marco."

"You sure about this? These boys are eleven. Twelve. They are maniacs with an endless supply of energy and jokes and pranks. It's chaos all the time."

My eyes drift to a group of kids who are doing stroke-drills under the careful watch of an assistant coach. Doubt creeps in. How will these kids respect me when I can't easily get in the water with them? How will I model proper form with only my upper body? Then I remind myself I'm more than just my body. I've got experience. Stuff to show them.

"I was like them once. Thought I knew everything."

He squats beside me. Deep scarring lines his hands from a boating accident when he was a kid. Regret flickers in his eyes. He knows that what he's going to say will wreck me. "Lot of people might think it's impossible for you."

A lump rises in my throat. "I know what it's like to think things only work a certain way. I've been living that for a while now. But there *is* another way."

"Something happen to you when you were stranded back there in the past?"

"Maybe I found out I'm a 'water whisperer.'"

He nods. "Yeah, I can see that."

"Mostly I'm seeing that who I am can't be defined by what body I have or what it can do. We're all more than that. I can show the kids that too."

"The pay here is good, not great. You'd probably make more if you went back to the courier company and begged to get your job back."

I shake my head. I've never been more certain of anything. "I want something more."

* * *

This is tougher than leaping large boulders and scrambling through rock scree at 14,000 feet in ninety-degree temperatures. The fifty feet separating me from the entrance of Celestine seem to stretch endlessly before me.

My heart is hammering so fast it's hard to breathe. Impossible to speak.

Stay focused. Commit.

I roll through the front door, and my heart skips a beat when I see Haley behind the bar. She places a pink cocktail in front of a blonde woman. It's probably something she does a hundred times a shift, but here it looks like ballet. Her lips curve into a smile, and then she glances in my direction. But of course, she doesn't recognize me.

I look away. Catch my breath.

I wheel up to the bar, and in a move I've practiced a thousand times, I raise myself on my arms and transfer from the wheelchair to the barstool.

Suddenly, she's in front of me. In real life. Present life.

"What can I get you?" she asks, wiping down the counter.

"Tacos?" I say, my voice catching. "Tacos are kind of my love language."

Her smile falters. The line landed as badly as it could have. Still, she saves me from embarrassment. "Would you like fish or chicken?"

"Which is better?" I ask.

"Have the fish," she says. "Anything to drink?"

"Water's good."

"You got it."

That's our entire conversation. Then she steps away. It was stupid to think I could get her attention now. I'm a stranger in a wheelchair. She's working and probably gets hit on all day.

But I know how to suffer. I've spent hours and hours in the dark gym sweating and building muscle at five in the morning, working to regain my strength. I know what it means to put in the work and the hours for something you want, but everyone else thinks is impossible.

I see her talking to the kitchen staff and vow to keep trying. Then worry creeps in. Maybe her attraction to me in the past was simply because I had two legs that could hike up a mountain with her, two legs that could kayak with her, and two legs to stand beside her when I kissed her.

What seems like forever later, but probably is only a minute, she comes back with the water.

"I've seen you before," she says, placing it in front of me.

"You sure about that?" I ask, rubbing my neck.

"I don't want to sound weird or anything, but I . . . I know who you are."

Heat rushes to my face. "You *do*?"

"You were in the accident with my neighbor, Sam." Her voice goes soft. "I still can't believe it sometimes. The reporters wrote a lot about you when they covered the accident. Before all this happened, weren't you one of the guys who climbed El Capitan in Yosemite in under two hours?"

"Yeah, I did that once."

"And not to sound creepy or anything," she says, smiling. I don't think she could sound creepy if she tried. "I saw you on the news. You're one of the Memory Collectors, right?"

I nod. This is the first time something positive has come out of all the media attention.

"What was that like being in the past for so long?"

I draw a deep breath and gather up the courage to say something bold. Something not like the usual me. "Not as good as it does to be right here with you in the present."

She meets my eyes for a second, then glances away. I've said too much. "Let me check if your order's up," she says, then heads back to the kitchen.

I messed that up.

Still, I'd never been brave enough to strike up a conversation with someone like her even when I had legs that worked, so I got to give myself points for that. And at least I'm not a stranger. She knows something about me. Something positive.

She returns with a plate of tacos. "I had them leave off the beans," she says. "They cook them kind of mushy here. I could have them give you a side order if you still want them."

"I trust your judgment. There's this food truck by the harbor that has great tacos and beans though—"

"José's?"

"That's the one. Would you . . ." I start, then stop. I think my heart is going to fly out of my chest. "Would you ever want to go there with me sometime?"

Her eyes widen in surprise.

"Yeah, I'm guessing that sounded wrong. Sorry, I didn't mean to make this awkward," I say.

"I might meet you there sometime," she says. "But I can see the owner looking at me so I'd better get back to work. Leave me your number and I'll text you." Then she's off to a trio of sunburned tourists.

Leave me your number and I'll text you. Sometimes fate steps in to steal things from you. And sometimes it sweeps in to take you places you only dreamed of going.

I write down my number. Will she really text me? I have the feeling this is just what she says when guys hit on her and she wants to say no.

Chapter Forty-Four

Andy

I awake with a jolt to the sound of banging on my front door. With bleary eyes, I glance at my watch. 7:12 AM. Probably not FedEx or the mail carrier at this hour. Whoever it is bangs again. More insistent this time.

My stomach lurches. My first thought is that it's Dane. He's Reynolds107 and has tracked me here to Ventura to confront me about why I'm on social media searching for him. I look around my room for anything to defend myself. Nothing. I don't even have a baseball bat, even though we writers always make sure our protagonists have one handy when they hear suspicious noises.

I throw on some jeans and tell myself I'm overreacting. It could be the neighbor who's always losing her cat. The banging continues. I muster the courage to peer through the curtains on the front window, not sure what to expect, and I'm surprised to see a dark-haired woman with an athletic build. I hope she's not one of my new fans on social media.

"Andy Schapiro," she shouts, pounding on the door again. She has the voice of someone who's used to getting what she wants. "Open up."

I fling open the door. "Can I help you?" I say gruffly.

She peers at me. "Are you Andy?"

I nod.

"You don't look like your author photo," she says, holding up a hardcover of *He's Gone*. She points to the photo on the back cover. It was taken five years ago when my hairline was a little lower.

"You realize what time it is?"

"I just met with the sheriff last night. You're going to want to let me in."

My heart rate soars. "The sheriff. What for?"

She moves toward me. "Let me inside and I'll explain."

I've read about scams where people let a seemingly helpless woman into their homes only to be robbed by her sturdy companions-in-hiding. I step on the porch and close the door behind me. "Anything you have to say, you can say out here."

"I want to talk to you about *He's Gone*."

I stare at the book and then back at her. "I appreciate your enthusiasm for my work, but I prefer discussing it in a public event. Sign up for my newsletter and—"

"I'm not one of your fans. You wrote some things in the book that have both the sheriff and me very interested."

My heart is hammering as I struggle to figure out what she wants. How the sheriff is involved. Or if he's involved, why I haven't heard from him.

I point to a table in the apartment complex courtyard. "Let me get my shoes. I'll meet you there."

I race inside and close the door behind me. Locking it. I text Jonathan and ask him to come over as backup in case something goes wrong. Thankfully, he agrees. Then I slip on my shoes and step outside, lock the door behind me and lift my shoulders, hoping I look calm and confident even as my heart is pounding.

From a distance she doesn't look all that intimidating. But her rigid posture and firm jaw tell me she's ready for battle—over what, though?

I step over to the café table and sit across from her.

"What can I help you with?" I say, hoping that by sounding friendly she'll dial down the glare she's giving me.

She sweeps away the avalanche of purple flowers that have fallen on the table from the towering jacaranda tree above. "Three years ago, the body of an unidentified man washed up at Ventura Pier," she says, matter-of-fact.

"Yes, I know. That's what that the novel is about."

"Advanced decomposition along with no identification meant the coroner couldn't identify him. Meanwhile, no missing person report was ever filed that matched the identity of the anonymous man. The coroner returned an open verdict and classified him as an Unidentified Person."

"Right," I say. "I assume you read this in the author notes at the back of the book?"

She ignores me. "The Sister Servants of Mary in Oxnard arranged for the body to be buried at Cemetery Memorial Park, which is about a mile from here. The unidentified man's headstone reads: 'The Man at the Pier. Found 25th October 2025. Name Not Known. Rest in Peace.'"

My head begins to spin. Is this woman a true crime fanatic who wants to talk about the story behind my book? I've met a few like her at book signings—overly enthusiastic, as we authors diplomatically put it. The kind who might even reach out to the sheriff.

She looks at notes on her phone. "California State Police entered his information into a database called NamUs—the National Missing and Unidentified Persons System—hoping that someone was looking for him. But no one was. That's why you wrote your story, wasn't it? To explain who this man was."

I sigh with relief. "Yes, I imagined a detective investigates the dead body and figures out who he was and how he was murdered."

"Except in the case of the real Man at the Pier, because of the nature of the gunshot wound to the neck, the coroner couldn't conclude whether it was a self-inflicted wound, an accident, or a homicide. Isn't that right?"

"That's my understanding, yes. But I write fiction and—"

"Yes, you write fiction. And you considered *all* those choices—an accident, suicide, a murder—and chose to make it a homicide."

"Murders do make compelling mysteries," I say glibly.

"Still. No one else knew his identity, but you did."

Heat rushes to my face. "I made it up. That's what authors do."

"And yet you're on social media looking for Dane Reynolds. Pretending you don't know that he's dead. Or that he's the Man at the Pier."

Shock slams through my body, stealing my breath. *Dane Reynolds is not the Man at the Pier.* Is he? If it's true, how could this person possibly know that?

The courtyard begins to spin, and I grip the table, trembling inside.

"Dane Reynolds is my brother," she says. "After you and I chatted on social media, I took your advice and read *He's Gone*."

I stare at her in disbelief. "You're Reynolds107?"

She nods. "Karen Fagan. My last name was Reynolds before I got married. A friend shared your post with me. She's one of your fans, I guess. After we texted, I read every word of *He's Gone*. Even highlighted some passages. And you know what? I kept wondering if the real Man at the Pier might be my brother."

She pushes her phone across the table and shows me a photo. "This is him." My heart stutters in my chest. It's Dane. "This is him."

She bites her lower lip. "So, I contacted your county sheriff—Eric Ingram—and shared photos of my brother. My photos of him matched the coroner's photos of the Man at the Pier."

I shake my head. "That's impossible. The body they found was bloated and completely unrecognizable."

"Except my brother and the Man at the Pier both had an identical scar down their left leg from a bike accident when he was a kid." She swipes right and shows me a photo of an uneven scar that starts below the knee of a man's leg and winds its way to the ankle.

Panic jolts my system. I'd interviewed the coroner about the body, heard about the scar, and made up an entirely different backstory. I'd imagined the man was wealthy and had injured his leg in a skiing accident in the Dolomites in Italy.

"This photo of Dane's leg matched the photos the coroner took," she says, bringing me back to the moment. "It was enough evidence for the sheriff to agree to exhume the body."

The air closes in around me. I can hear my heart pounding in my ears. Every detail of the crime scene report had been seared into my mind—the massive swelling, the awful discoloration, the way every feature of the man had been distorted beyond recognition. That the body was Dane Reynolds seems impossible.

"They'll compare the DNA to get a final confirmation. And I don't doubt—and neither does the sheriff—that they'll confirm it's my brother."

"So, you're getting the answers you need," I say, sounding calm even as my pulse is racing. "I'm glad my book was able to help in some small way."

She narrows her eyes. "Don't pretend, Andy."

I meet her gaze. "I'm not. Pretending."

"You expect me to believe that you wrote this novel about the unidentified Man at the Pier, and three years later you just happen to be on social media looking for a man named Dane Reynolds? You must have known who the dead body was when you wrote your novel."

I stare at her and think about telling her the truth about her brother. That he was in Ventura to track down Kate. I consider telling her every lurid detail I know of what he did to Kate. The threats he made. But something is holding me back. A single irrational thought that if I reveal too much, I'll regret it later.

My face reddens. "I didn't know."

"I'm betting you even know how he died. Suicide? Accident? Homicide? You know that too."

My heart is pounding. One question is nagging at me, begging to be answered even as this woman sits before me with questions of her own.

Did Kate kill Dane?

If she did, she couldn't have shot him on the crowded pier where his body was later discovered. Too many people would've seen it happen. And his body would've surfaced days later, not weeks.

No, Dane's bloated body had to be in the ocean for weeks before its discovery at the pier.

In the haze of my confusion, there's only one possibility that makes sense. Kate made it to Sam's boat. She reached Anacapa Island.

"Look," I manage to say. "It's all a strange coincidence. Kind of crazy, you know? But I don't know anything about what happened to your brother. And, until now, I had no idea that he might be the Man at the Pier."

She looks at me like she doesn't believe me. Inside, my stomach roils, because the sheriff might also not believe my story and want to investigate whether I had something to do with Dane's death.

Kate did it.

Karen lowers her voice. "I know my brother wasn't, you know, a good guy. I've heard scary things about him over the years. We'd lost touch, which sometimes happens when parents die, and when I'd tried to reconnect with him, I never could find him. Maybe that's why I never put out a missing person report, thinking maybe he was in hiding for whatever things he'd done." She leans forward on her elbows, her eyes searching mine. "Tell me the truth. When he was out here in Ventura, you knew him, didn't you?"

I don't answer. I can't.

I'm imagining what must've happened. Dane must have followed Kate to Anacapa Island. When she arrived there, maybe she waited for Dane, gun loaded. Or had he managed to hurt her once more in the quiet of that desolate island and she'd fought back, this time armed and ready?

"I never knew Dane," I say forcefully.

"Then maybe he was out here because of someone you *do* know."

I shake my head and lie. "No."

I close my eyes for a split second and imagine Kate pulling the trigger, the recoil slamming against her shoulder.

"I don't think it was suicide," Karen says, snapping me back to the moment. "Or an accident. I think someone killed him."

I don't answer. I can't form any words, my mind racing to fill in the blanks. After Kate shot him, what did she do? The most plausible answer is that she escaped on Sam's boat, not knowing if he was dead or alive. She had no idea that the ocean would claim him, that nature would take its course.

She rubs her forehead, closing her eyes. "You expect me to believe that you wrote *He's Gone* about the unidentified Man at the Pier *not* knowing who he was and then three years later, you're on social media looking for a man named Dane Reynolds, who just so happens to be the Man at the Pier?"

I struggle to focus on her question. Her words become a distant echo as my heart pounds with a singular, overpowering thought.

Kate could still be alive.

* * *

Chapter Forty-Five

Brooke

I'm the same person who walked into Aeon Expeditions a week ago. I have the same body. The same memories. But I feel different as I leave Celestine.

On my way home from the restaurant tonight, I pass the entrance to the PCH, and as always since the accident, my heart races. But this time, I wonder—how much longer will I let what happened on this highway haunt me?

I grip the wheel tightly, pull a U-turn, merge onto the highway, then immediately regret it. The rush of the cars zooming by fills me with panic. This is a mistake.

Then a strange sense of calm takes hold. I manage a mile on the highway. Then a second mile. My nerves on edge, I drive along the curved stretch of road where the accident occurred, expecting to see the vague but imaginary figures that have always haunted me on deserted roads since the accident. When none appear, my breathing gradually slows.

I finally pull into my own driveway. A sigh of relief. As I step out of the car, the scent of cut grass hangs heavy in the air. It smells like home.

I head into the house and call out, "James? Olivia?"

Instead of the usual sounds of home—James talking on the phone, Olivia playing with her friends—silence greets me.

The kitchen is still. The dining table untouched. Did they even eat dinner? I'd left them a meal in the freezer and it's still there, uncooked. I head to Olivia's room. Her desk, scattered with her drawings, stands deserted.

Am I now so invisible in this family that they make plans to go out without telling me?

Then I hear laughter. Olivia's high-pitched giggle. But from where?

I follow the sound, then rush outdoors. It's coming from the garage. My steps quicken as I approach the door, slightly ajar.

Bathed in the soft glow of a single bulb hanging from the rafters, James kneels beside Olivia, who's deeply engrossed in painting a wooden box resting on a drop cloth on the floor. Dust particles dance lazily in the faint beams of light. It's an ordinary scene, one I would've once taken for granted: James and Olivia surrounded by a clutter of forgotten cardboard boxes, old bicycles, and the pungent smell of paint.

James looks up. "You're home," he says brightly.

I step inside. "What're you two up to?"

"This is for a social studies project," Olivia says. "We're collecting things that're part of our family history. Photos. Artifacts. Maps. Treasures."

"I doubt we have any treasures to put in," I say.

"I was hoping you'd make some of my favorite cookies. That could be the treasure."

My eyes meet James's, and I tremble, on the edge of tears. This moment is filled with possibility. I will look back upon it as a memory someday, I'm sure, and regret what I didn't say and what I didn't do. Or I'll relive it again and again for all the ways I used it to change my life. And theirs.

I pause, gathering my courage. Why is it so hard to tell them what's in my heart? I'm afraid that if I say the truth aloud, they'll no longer see me for who I always wanted to be: the wife and mother who did it right. Who didn't make big mistakes.

I'd defined myself by what happened that one night in August, reliving it in every thought and action since then. *I may think I'm a good person, but when it comes down to it . . .*

Maybe I can let that go?

"There's something I want to say to you," I say, my voice wavering. From here I can say anything. I can regale them with every detail of the jump. I can share with them what it was like to relive our halcyon days together. I can remain, as I have been, fixated on a past that I cannot undo.

But this moment, like every moment, is too precious to waste on yesterdays.

I think about walking them through my discovery, thanks to the other Memory Collectors, of what really happened that night. I could explain that I'd been jolted by two people running across the dark highway and gently swerved to miss them only to hit two others in the bike lane. I could make the case that the mistake wasn't entirely my fault. It was an accident.

All of that is true. But something inside me is changing. A new version of me is emerging from the past and from the dinner with the Memory Collectors. One that's stronger and wiser. I'm moving to a place of forgiving myself.

I sit on the floor with them, crossing my legs. I look at them, my eyes glistening with unshed tears, and I force myself to do what my heart already knows. *I can change what happens next.*

The moment hangs in the air. A musty garage is hardly a place to hope for redemption, but if I do this right, it could become one.

"I'm sorry," I say, my voice spilling out. "For not being truthful with myself. Or with you. I'm sorry for all of it. Can you ever forgive me?"

"Brooke," James says, his voice breaking.

Olivia puts down her paintbrush.

"All this time, I've been pretending I'm okay while inside I've been a mess," I continue. "I'm wrecked by what I did. I promise you both that I'm going to do better. I'm going to rebuild trust between us."

The next moment James takes my hand in his, and Olivia wraps her arms around my waist. The moment is so surreal, it feels like I'm not in the present at all, but somehow still in the past.

As I sit with them and share the story of the past, I sense a shift in them. And in me. I brought darkness into their lives, but they're standing on the doorstep of forgiveness. They're finding a way back to me.

Chapter Forty-Six

Andy

~

"I think Kate is still alive," I say, my voice trembling.

The four of us Memory Collectors sit huddled around a table at Celestine. The dim lighting casts long shadows over the untouched plates, making the rockfish, branzino, and shrimp laid out before us seem strangely out of place, like a feast at the wrong time. Brooke had put so much care into the spread, but now it just sits there, as everyone focuses on the reasons I asked them to meet me here.

"I think she escaped from Dane," I add.

I can see in their eyes that they *want* to believe me, to hope that Kate is alive—but after everything they saw that night, they're all skeptical.

Brooke speaks first, her fingers tracing the edge of her plate as if she's searching for something to anchor her. "Why do you think that, Andy?"

"The body that washed up a few months after Kate disappeared—the Man at the Pier? They've identified him. It's her ex, Dane Reynolds."

"What?" Brooke says, stunned. "It's *him*?"

I nod. "The sheriff is confirming it now. May be a while before they announce it officially. But his sister identified the body as his. If you remember, the man died of a gunshot wound to his neck. I think this is proof that Kate made it to Anacapa Island, shot him, and escaped."

"Or—" Elizabeth hesitates, her gaze drifting to her half-empty wineglass. "It could simply mean that *someone* shot him. Not necessarily her."

"And even if she did, there's a good chance she still didn't . . . make it," Logan says, finishing her thought.

"Why do you say that?"

Logan's expression hardens, muscles straining in his neck. "I saw firsthand just how dangerous Dane is."

His words hang in the air, the clink of silverware from nearby tables emphasizing our silence.

Brooke's initial disbelief softens into something more thoughtful. "If she shot him and escaped—and, just for the moment, let's say that's true—where is she? Why haven't you heard from her?"

"She might be in hiding," I say. "She doesn't know he's gone."

Brooke's voice tightens. "I think Logan's right. It's most likely she didn't make it. You probably don't want to hear this, but knowing that the Man at the Pier is Dane Reynolds doesn't prove that Kate's alive."

"Right. We can't assume she escaped," Logan says, his voice low. "Sam and I were no match for him. She probably wasn't either."

Outside, the distant sound of the ocean crashing against the shore filters through the restaurant's open windows, a reminder that the world keeps moving, indifferent to all our questions.

"And if she's in hiding," Logan continues, "how would we even find her after all this time? Everything's gone cold—there's no trail left."

"I suppose you could file a new missing person report for Kate and see if the police can find her," Elizabeth offers.

"Three years later? It won't get far," Logan counters.

I cross my arms on my chest. "I'll have to figure out how to bring her out of hiding."

"How, though?" Logan asks.

Brooke leans in. "Andy, the Aeon press conference . . . I know we all said no. But maybe you do it and ask the reporters for help finding Kate."

Just thinking about the journalists hounding me about Kate makes my breath catch. What if they connect her to Dane's death? The sheriff would have no choice but to investigate. Kate would become a murder suspect.

"People pay attention to press conferences," Brooke continues. "Especially if you're the only Memory Collector to do one."

Logan shakes his head. "I don't know. You get out there and talk about Kate and the press is going to do some digging. I can already hear the headline: Memory Collector jumps to the past to find the 'Lost Love Who Got Away'—and discovers she's a murderer."

"Not a murderer," Elizabeth interjects. "This could easily be considered self-defense."

"The self-defense claim is so much harder than you think," Brooke counters. "She'd have to prove she was in real danger, beyond any doubt. They could argue she overreacted or that she could've gotten away if she tried. If they decide she used 'too much force,' it could ruin her case. Then they'd dig into her past, looking for anything that suggests she's capable of losing control. They'd question why she didn't go to the police when he first arrived in Ventura. It could take years to clear her name, and even then, she might still face a civil suit from Dane's family."

I struggle to process everything they're saying, and then a thought crystallizes. "The only way anyone could connect her to Dane is if they knew he was her ex," I say. "And so far, the only ones who know that for sure are the people around this table."

Elizabeth's expression shifts, realization dawning. "If we all make a pact never to tell anyone what we saw the night of August 25 . . ."

Brooke exhales sharply. "Are you suggesting we lie?"

"This isn't just a little lie," Logan says, turning pale. "It's breaking the law. I mean, we'd be accomplices to murder. That kind of stuff lands you in jail. All of us."

"We all lost something that night," Elizabeth says softly. "If there's any way we can make things right for Kate, I say we do it."

One by one, they each give a single, slow nod. Elizabeth first, her fingers drumming against the table. Brooke takes longer, her eyes darting between Logan and Elizabeth, then her chin dips in agreement. Logan is last, his crossed arms gradually loosening as he studies each face around the table. "Yeah. Okay."

"We won't say anything to the police," Brooke says. "We didn't see what happened. We don't know anything about Kate or Dane. We'll keep your secret, Andy."

Her words create an unspoken instant agreement between the four of us. Maybe it's a response to years of violence against women.

Or maybe our decision is because we're all still reeling from the pain and loss of August 25. But there's no doubt we're desperate to do something—anything—to change the outcome of that night.

"Do the press conference, Andy," Brooke whispers. "Find Kate."

* * *

"I'll be right here if you need me," Jamie, the head of PR for Aeon Expeditions says to me as I stand outside a conference room at the Crowne Plaza Ventura Beach Hotel. Eleven o'clock sharp.

Media scrutiny of Aeon's safety procedures has reached a fever pitch with headlines blaring: "Is Aeon Expeditions Safe?" "Aeon Under Scrutiny: Safety in Question." "Experts Question Safety of Time Travel Technology."

Aeon is grateful for my participation in the press conference, and Jamie has coached me on how to shift the narrative, aiming to reassure the public and restore faith in the technology. But I have my own agenda—one that diverges sharply from hers.

Her assistant hands me a bottle of Fiji water, then Jamie swings open the door to the ballroom, and the quiet of the hallway is swallowed by the bustling energy of a room filled with at least a hundred reporters, their cameras already whirring.

I wasn't expecting so many. The bright overhead lights flood the space, and I squint for a moment, hoping my eyes will adjust. It's so bright that aside from the front row of reporters, I can't make out the faces of anyone else in the room.

As we make our way over to the podium, I can feel their stares, scrutinizing my every move. A few of them peer at me as though I'm a strange creature. Do I look healthy? Do I appear traumatized? A young reporter nervously fiddles with his collar, surprising me. Are they as anxious about this press conference as I am?

The room is tightly packed, with reporters squeezed shoulder to shoulder, some standing on tiptoe, others leaning against the walls. All eyes on me. They're here for answers, but I carry a different message—one they're not prepared for.

As I take my place behind the microphone, the room falls silent. I expect Jamie to introduce me, but instead, she steps to the microphone and says, "Thank you for joining us to speak with one of the Memory Collectors. Pat yourselves on the back for getting into this room, because for every one of you here, there are at least a hundred other reporters vying for a spot."

The air buzzes with electric energy, and suddenly the room erupts with a cacophony of voices. Jamie raises her hand. The effect is almost immediate. Silence washes over the crowd.

"To make this go smoothly, I've already given each of you a number and you'll ask your questions in numerical order. And yes, just in case you're not sure, we start with the number one."

Laughter ripples through the audience, and a woman with dark hair cascading in loose waves, stands. "Kate Bradley, Channel Eleven News. A lot of people think it makes absolutely no sense to relive *any time* in our past. Whatever happened to us is behind us. Done. What is the point of traveling back?"

I lean forward. "Many of us are stumbling through life. The first time around, we don't always know what to do with a moment. We're distracted or we waste it, not seeing its full value.

Thinking there'll be more. The second time around, we've gained perspective, we understand the significance of a moment, a gesture, or a word said. We know what's at stake. What's ahead that we may lose. We notice things we didn't see before."

A thin reporter with a razor-sharp bob and an equally shrill voice chimes in. "Alice Williams, *New York Times*. What did you take away from your week in the past?"

I freeze. I'd written down what I wanted to say and rehearsed it, but now that the moment is here, I'm not sure I can go through with it.

"I went back to find a lost love," I say. "I spent a week with her. I realized that the reason I could never get over her wasn't because I was unable to let go of the past or because I'd idealized our relationship. What I discovered was that I haven't been able to forget her because . . . because she *is* the one for me. When I'm with her, everything makes sense."

The room is charged with sudden energy. Several reporters start lobbing follow-up questions at me. I see Jamie step to the microphone to restore order, and I push forward. "I'd like to finish my answer, if you'll allow me," I say, and the room quiets again. "This next part is crucial."

A few reporters lean forward, their eyes locked on me. My hands are clammy as they grip the table's edge, my heart pounding.

"I'm searching for Kate Montano—she also goes by Sarah Canford—in the present with the same determination I had in the past," I say, my voice cracking slightly as I try to hold it steady. "Please, help me bring Kate home. I believe she's still out there, maybe even hearing me right now, unaware that I've never forgotten her. I want her to know that I am still in love with her and always will be. And I need her to know that it's safe for her to come out."

Cameras flash, and a blonde reporter in a turquoise dress shouts, "Safe? What do you mean by safe?"

"Kate, if you're hearing me," I continue, my voice raw with emotion, "he's gone."

Chapter Forty-Seven

Elizabeth

~

"Did you see me?"

This is the question everyone asks me. "Did you see me in the past? What was I like? Have I changed?"

They're fascinated with what secrets the past holds, what memories they're holding on to that might shift in the light of reliving them again. They're curious if what they remember about themselves is really how it was.

Mark is no exception. He may have created this technology and labored over it for years on the granular level, but his wonder about my experience in the past seems endless.

"Did you see me?"

"Yes," I tell him. We're on the deck facing the ocean in the same chairs we sat in when we were married. Perhaps it's muscle memory, but he's sitting on the right and I'm on the left. Like we always did.

"And?"

"You told me every detail of our first date."

He smiles. "What? I sound like a hopeless romantic. What else did I say?"

"You asked me to choose *us* in the future."

His jaw slackens. "I was a smart guy. I still want that, Elizabeth. With all the problems surrounding the extraction, what truly wrecked me was that I could *lose you*," he says softly. "It forced me to wake up to what's always been the most important. And that's you."

Tears well up in my eyes.

"How did I mess this up?" He glances out at the waves, his hair lifting in the breeze, revealing a face lined with worry. "I always believed that my life would get better and better. For a long time, it did. I met you, we got married, we had Sam. I had the beginnings of a groundbreaking invention. Then everything came crashing down around us. I was dead inside when Sam died. I was no longer Sam's dad. I didn't know who I was. Honestly, I was lost. Everything felt meaningless. I hid in my work, untethered from everything else. I was terrified to be here with you, in this empty, quiet house with all its reminders of our life with Sam. I became obsessed with finishing this invention that would help us find our way back to him. And in the process, I did all the wrong things."

As the waves beat a steady rhythm in the distance, I feel the weight of his grief, as if his pain is becoming part of my own story.

"I wasn't here for Sam either," he continues. "I was gone all the time. It's my fault he was on that deserted highway with a drug dealer. If I'd been around more, maybe I could've—"

"Sam wasn't on that highway to meet Logan. They didn't even know each other. Logan had left his drug-dealing days behind and was focused on staying clean."

"Then why was Sam there?"

"He had a reason. A good one," I say hoarsely. "He was protecting his friend Kate, who was in danger from her ex-boyfriend. That night by the highway, her ex came after her. Sam charged in, giving Kate the chance to break free and run across the highway. Her ex sprinted after her, and Sam chased him down, trying to stop him. But . . . we both know what happened after that."

He blinks back tears. "All this time . . . All those nights we worried about him, not knowing who he was with. I'd always feared the worst, believing that the accident was proof that we'd failed him."

"We were wrong about Sam. We should've trusted what we already knew and loved about him. He was kind and brave and a true friend. He was so much more than we ever realized."

In the silence, we both grapple with two truths. Grief for the son we'd lost but pride for man he'd become. "Remember the night we lectured him, frustrated that he was always going places and doing things and not telling us anything? We thought we were steering him back on the right path."

"Sam already knew the way."

He turns away from the ocean and looks at me. "I was a terrible husband when Sam died," he says, his voice catching. "I didn't say or do any of the right things. I saw how wrecked you were when he died and I . . . I wasn't there for you."

I see it all clearly now. My trip to the past didn't change anything. Sam is still gone. But the jump has opened a portal of sorts. A gateway to understanding Mark. "You were launching Aeon—"

"Don't go easy on me. I want to be better than I was."

My heart is filled with painful tenderness. It's as if the uncrossable barrier that's separated us in the three years since Sam died is lifting and I'm seeing Mark for the first time: the brilliant Type A genius I fell in love with, now layered with a heartache I hadn't grasped before.

"You used this invention, this thing that broke us apart, to give me more time with Sam."

"But I lost *you* in the process." His gaze holds mine. "And now I want to get you back."

Get me back. I feel a breath of magic from another place and time. The past perhaps. Or is it a glimpse of a future that had once seemed out of reach? I glance away, grappling with the implications of what he just said. Memories flash through my mind: laughter shared over coffee, late-night conversations, and the quiet moments together where everything felt right. But I also see the cracks, the misunderstandings, and the hurt that led us to this point.

"This might be too much to ask." His gaze holds steady, a flicker of fear just beneath the surface. "But . . . would you ever take a chance on us again?"

The question is simple, yet I'm overwhelmed by how we'd do that. How do we navigate the fragile landscape of our past while trying to build something new? There are feelings to sort out—grief, love, anger, and lingering resentment.

What if we slip back into old patterns, the same misunderstandings and distance that drove us apart? I can envision the steps, the tentative conversations, the slow rebuilding of trust. Every twist and turn holds the potential for both joy and heartache.

Yet within that uncertainty, I feel a flicker of hope. And beneath the fear lies a whisper of excitement at what could be.

"Maybe," I say. "Maybe I would."

"Maybe is good," he says as he takes my hand in his. "Everything good begins with a maybe."

I'll be forever broken by Sam's death, but for the first time I realize I might still be capable of hope and wonder.

Chapter Forty-Eight

Andy

In the days after the press conference, my phone dings all day. Every day. Messages, tags, and comments stream in like a relentless tide. My story is splashed across newsfeeds and headlines, the details of my lost love laid bare for all to dissect.

Most were positive. Nina Jarrett posted on X: *Brb, melting into a puddle of emotions over here. Andy Schapiro's longing for Kate Montano/Sarah Canford is everything. #hopelessromantic*

Of course, there are lots of cynics too, including Colin Bex complaining to his 23,000 followers:

@AndySchapiro, maybe instead of making your heartbreak a public spectacle, try dealing with it privately? Your declaration is giving me "red flags" vibes. Dude, she might have moved on for a reason.

He might be right.

I keep replaying the press conference in my mind, every word, every glance into the camera. I remind myself this was it—my one chance to speak in front of countless news outlets, knowing Kate might hear me.

And now I'm just waiting. Scrolling through my phone, checking for anything that might be from her.

The hours drag. I check every platform she might use—emails, messages, texts, social media, even some accounts I haven't opened in years. I scour through every notification. And when I finally tear myself away from the screen, I barely make it out of my bedroom before turning back, convinced I might've missed something.

Every time I get a notification, my pulse spikes. It's ridiculous how much weight I've placed on every buzz, every vibration. I go through the same cycle every day: scanning social feeds, obsessing over any mention that might somehow be her. But every lead I chase turns into a mirage.

A guy on TikTok swears he met someone named Kate Montano last month at a beach town up north, but the picture is grainy, and the more I stare at it, the more I realize it's not her. Another woman on Instagram claims she met Sarah Canford at a bookstore in Ventura and swears she was buying one of my books. But it's all wrong.

Dozens of reporters try to track me down too, leaving questions in private messages on social media. A few have figured out my private email address. One journalist from an online paper found a second cousin I met once at a family reunion and asked her to put us in touch. I get a message from her: "Hey, this guy reached out; thought you might want to talk to him?" Another reporter who'd been at the press conference—Kate Bradley—even went so far as to slip a note under my door.

"What did you mean by 'It's safe. He's gone'?" is the one question they all ask. They also want to know why Kate has two names. *Did she change her identity? Was I part of some cover-up?*

I try to stay hopeful, telling myself each new lead might be the one. Brooke even texts me every few days, "Don't give up, she's out there" or something similar, but her optimism fades as the weeks fly by with no response.

I try to get out of my own head, to write—to pour this mess into words. But every sentence is riddled with clichés and tired tropes. I try different approaches, but nothing works. It's all just . . . hollow.

Some reader sends me a clip from the press conference, and I replay it on my laptop, thinking maybe I missed something. I listen to my words and cringe. That man was clinging to hope. Stupidly naïve.

It wears on me, the constant strain of looking and hoping. As the days pass and there's no word from her, I start to believe maybe she knows I'm looking for her—and has decided not to respond. That thought eats away at me. Maybe she heard everything I said and feels nothing. Or maybe she doesn't want to be found. By me, anyway.

And the thought that's been circling in the back of my mind, the one I've been pushing away, comes back stronger than ever. What if Logan is right? What if she's . . . gone? The longer I go without a response, the more her silence feels like an answer itself.

One afternoon, my phone buzzes with a FaceTime from Jonathan. I almost let it go to voicemail, but then swipe to answer. Behind me he sees the piles of papers, coffee mugs left cold and untouched, clothing strewn about.

"Have you left your apartment even once this week?" he asks.

I look away, shifting the phone so he can't see the worst of it, and he sighs. "I'm serious, man. You need to get out of there. Just . . . breathe some fresh air."

"I will," I say, but it's a lie.

"Don't make me call you again in another week just to see your place looking like something out of a crime documentary."

I let out a weak laugh. "Okay."

Later that day, I finally get the energy to head out the door. The cool ocean breeze hits me like a reset button, clearing some of the cobwebs from my head. I walk aimlessly, passing people chatting outside cafés, couples laughing on the beach. Everyone has someone.

The next thing I know, I'm on the beach in the same place where I once told Kate I was falling for her. Mistake.

I notice the surfers out in the water, bobbing up and down on their boards as they catch the last waves of the day. Their graceful arcs in the water feel like poetry in motion. It shifts my focus from my own worries, even if just for a moment.

The waves roll in, the water a deep blue flecked with white foam, bringing with them a collection of shells and stones scattered along the shoreline. I stoop to pick up a smooth, flat rock, feel the coolness of it against my fingertips, and skip the rock across the water, watching as it bounces before sinking beneath the waves. When I look up, I see someone standing a few yards away.

Kate.

Shock slams through my body, stealing my breath. She stands before me, a vision in a blue sundress that dances around her legs in the ocean breeze. Her hair is darker, but there's no mistaking the almond-shaped eyes, the gentle curve of her chin.

I try to call out her name, but my voice is locked in my throat.

This is a dream. It has to be. How else to explain why it feels like I'm falling and flying all at the same time? My trembling knees threaten to topple me into the sand.

She drifts toward me, as if she thinks she's dreaming too.

I have so many questions, so many things I want to ask. Where to begin?

"I've looked everywhere for you," I say, and then my voice collapses. I hear how desperate I sound. I'm doing this all wrong.

She draws a breath and straightens her shoulders. With her sun-kissed skin, she's spellbinding. Her face is fuller. Her hair is loose and carefree. And something else. There's a self-assurance about her that's been brought out by the passage of time.

"I heard what you said about me on the news," she says, quietly. "For weeks I've thought about reaching out to you. But I can't risk going on social media. I can't have a digital footprint. I came to Ventura and walked down the street in front of your apartment building a couple of times, but there were always too many people around. With all the media attention, I thought I'd be far too easy to spot. Then I had an idea to come to the beach, the place where I saw you last, and here you are."

A tight ache builds in my chest. After all the years I've spent searching for her, she's the one who found me. I've dreamed of this moment, played it over and over in my mind, but now that it's here, words fail me.

"I didn't know you still felt this way about me," she says softly.

I hear the delicate rawness of her voice, and it seems impossible that I'm here with her. "I can't imagine life without you in it," I say, then immediately regret it. I'll scare her off.

It doesn't seem to faze her. "Everywhere I turned, the news media was buzzing about 'he's gone,' trying to figure out who you meant. I wondered if you were talking about Dane. But how could you when I never told you about him? I watched the clip a hundred times, and all I could figure is that you learned about Dane when you jumped to the past. Did you?"

I nod. "When I saw you last, you were trying to get to Sam's boat to escape to Anacapa Island."

"So then you know . . ." she says, softly. Her gaze meets mine. "But how can you be sure it's safe for me to come out of hiding now?"

"They found Dane's body."

I watch her eyes widen in surprise.

"He's the unidentified body they found at the pier three years ago," I continue. "His sister says it's definitely him."

She tilts her head. "I haven't seen anything about that in the news."

"It will be soon. The coroner is confirming it. But it's Dane. I'm sure of it."

She walks to the water's edge. Silent. As the tide rolls in, the waves are gaining strength, large and powerful, churning and frothing around her feet. I follow her deep into the surf, feeling the raw power of the ocean and all its unpredictability.

"I've been hiding from him for so long," she says, her voice barely above the roar of the waves. "Living far away from here. Every day on high alert. Every moment feeling like I'm in danger."

"You can let go of that now. He's gone."

"I don't know how to live in a world where I don't have to worry that he's going to come after me again. How can I be sure he's really gone?"

"He died of a gunshot wound to the neck. He's not coming back."

She turns to me, fear in her eyes. "Then you'll need to turn me in to the police."

"What do you mean?"

Her voice falters. "You know I was headed to Anacapa Island, but what you don't know is that I made it. As I was setting up my tent that night, I heard slow, quiet footsteps coming up the gravel road to the campground. They stopped and started again, like someone was searching. I just knew it was Dane. I turned off my lantern, grabbed the gun, and hid behind some tall rocks nearby. Waiting. After a long time with nothing, I thought I'd imagined it all. But when I headed back to the tent, he charged at me. Somehow, I shot at him. My hands were shaking so hard I was sure I'd missed. I ran—faster than I've ever run—back to the boat."

She hesitates, her lips trembling. "But if the dead body is his . . . I killed him, Andy." She watches me, her eyes searching for shock or disgust.

"I won't turn you in."

"How can you say that? If anyone finds out that you know that I killed him, you'd be—"

"I know."

"You'd be an accomplice to murder," she finishes, her voice dropping to a whisper.

I consider telling her that the violent merry-go-round of images from the encounter with Dane will be forever burned in my memory. That I don't need a time machine to remember Dane's shadowed figure on the beach, his hand covering her mouth, her eyes wide and filled with terror. When she finally broke free, I remember the split-second glance she threw over her shoulder, like she was making sure I was still there, before she ran.

"I still remember every minute of that night on the beach as if it happened seconds ago," I tell her. "I saw what he did. And I know what terrible things he was capable of."

"You'd be risking everything," she insists. "Why would you do that for someone you knew for what—five days?"

I step closer. "The first time we met—at Jonathan's birthday—it felt as if fate had arranged our meeting." I look away, the crash of waves helping me steady my voice. "Before you, I thought love was just another product, marketed to us like any other commodity. Yet, within days, I found myself falling for you. I wondered if it was like lightning in a bottle—if we didn't meet exactly that way, maybe we'd never have fallen for each other. But then I took the Aeon trip. This time I met you a few days *before* Jonathan's birthday party. Even under entirely different circumstances, we fell for each other. I know now that what we have is rare, and I've felt the pain of losing you—twice." The ocean's roar fills the silence. "So, yes, I'll keep your secret."

She blinks back tears. We watch the setting sun paint the sky a riot of colors: orange, pink, and purple. Waves crash against the shore, sending up a misty spray, and I see her shoulders relax. I stand beside her in the swirling waters, and I feel the powerful energy of the waves washing us clean of the past.

The sun sinks lower in the sky, and the waves are brushed by gold as the final rays disappear over the horizon. The effect doesn't last long. Everything out here on the ocean moves and changes from moment to moment.

"Look, a lot of time has passed since we . . ." I say, then trail off. "And I imagine you're in a relationship. Maybe even have a couple of kids by now."

She laughs and shakes her head. "None of that. But I often think about the last time we were together," she says softly. "And I envy that you got to experience it all again. I really liked you, but my life then . . . it was never my own. I was always afraid. Until I met you. But that was so long ago, Andy."

I nod, keeping my voice steady, though I'm not sure how long I can keep that up. "I don't want to go back to what we had. I already did that. I want to move forward."

She's silent for a moment, her eyes drifting past me toward the water, like she's looking for answers in the waves.

"I'm not the person I was back then," she says quietly, as if she's warning me. "I lied to you. Kept secrets. I'm not proud of that."

She looks away again, and I think she might be getting ready to say goodbye. But then she looks up. "I wanted so badly for you to like me. Not to see me as a broken person. A victim."

"You're strong, Kate. You didn't just stand there when Dane had you. You fought. I saw you take control when most people would've crumbled."

My hand reaches for hers, and when our fingers touch, I feel an electric charge as if someone just jolted me alive again. Everything I want, and everything I experienced in the past, comes down to this moment. Things can stay exactly as they've been. Or I can make them change.

"What if we do something simple now? Maybe dinner?"

She isn't sure. I can see it in her eyes. She doesn't know if she can trust me with her secret. Then, "I'm starving, actually."

"Okay, then. We'll also order a bottle of Dom Perignon."

She steps back. A playful smile tugs at her lips. "Wait. Why are you suggesting Dom Perignon?"

"From *Sleepless in Seattle*, of course. Only Bill Pullman called it Dom DeLuise."

Her smile morphs into astonishment. "Are you saying that years ago when we first met and we watched *Sleepless in Seattle* in my apartment and I said I really wanted to try Dom Perignon someday, you *still* remember that?"

I glance down at our hands, still touching. I remember watching the movie with her that first time—and how incredible it felt all over again the second time. "I remember everything about you, Kate."

She looks at me in surprise. "Seriously? Were you really paying attention to a minor detail like that?"

I glance up. In the hushed colors that stretch across the horizon, I see it all. Our past together. Our present. Our future. I want all of it.

"To you? Always."

Chapter Forty-Nine

Logan

It takes Haley over a week to text me. Eight agonizing days while I ruminated about popping back into Celestine to remind her who I was. Eight grueling days while I checked my phone every fifteen minutes in case a text had slipped through, and I'd somehow missed the sound of its high-pitched chime.

When the notification finally swoops across my phone, I stare at it as if I'd just been handed a bomb. Whatever words she might say will blow up my heart.

Hey Logan. It's Haley.

I wait, my heart pounding. The tiny ellipses pulse on the screen, indicating she's typing. Thoughts swirl in my head, bracing myself for the possible blow. She's found someone else. She misspoke when she said she might go for tacos. She's leaving town.

The seconds stretch into eternity. This is the moment everything changes. My hopes dashed. An ending before there was a chance of a beginning.

I get off at 7.

It's not flirty, but it's a beginning.

Want to meet at José's tonight? 7:15?

Relief floods through me, and I reread her response, making sure I read it right. Still, I don't want to seem too eager, so I wait five minutes to answer. Then:

You bet! See you there!

Before I press Send, I erase the exclamation marks. But then it looks too laid back—too cool—so I write:

You bet! See you there.

I press Send before I can overthink it some more.

Now I'm wheeling my way there, wearing a blue button-down and brand-new jeans that took me ten minutes to choose. I'm probably overdressed for tacos, but I want my clothes to tell her that this date—or whatever this is—means something to me.

José's food truck is parked a block from the harbor, so even when guests are eating tacos that cost four dollars, we can watch the sunset over this million-dollar view of sailboats, old sea ships, and yachts.

I glance up and see Haley coming toward me. Her brown hair, released from her work ponytail, now falls to her shoulders, framing her face with soft waves.

Her eyes click onto my face and the breath whooshes out of my body. "Hey," she says.

I've waited so long for this moment, and this is when my brain freezes. "You made it," I manage.

"I've never done this before," she says. "Go out with a stranger I met at the bar."

"Me neither."

"No, I know people say that, but I really . . . Well, I haven't."

"Maybe I'm not a stranger?"

"Maybe you're right about that."

"Want to order?" I sound like a nervous teen on his first date.

"Sure. What do you love on the menu?"

My heart is pounding, my hands moist, but I know the answer to this. If only I could calm down. "Chicken tacos. Agua Verde."

Agua Verde is a green juice made from spinach and secret other ingredients José won't divulge, despite everyone's attempts to coax it out of him. It tastes healthy, but I know brown sugar is one of the ingredients, so it probably isn't. We order a couple of tacos and Agua Verde, then head to one of the picnic tables in the plaza and wait for our order to get called out.

"What was it like being in the past for almost a week?" she asks.

What was it like? How do I answer that without telling her how we met or what we did together? The story of us.

"It's crazy. You see everything with fresh eyes—all the small stuff you once took for granted. All those moments, big and small, that shaped who we are. Back then, we were always striving for more of everything, but going back you realize how much you already had."

"So, it's more than reliving a memory?"

"Far more. You see your life as it was, and you realize there's so many more possibilities for your future than you ever imagined. Thousands of choices you can make."

"Like?"

I shrug. "For me, I could see that I spent too much time thinking that all I am is what other people see. I'd limited myself to only what's on the surface."

Her eyes search mine. "Five days in the past is a long time. What did you do with all that time?"

"I tried things I never thought I would. And met people I wouldn't otherwise. I had these plans to swim, surf, hike, and bike every moment, but then other things happened."

"Like what?"

José calls out our order, and I start to wheel my chair over to the truck. "Race you," I say, and then we both take off. For a girl who loves puzzles, she's fast. But I'm faster. Maybe it's the adrenaline at work, but I feel invincible. Still, I let her win by a foot.

Then I catch her smiling at me and it feels like before. Only better. Because I'm part of something that's happening right now. My body is broken, but the world tastes of blue skies. And hope.

The tacos kickstart our conversation. We have something to look at. To rave about together. We cover a lot of ground. Some stuff I knew from talking to her in the past. Other things are new to me.

She tells me she's going back to school to become a licensed vocational nurse. She thinks she can become a travel nurse and see more of the world. She's growing hydroponic tomatoes on her apartment balcony. No soil, just water, but the approach makes them grow faster so now she has too many tomatoes, and she's teaching herself how to make and can tomato sauce.

"I've got an entire cabinet full. Chunky and pureed."

"I guess they'll come in handy if the apocalypse happens."

She laughs, like she thinks that was funny. Then she asks me what I do for a living, and I tell her that I quit my job at the courier company and started a new gig at the Y, coaching swimming for middle school kids.

"That's ambitious," she says.

"I came back, you know, with all these questions."

"Questions?"

"What more can I do with my time? What more can I bring out in myself?"

"You found answers yet?"

"Beginning to."

The sun has set over the still harbor waters and the streetlights are flicking on in the plaza. The dinner crowds that had gathered here have begun to thin out. I dig into my backpack and pull out a bag of Belgian chocolate I bought on Amazon. The price was eye-popping—the cost of an entire meal—but it seemed like a cool move at the time.

I place the bag on the table. "You interested in some dessert?"

She picks up the bag and smiles. "Belgian chocolate? Milk chocolate to boot. How did you know this is my absolute favorite—?"

She stops midsentence and her expression shifts. I see the wheels turning. "Unless . . ."

"Unless what?" I ask, but I can see she's putting all the puzzle pieces together. She's figured it out.

"Unless you spent time with me in the past."

It's come to this. What do I say? A lie feels like the easy choice, but it would destroy any trust she might have in me. Now I've waited too long to answer. A denial is just gonna sound like a lie.

"You met me in the past, didn't you?" she asks in a half whisper.

I nod. "Three years ago."

She has no idea what to do with that. Her eyes dart toward me, questioning. Then she seems overwhelmed, as if it's dawning on her why I sought her out at Celestine.

"Were we . . . ?"

"We were."

Her eyes widen in surprise.

"I thought I was going back in time to use my body for whatever wild cliffs, fierce waves, or tough trails I could find—but it turns out, I came alive in a whole different way. I met you. And none of that mattered anymore."

There. I said it. I feel like I'm exploding everything that was fun or breezy about the night so far.

"You don't expect . . ." she says.

"I don't expect anything."

"Did you ask me out because . . ."

"I came to find you. And what happens . . . or doesn't happen . . . well, that's okay with me."

Except that it isn't true. If she decides that this whole situation is too strange or that I'm not a good match because I'm in a wheelchair or not what she's looking for or whatever excuse she comes up with, it will feel like a bullet straight to my heart.

"That's not entirely true." My face is hot. Flushed. "What I'm trying to say is that the past isn't the future. What happens next is entirely in our hands. Every moment, we get to live all the possibilities."

She sits back in her chair. I can't read her smile. Is this the pleasant smile that's going to precede a quick exit? Or does she find me amusing? Maybe a little pathetic?

"I'm still stuck on the idea that we had a relationship. What was I like—what were *we* like? How did we even meet?"

"We hiked Mount Whitney. I shared my chocolate with you and helped you reach the summit. Then we ended up spending nearly every minute together."

"So you know everything about me, then?"

"Not everything. There's so much more I want to know."

"I know so little about you."

"We can change that," I say, quickly, hoping I sound quick-witted, not pushy.

She leans back in her chair. "I'm in different place in my life than I was three years ago."

I feel the door closing between us. Although it feels like yesterday to me, a lot has happened to both of us in those three years. Maybe what we had was truly lightning in a bottle, crackling bright, but ultimately temporary.

The words fly out of my mouth. "I'd like to see what the future holds for us." I feel like I've taken a giant leap from which there can be no recovery. No soft landing. All she has to say is "I don't" and there can be nothing ahead for us. We'll become a dusty memory that only I carry with me.

She releases a breath. "Just because we had a relationship in the past doesn't mean we have a future."

"I think you underestimate us."

"Have you always been like this? So sure of . . . everything?"

"Actually? No. The old me would've never had the nerve to even talk to you. Or ask you out. Then I met you and . . . everything changed. *I* changed."

She leans in. "If we try this, there have to be rules."

I sort of inhale her words and repeat them in my head. *If we try this.* "Rules? Bring 'em on."

"I don't know how I can compare to whatever happened between us before. It might be a lot to live up to. Probably impossible. So, no talking about it."

"Never? You don't want to know what happened between us?"

She studies me for a beat. "I want to get to know the person you are today. Same for you getting to know me."

"Okay." My heart is racing a million beats a minute. "Seriously, you really don't want to know?"

A hint of a smile plays on her lips. "Even if I beg you, never tell me. Promise me that."

"Okay. I'll never say a word. Until we have to explain to the grandkids how we met."

THE END

Acknowledgements

I'm someone who vividly remembers my dreams. I write them down, reflect on them, and share them with my husband and kids. One night, I had a dream so real that I rushed to write it down the moment I woke up. In this dream, I turned to see my son, Jake, as he was twenty years ago—four years old, with strawberry blonde hair, and big brown eyes. His cheeks were flushed from the sun, and I leaned in to kiss his hair, inhaling that familiar little-boy scent. In that moment, I was convinced I'd traveled twenty years into the past.

The dream lingered with me for days, blurring the lines between reality and imagination, making me wonder: *What if we could truly revisit our past? How would we be changed by our experience?*

My passion for science, which has led me to produce hundreds of science-focused TV episodes, naturally pushed me to dive into research on time travel. Most theories suggested that traveling to the past would alter the future, creating ripples with unpredictable consequences.

Then I discovered the work of renowned physicist Dr. Fabio Costa at the University of Queensland. His research on closed time-like curves (CTCs) proposed that time travel could occur without paradoxes. According to his theory, if someone tried to change the past, the timeline would adjust to prevent any lasting impact on the future.

This revelation sparked another question: What if we *could* spend an hour in our past, fully knowing it couldn't affect the future? I shared the idea on social media, and the overwhelming response convinced me there were countless stories waiting to be told. It took years to develop this novel—partly because I was balancing raising kids with producing television series and a feature film—but also because the story itself needed time to fully take shape.

I'm deeply grateful to my talented agent, Christina Hogrebe at the Jane Rotrosen Agency, who believed in this story from the start. Thanks to Christina, I was fortunate to get *The Memory Collectors* into the hands of editor Holly Ingraham at Alcove Press, who's been an incredible partner in bringing this book to readers.

A special thanks goes to my friend Kes Trester, whose home in Ventura, California, inspired the setting of this story. Its sun-drenched beaches and serene waves contrast beautifully with the winding highways that vanish into pitch-black nights, making it the perfect backdrop for this story.

Most importantly, thank you to my readers who take the time to reach out. I cherish your comments on Facebook, your emails, and your messages. I truly believe I have the most amazing and generous readers in the world!

Discussion Questions

~

1. <u>The Unanswered Question</u>: All four of the Memory Collectors had an unresolved question from their past. Is there a mystery or secret from your past that still haunts you? How would you spend an hour going back to that moment to seek the answers you never got?
2. <u>The One Who Got Away</u>: Andy wanted to find his first love, Kate, who disappeared after a whirlwind romance. Who in your life did you lose touch with but wish you could speak to again? What would you say or ask if you had just one hour with them?
3. <u>The Unforgivable Mistake</u>: Brooke looks for an hour of relief from the guilt of an unforgivable mistake. Is there something you regret that you wish you could take back? How would going back to that hour change things for you now?
4. <u>An Hour of Adventure</u>: Logan craves the rush of adrenaline from surfing and mountain climbing, yearning to

reclaim the freedom he lost. Is there a spontaneous adventure you took that you'd like to revisit?

5. <u>A Second Chance</u>: Nearly all the Memory Collectors get a second chance at relationships that had gone awry. Is there a person or relationship you let go of too soon that you'd like to revisit?

6. <u>A Moment of Joy</u>: Recall an hour when you felt pure happiness. What was that moment, and how would you relive it differently knowing what you know now?

7. <u>A Conversation</u>: If you could have one more conversation with someone from your past, who would it be and why? What would you say to them?

8. <u>An Hour of Courage</u>: Think of a moment when fear held you back. If you could return to that moment for an hour, how would you face your fear differently?

9. <u>The Question Left Unasked</u>: Is there a question you've always wished you had asked someone? If you could go back and ask it, what do you think or hope the answer would be?

10. <u>An Hour of Gratitude</u>: Is there someone in your past who helped shape your life, but you never had the chance to thank? How would you use an hour to express your gratitude?

11. <u>An Hour with Your Younger Self</u>: If you could spend an hour with a younger version of yourself, what advice, comfort, or warning would you give them?